Old
Maid's
Puzzle

A QUILTING MYSTERY

Old Maid's Puzzle

Terri Thayer

MIDNIGHT INK
WOODBURY, MINNESOTA

MIDNIGHT
INK

First Edition
First Printing, 2008

Book design and format by Donna Burch
Cover design by Lisa Novak
Cover illustration © Cheryl Chalmers—The July Group
Editing by Connie Hill

Midnight Ink, an imprint of Llewellyn Publications

Library of Congress Cataloging-in-Publication Data:

Thayer, Terri.
 Old maid's puzzle : a quilting mystery / Terri Thayer. — 1st ed.
   p. cm.
 ISBN 978-0-7387-1218-5
 1. Quiltmakers—Fiction. 2. Quilting—Fiction. 3. Quilts—Fiction.
 4. Santa Clara Valley (Santa Clara County, Calif.)—Fiction. I. Title.

PS3620.H393O44   2008
813'.6—dc22

                                                    2008010940

Midnight Ink
Llewellyn Publications
2143 Wooddale Drive, Dept. 978-0-7387-1218-5
Woodbury, MN 55125-2989 USA
www.midnightinkbooks.com

Printed in the United States of America

ACKNOWLEDGMENTS

Old Maid's Puzzle wouldn't have been possible without the support of my super critiquers, Beth Proudfoot and Becky Levine. They keep me grounded and on track. They keep Dewey moving forward, and Kym in our sights.

Technical help came from Mike Hahn of the San Jose Police Department, and John Howsden, retired from Fremont Police Department. I picked a very small portion of their vast knowledge to help my story along. I greatly appreciate their generosity.

To Mary Hernan, thanks for the bagels and brainstorming.

Thanks to the fans who enjoyed Wild Goose Chase. This one is for you! It's nice to have an audience.

To all the Midnight Ink staff, a hearty thank you. You make me look good!

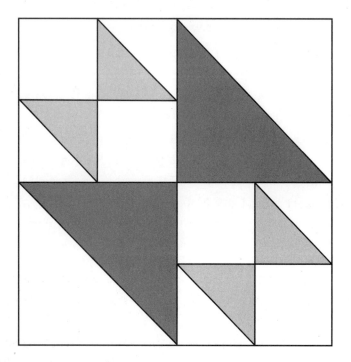

Old Maid's Puzzle block is an old design, sometimes called Hour Glass, School Girl's Puzzle, or Double X. The basic nine-patch block is made from six half-square triangles and 3 plain blocks. When set side by side, lovely secondary patterns emerge. Change the position of the light, dark, and medium fabrics for endless possibilities.

ONE

"You've got a finely honed definition of celibacy, Healy," I gasped through gritted teeth. Buster Healy leaned back on the arm of the couch and grinned.

His shirt was draped over the slatted rocker. My T-shirt was acting as a dust magnet on the oak floor and my bra was slung over the beaded lampshade. His jeans were firmly zipped up. Mine were unzipped but still on my hips—barely.

We were playing at our nightly activity of refraining from sex. Buster's definition of celibacy was that his body was off-limits but mine was fair game.

We were supposed to be renovating. I owned a tiny bungalow on the verge of a nice neighborhood in San Jose. A definite work-in-progress. A UFO, my quilter customers would call it. Unfinished Object.

Tonight Buster and I had stained the twin built-in corner cabinets in the dining room. We'd finished early and found ourselves with time on our hands. Play time.

A deep breath restored some equilibrium. A guy as virile and handsome as Buster choosing to be chaste, that was a major turn-on. His celibacy was a one-way street, though, with him having the right-of-way to my cul-de-sac. And I was denied through access. I wanted our deal to end tonight.

My body pulsed with sensation. "I can't take much more of this."

He nuzzled the end of my nose. "That's where you're wrong. The beauty of a woman's body is that she can withstand more excitement than a man."

I'd never met a guy with that particular theory about sex before.

"Did I even agree to this ban?" I asked.

I knew that I had. I'd even conceded that we might have gotten off to too quick a start the first time we reconnected, by jumping into bed. Twice. In two days.

That was nearly six months ago. Since then, we'd taken things slowly, dating as though we'd just met and hadn't grown up together. As though we hadn't had sex the first time we'd noticed each other as adults. The dating had progressed and I was ready to take things to the next stage. Buster was balking, sticking to the original deadline, which was still two weeks away. My plan required his full cooperation.

I continued my argument for breaking the boycott. "I thought the ban was on all forms. Any public service announcement will tell you that sex is sex. Just because it doesn't involve actual..."

"I know, I saw that After School Special, too."

"And?"

"Aren't you having fun?" His fingertips danced up my spine.

Hard to argue with that. Sometimes I had fun twice a night.

2

But I wasn't going to give up. My father had been sure I'd grow up to be a lawyer, since I loved to debate. Being a quilt shop owner didn't give me much opportunity to argue, unless I counted every conversation with my sister-in-law. I took in a deep breath.

"If 'no means no,' it only follows that 'yes means yes.' Yes?" I said.

"No." Buster moved behind me, kneading the muscles between my shoulder blades. I was like a guitar string. He knew just when to tighten and when to slacken. He rested his chin on my shoulder. The point of his jaw dug into the tender flesh, but I welcomed the pain.

I knew when to back off, too. I nestled into his chest, being sure to give an extra grind with my hip. "You do remember that Saturday is the anniversary sale? And that you promised to work."

"When did I promise that?"

"Probably the same night I agreed that not having sex was a good idea."

He grinned and moved in on my neck, planting tiny kisses. His stubble tickled my chin. I felt heat rise and my brain start to muddle. He always won this argument in the same way. By driving me out of my mind.

"Let's end this now," I said, reaching for his belt.

"Two more weeks. I'm a man of my word."

I said, "Save your integrity for someone who cares."

"You don't mean that."

He knew I didn't. I loved his overdeveloped sense of honesty. That was what made him a great homicide detective, the youngest in the San Jose Police Department.

"We could put on another coat of stain," he said, pointing with his chin to the dining room. I followed his direction. My collection of art pottery was spread over the dining room table. We'd propped up the glass shelves of the cabinet against the wall. I couldn't wait to see my pots inside the cupboards. The colorful glazes were going to pop against the rich mahogany stain.

I'd been trying to get to this for months. My renovations were behind schedule. My attention had been focused on the quilt shop, for all the good that did me. The shop was barely staying open.

I sat up, flinging my arms open wide. My voice carried in the small house. "I'm out of stain and out of budget. I can't buy what I need for the house, because the store isn't making a profit. The store's not making a profit, because I can't afford Kym, but I can't fire my sister-in-law. I can't have sex, because my boyfriend has this silly idea that we need to get to know each other better. I know you, I *know* you. Let me get some satisfaction in this one aspect of my life." I leaned in and kissed him, giving him an adoring look.

Buster ignored my batting eyelashes and said, "I might have to work on Saturday."

I squinted. "Since when do you work weekends?"

The SJPD had moved him up to homicide a year ago to take advantage of his computer skills, then, to his endless frustration, put him on cold cases. He spent most of his days at a desk, reading old files. Good because his nights and weekends were free, but not what he'd signed on for.

"I'm close to identifying an inmate in SoCal as a suspect for the Jenkins murder. I need to go down and see him. Get a look at him myself. If he'll let me, I'll get a new photo to scan into the facial recognition software for comparison."

"That was twenty-five years ago, wasn't it?" I wasn't old enough to remember when the young Traci Jenkins had gone missing after a blind date, but the *Merc* did an update nearly every year. "The murderer would be a lot older. Would he look the same?"

"The computer doesn't care. It tracks landmarks, plots points. Underlying bone structure doesn't change." Buster traced a line on my face. "For example, even when you're old and wrinkled, these cheekbones will still have the same beautiful shape."

I batted his finger and the left-handed compliment away. "I remember that from anthro class in college. We did a unit on identifying indigenous people by their facial similarities. They can tell who came from Asia originally and who came from North America."

I loved talking about Buster's work. I settled next to him on the couch, feeling his warmth as I listened.

"Like that. The software maps the face, in this case, the suspect's mug shot, and then we can overlay it on another photo to see if they match. The trouble is, the old picture of this guy is not a full shot, and it's not conclusive. There's no DNA to test, so I've got to go down and see if the suspect will talk to me. I'll try to do it before Saturday."

"I'd like to have you around at the sale," I said. Worry about the shop crept into my voice and Buster heard it. He squeezed my waist with his arm and kissed my neck.

"It's going to be fine."

"This sale is make or break for the shop," I said. He knew this as well as I did.

His voice was muffled by my hair. "You've done everything you can, right? Ordered lots of new things, advertised the sale, prettied up the place?"

I nodded.

"So. Relax." He punctuated his command with a kiss. "The customers will come and spend a lot of money. Even if I have to drag people in off the streets," he said.

The picture of Buster pulling quilters out of their cars made me laugh. It was so nice to have someone completely on my side. Buster made my heart lighter.

That made me feel hornier.

I pulled on his belt buckle, rubbing my body along his and tried one last tactic. "Every fireworks show has a grand ending. I mean, all those waterfalls, palms, and chrysanthemums are spectacular, but the best part is always the finale. How about my finale?"

I'd been working on this fireworks analogy for a week, but Buster was unmoved. His kissed me quickly, throwing on his shirt and buckling his belt. I hated that he was covering up his beautiful shoulders.

"Nice try," he said.

"Aren't you worried that by the time we actually do it, it won't be any good?" I asked.

Frank Sinatra was singing "Nice and easy does it every time." Buster barely tolerated my CD collection. As his idea of mood music was Metallica, I played what I wanted to hear.

"Are you?" He kissed my palm and sucked on my finger. I felt myself sink.

"Well, I mean, if I get used to a certain level of …" I couldn't think of the word I wanted. He had two of my fingers in his mouth and, unlike me, words wouldn't come.

"Foreplay? Arousal?" he said.

Just hearing the words was stopping my breath. I nodded. His mouth moved off my fingers. I felt cold where his lips had been. Then I felt his hot breath on my ear as he whispered. "Why would I stop? I'm having a grand time."

I fell onto the couch. "Well, for one thing, who has time for this?"

Buster continued huskily, "Did you know the average person watches four hours of television every night? Who needs that?"

He leaned over and slipped a wet finger along my ribs.

I leaned back away from his one-sided gestures. "No way. I'm not going there unless you go with me."

He straightened, and said, "My work is done here tonight."

I pushed him toward the door. "That's the last time, Healy. Next time it's all or nothing."

"Don't forget this week is my Date Night. I get to chose what we do," Buster said with a grin. "My choice."

"I better like it," I said.

He laughed. "Oh, you will."

TWO

THE NEXT DAY AT work, I was making my job list on the whiteboard when Pearl Nakamura skated into the classroom.

"Hey kiddo," she said.

Dropping the Kenyan market basket she was carrying on a table, she retracted the wheels on her Heelies and walked over to me. Seventy-two years old, barely five feet tall, Pearl just cleared my shoulder as I stood at the whiteboard. Her black hair was cut short with a stubborn cowlick that rose from the back of her head like a broken feather.

Pearl looked like she'd been shopping at the Gilroy outlets with Vangie again. The fifty-year age difference did not matter to those two kindred spirits. Pearl eschewed grandmotherly garb for rolled-up jeans and layers of brightly colored T-shirts. Her sunglasses were tucked into the neck of today's sunny yellow one. They were rose-colored, of course.

She scrutinized the to-do list I was writing. I was pretty happy with it. Jobs that needed to be done before the sale were color-coordinated to indicate their priority. Red for must-get-done, blue for should-get-done, and pink for nice-if-we-get-to-it. One column was designated for the responsible party to initial when the job was finished. Accountability. Responsibility. Organization. Welcome to the new Quilter Paradiso.

Pearl frowned. "Do you really expect Kym to work your system?" she asked.

I shot her a don't-start-with-me look. "This is all for her benefit. You know she doesn't like taking direct orders from me, so I figured if I write all the jobs down and let *all* of my employees have their choice, the work will get done and I can avoid some drama."

My vision of the quilt shop had changed in the last six months. When I'd first inherited the shop a year ago, I'd stalled, trying to decide what I wanted to do with the place. After a failed attempt to sell, I'd decided I would make the shop into a place I wanted to work. To Kym's despair, that meant letting go of the old ways.

My mother had started Quilter Paradiso in the early eighties with a few bolts of calico in a corner of her father's hardware store and had grown it accidentally into a million-dollar-a-year business. That had been at the beginning of the quilting boom. Customers, and money, flowed into the store without much effort. But the quilting business had changed. Competition had gotten fierce. By the time I took the store over last year, there were eight quilt shops within twenty miles, and I had to fight for every consumer dollar.

In my mother's time, the shop had been a gathering place for friends. Her employees were her quilting buddies, whose schedules were as flexible as their joints weren't. They gossiped between customers, sewed on their quilts when the store was slow, closed every day for lunch. Kym had fit right in, even though she was far younger than Mom and her friends. The hand-appliquéd quilts she'd made back then were exquisite—with ruched flowers, sawtooth borders and other time-consuming detail.

I'd computerized the inventory, instituted regular staffing hours, and lured the lucrative lunchtime buyers by staying open and running specials. Any time customers weren't in the store, my employees were kept busy—assembling quilt kits, reordering books, or making store samples. Time was money.

I'd lost several employees and a few customers, and the shop was still not making the profit I needed. The regime had to start paying off soon—if just to shut up Kym.

Pearl snickered. "It's good to have a dream, girly."

I bumped her with my hip, and she laughed harder. "I have a dream, too," she said. "That the Stitch 'n' Bitch group will show up today." She skated a few feet away and circled back.

"Just because you're on time …" I teased.

"For the first time ever," Pearl finished for me. "I know."

According to the oversized schoolhouse clock on the wall, it was a little after nine. The Stitch 'n' Bitchers had been meeting here Tuesdays at nine since my mother had first opened twenty years ago. They came early and stayed all day, working on their projects. Lately, though, the members had been straggling in later and later. Most of them were Pearl's contemporaries. Women of a certain age, and then some. Seventy was the new forty-five and a half.

"Everyone's not like you, Pearl. Some people slow down as they get older," I said.

"I keep telling them, 'You rest, you rust,' but they don't believe me. Gussie came to my yoga class. She only lasted fifteen minutes," Pearl snorted. "I've never seen anyone turn that color purple before."

"Poor Gussie. She's no match for you." Gussie Johnston, a charter member of this group, was one of my favorite customers. Naturally frugal and living on a fixed income, she was a careful spender, never adding much to my bottom line, but her sweet disposition and smiling countenance always brightened my day. It didn't hurt that I could do no wrong in her eyes. She treated me like a favored, spoiled granddaughter.

Pearl spread out a multi-colored quilt top, as bright as Mexican pottery, and pointed to a particularly virulent violet patch. "Seriously, she was like this color."

"Is that the raffle quilt?" I asked. The Stitch 'n' Bitch group was selling tickets at the sale on Saturday to benefit Women First, the local women's shelter.

"Yup. Old Maid's Puzzle."

Old Maid. I chuckled, and Pearl looked up from digging in her basket.

"What?" she said.

I held the marker in my hand, and remembered. "My brother Kevin was one of those kids who took every word uttered at its literal meaning. This one day, Mom was driving a bunch of my friends to soccer practice, and Kevin was in the back seat, scrunched between me, Janie Rizzo, and Debra Lupo. When we went over the railroad tracks, the girls lifted their feet off the floor. Kevin said, 'Why'd you do that?' Janie Rizzo told him it was a superstition. Over the tracks, raise your feet up or you'll become an old maid. The next set of tracks, up come Kevin's little legs. We all looked at him. 'I don't want to be an old butler,' he said."

Pearl laughed. "Old butler, heh. No one wants that."

She unpacked her sewing supplies. I went back to my list. Thinking about Kevin, a small twinge of sadness passed through me. We were no longer those carefree kids. Ever since he'd married Kym, we'd grown apart. Maybe we'd have a few laughs at the sale on Saturday. He always worked the big events at the store.

After a few minutes, Pearl cast a significant look around the too-messy classroom. A huge pile of quilts took up the table under the windows. A shipment of notions, rulers, and books was spread over the three tables nearest the door, right where the UPS man had dropped them yesterday. Half-finished quilt kits littered the rest of the tables. With three full-time employees, and several part-timers and a phalanx of teachers all sharing the space, it was a never-ending struggle to keep this room neat. As soon as an empty spot appeared, someone dropped something on it. With the anniversary sale in just four days, the chaos had reached new heights.

Pearl said, "We're going to need these tables out of the way."

"Wait until Vangie or Jenn gets here. We'll clear a space," I assured her.

I added that job and more to my to-do list. *Clear out classroom. Bring down more bags from the loft. Scrub the bathroom.*

"Celeste is bringing the quilt frame," Pearl said. "It'll take up half the classroom."

Ever since I'd found the old quilting frame in the loft, I'd wanted my customers to see how a quilt was hand quilted. Many sewers new to quilting used professional long-arm machine quilters to finish their projects, and had never even seen handwork done. I'd asked this group to demonstrate at Saturday's sale. Celeste had volunteered to re-stain the wood and make sure that all the moving parts moved.

"Did Celeste do a good job of restoring it?" I asked.

Pearl looked over her glasses at me. "What do you think? We're talking about Celeste. We would not be using it if it were not perfect. As soon as the others get here, we'll get the Old Maid's Puzzle into the frame, and start quilting it," Pearl said.

"Are you okay with that?" I asked. Pearl was a whiz with her sewing machine.

"My hand skills are kind of rusty, but it'll come back to me."

"Don't do too much. Save some quilting for Saturday."

Pearl smiled at my naiveté. "No worries. It would take weeks to hand quilt anything this size. We'll just get it started so people can see how the stitching looks. We'll sell more tickets that way."

A new voice entered the conversation. "If you were so worried about selling tickets, you should have let me pick the colors."

Celeste Radcliffe came through the door, snowy eyebrows furrowed. Her words were clipped, her cadence that of an old-time actress in a black-and-white movie, the result of being a native Californian educated at New England boarding schools.

I sucked in my stomach and straightened my spine. Celeste had the effect of making me feel like I was permanently slouching.

Pearl pulled out a chair next to Celeste. "Oh sit down, you old grouch. People love a bright-colored quilt. Not everything has to be turkey reds and browns, you know."

Celeste said to me, "If you'd had those Civil War prints while we were choosing the fabric, they would have been perfect. We'll be lucky now if this quilt sells a hundred tickets."

"Do you think?" I said. "That reproduction line isn't moving very well. This is sunny California after all. My customers don't like those dull colors."

"Historically accurate colors," Celeste sniffed. "Shows what you know."

"The computer doesn't lie," I protested. "My inventory tracks what's selling and what's not."

"Computers can't tell you everything," Celeste insisted.

I bit back a retort. These women were half a century older than me. They'd lived lives I could only imagine, with changes in technology that dwarfed anything in my experience. If they didn't want to carry cell phones, watch TV on an iPod, or trust the information from my computer, I had to respect that.

Celeste was staring at my list. "You've misspelled inventory," she said.

I took a step back. She was right. Right there, after #2, *Make pretty fat-quarter bundles,* was #3, *Check in new inventorry.*

"It's just a to-do list," I grumbled, even as I erased the offender. Celeste had been brought up in the days when education meant memorizing epic poems and long lists of vocabulary words. When I'd been a kid doing homework in this room, she'd happily drilled me for hours for the school's weekly spelling tests.

"I don't know how you expect to gain respect from your employees if you can't spell," Celeste said, opening her handled clear-plastic block organizer box and taking out her redwork embroidery. She opened her tapestry bag that was fitted with a half-dozen zippered compartments. Inside, needles were divided by size and use, floss was wound onto individual bobbins, and scissors tips were protected with tiny sleeves. Celeste was one of those quilters who spent nearly as much time in Organized Living as the quilt shop. She believed in everything having a place.

She took the seat across from Pearl, her back to me, her fingers already stabbing the needle into the fabric. These women were never without something to do.

As usual, Celeste was wearing expensive knit clothing that complemented her white hair, mostly purples and reds. I'd never seen her in anything but pants, but the hems were perfectly tailored to her extra-long inseam.

The back of her head was covered with a staid-looking bun that had swirls and whorls like a complex mandala.

"I can spell," I muttered. "I just had a flash of dyslexia."

Celeste frowned at my flimsy excuse, pulling the red embroidery floss roughly through the hooped fabric. Redwork was hand embroidery done on muslin. Celeste had drawn a picture on the fabric with a mechanical pencil. She would use the stem stitch to outline the drawing. The result was a perfectly rendered image of the object—in this case, plants with the Latin names underneath. Celeste had been a botanical illustrator before she retired when her children were young. Her drawings were full of authentic detail.

"You need to have one of your people get the quilting frame out of my car," Celeste said.

"Where's Gussie? Didn't Gussie pick you up?" Pearl asked Celeste.

Celeste shook her head. Her mouth was a grim line as she bent over her embroidery hoop. Never a ray of sunshine, today she seemed extra uptight. Gussie and Celeste were best friends. Something wasn't right.

I tried some flattery. "Is that a new quilt you're working on?" I asked. "Celeste's Garden, Part Two?"

The most exciting part about the sale was the launch of our Quilter Paradiso Originals line. I'd asked friends of QP to create original quilt designs. Once the quilts were made, Vangie had produced colorful, easy-to-read instructions and created a pattern for each quilt. We'd made up kits with fabrics similar to the ones used in the original so the customer could take the kit home and reproduce the quilt.

Publishing patterns could become a lucrative sideline for the store, if Vangie and I could find the time to develop more. With the free labor, and the store as our outlet, we'd managed to keep the patterns and kits at a competitive price. I was thinking about taking out an ad in the next issue of *Quilter's Home Magazine*. If we could get national exposure, I was sure the QP Original line would take off.

"My quilt is nearly finished," Pearl said, holding up her QPO quilt, a simple landscape of sea, sun, and beach, a blend of color and curved lines. Pearl's quilts were unique, not easily reproducible, but she'd come up with an easy rendition of one of her more complex quilts and included some of her hand dyes in the kits. "I just need to fuse my binding."

Celeste flinched as though stuck by a needle. "Ironing on your binding," she shuddered. "You ought to be shot."

Pearl smiled at me, a sly smile that told me she knew she was winding her friend up. "Times are a-changin,' my friend, just like Bob Dylan said."

Celeste sniffed. "I don't know who that is, but he doesn't know the first thing about quilting. Bindings should finish at exactly one-quarter-inch, be filled with batting, and be hand sewn to the backing."

"Different strokes for different folks," Vangie said, appearing at my elbow, her long, lush brown hair slightly damp and curling at her neck, and cheeks flushed from her bike ride to work. Vangie Estrada had been my mother's last and best hire. Only twenty-one-years old, she'd been brought on to do the heavy lifting. Moving fabric bolts is hard labor. I'd found other ways to use her, though. She had innate design ability and great computer skills, the result of time spent in juvvy as a rebellious teen. She was becoming a good quilter too. Her paper-pieced Starry Night QPO quilt was bound to be a best seller.

"Right on, sister," Pearl said, standing and exchanging a hip bump with Vangie. They'd become fast friends when Vangie'd found out Pearl had been at the 1967 Monterey Pop Festival and seen Janis Joplin, Vangie's hero. Their age difference disappeared when talk turned to rock and roll.

"Hey, Vang, have I got a treat for you," Pearl said. "Hiro and I found a box of old Janis bootlegs on eBay. He figured out how to put them on CDs. Don't ask me how," she said, handing Vangie a stack of jewel cases she produced from her basket.

Vangie broke into a huge grin, her eyes crinkling with pleasure. "Far out," she said, her voice fading as she flipped through the CDs.

"And some brownies." Pearl's eyes twinkled. "Special for you."

"What about the rest of us?" I asked. Why did Vangie rate special ones?

"There's another batch in the kitchen for general consumption, Dewey," Pearl said.

Vangie rubbed her hands together in anticipation. Whether for the CDs or the brownies, I couldn't tell.

Pearl skated back to her seat.

Celeste's eyes followed her friend, and she snapped, "Could you please hold still for one moment, Pearl?"

"Oh, Dewey, telephone," Vangie said, eyes still on the CDs.

I hadn't heard the phone ring. I hated to keep people on hold too long.

I said to Vangie, "Thanks for telling me." My sarcasm hit deaf ears. She was lost somewhere in the sixties.

"Who's on the phone, Vang?"

She came out of her purple haze for a moment. "It's Lark," she said.

I *really* didn't want to keep *her* waiting. Lark Gordon was the hostess of the best-known cable quilting show, *Wonderful World of Quilts*. She was extremely popular and very influential.

"I'll take it in the office." I hurried out the door and across the hall into the office I shared with Vangie. Her computer was booting up without her as I plopped down in my chair and picked up the phone.

Last week Lark had taped a segment in Quilter Paradiso. I'd promised Kym she could be on TV, so she was the one featured. The taping had taken place on a day that both Vangie and I were out of the office. I was sorry to miss seeing Lark, but we'd already paid for our spots at How-to-Run-Your-Small-Business Successfully. We'd had the seminar on the calendar for weeks.

I had an awful thought. What if they needed to reshoot part of the show? If so, her timing was terrible. It had taken the whole day to set up and shoot what they did. My stomach tightened. I couldn't let anything interfere with the sale.

"Sorry to keep you hanging, Lark." I picked up a pencil and tapped it nervously on the desk.

"It's okay, doll. I'm on my cell waiting in line at Starbucks anyhow. Can I have a nine-pump, nonfat chai, please?"

"What can I do for you?" I asked. "Did your piece on the shop come out okay?"

I girded myself for bad news, doodling circles on my desk calendar.

"It's great. So great, in fact, it's going to air this Friday."

The pencil lifted. "Are you kidding?" I gasped. "We're having a huge sale on Saturday."

"I hope you have plenty of staff. Your store is about to go on national TV."

Quilter Paradiso on the airwaves. "Wow. I mean, thanks."

"No problemo. Next time I'm up there, you owe me a coffee."

Or a nine-pump something or other. I said my goodbyes to Lark and hung up. My stomach was still doing flips, but in a good way now.

Vangie had seated herself at her desk and was clicking furiously. She was downloading the music onto her MP3 player already.

I said, "You're not going to believe this."

She wasn't listening.

"Vang!" I yelled.

I waited until she pulled out her earphones, and spread my arms wide. "We're going to be on *Wonderful World of Quilts* Friday morning."

She jumped out of her chair. I grinned at her.

Vangie grabbed me and we bounced up and down. "That's so far out."

Far out indeed.

"We are on TV," Vangie sang to the tune of Sly and the Family Stone's, "We are Family."

"'I've got all my brothers with me,'" I sang.

"What's all the commotion?" Jenn poked her head in the office, a hot-pink, fuzzy scarf dangling from her neck. I glanced at the clock. She was right on time. The store was due to open in a few moments. She was on her way to the kitchen to stash her belongings in the cubbyhole and get to work. She would be working on the floor today, selling fabric.

Jenn was the typical Silicon Valley soccer mom and looked the part. Her blonde hair was pulled back into a perky ponytail. She had two pre-teens and worked part-time during their school hours. She'd been with my mother too. She wasn't crazy about some of the changes I'd implemented, but she was going along with most of them. She was reliable and great at helping customers chose fabrics for their projects.

"We're going to be on *Wonderful World of Quilts*," I said, gratified by her eyes opening wide.

"On *Friday* morning," Vangie said.

Jenn looked from me to Vangie and back. "Omigod, think of all the people that'll see it," Jenn said. "Millions."

Jenn hugged Vangie, then me. She squeezed my shoulders. I felt my eyes fill with tears. This was a huge week for Quilter Paradiso. Our twentieth anniversary, our first appearance on TV. And the sale that was going to keep us in business. Maybe things would turn out okay after all.

I broke away from the group hug. "Okay, enough celebrating. We've got a lot to do. More than we did ten minutes ago."

I remembered the Stitch 'n' Bitch request. "I need you two to get the quilt frame out of Celeste's car and go move tables around for the group. While you're in the classroom, sign up for your assignments on the whiteboard. You know yours already, Vangie. Update the database; send out e-mails about the sale Thursday. Now you can include a news flash about the TV show."

"Let me go stash my purse," Jenn said, slipping into the kitchen next to the office to drop her designer purse. A set of cubbyholes just inside the door held our personal items.

Vangie watched her leave, but didn't move toward the classroom. "You know what this means?"

I was thinking about the sale on Saturday. Business was likely to increase. "That I'm going to need temporary help for Saturday? And we'll sell out our inventory? That I now stand a chance of keeping the store open past next week?" I couldn't help but project a little.

She nodded. "Yes, all that. And one more thing. Think computers."

I tried to settle my brain down long enough to think. Computers?

Vangie filled in the blank. "We're going to have to get the online store up and running sooner rather than later."

My hairline tightened. I glanced in the hall. No one was there. I closed the office door. QP Online was not for general consumption. Vangie was the only one who knew about my plan for an online store.

My voice squeaked. "We're ..." I started again. "We're not ready for that. We don't have the inventory."

Vangie frowned. "You can't let this opportunity get away from us. QP is going to be beamed into thousands of homes. Hits to our website will be crazy as soon as that show is over."

"But we've got so much else to do before Saturday."

Vangie said, "We can do it." She went into her overdrive mode, talking fast, her voice rising, spit flying. "You take over sending the e-mails out to the customers and updating the database. I've been taking pictures of fabric as it comes in. I just need to load the files and take pictures of some of the older stuff. I'll set up a special e-mail address to handle the traffic. I'll concentrate on getting our webpage more user-friendly."

"Vangie, it's not possible." My head swam with the to-dos on my list. Adding her list to mine was nuts.

"That's what I'm telling you. It is. I can get the webpage ready to accept orders. We won't have all the fabric online, but we can get started."

I nodded, but she wasn't done yet. Her hands were clicking around the computer. I felt her excitement and began to believe her. Maybe we could pull this off.

"I've been talking to PayOne about using their system for collecting the money. They're just waiting for our say-so."

This was about four months earlier than I'd planned. But Vangie was right. It was time to strike. "Are you sure you can do all that?"

Vangie nodded. "Positive." She stopped her mouse and looked at me. "Absolutely."

I blew out a big breath. "Okay. I'll correct the database and send out the e-mails about the sale. You just work on the online store."

She hugged me.

"Promise me one thing. Don't tell anyone yet," I said. This was news my sister-in-law would need to be prepared for.

THREE

We headed for the classroom. My heart sank, because the room was in more disarray than it had been a few moments earlier. Piles of fabric scraps were laid out in between empty soda cans and water bottles littering the tabletop.

Gussie Johnston was on her usual scavenger hunt. She and Ina Schaeffer made up the remainder of the Stitch 'n' Bitch group. Ina was muttering. Damn. I'd hoped we'd have had the place cleared out before she got here. I hated it when she was annoyed with me.

Gussie, on the other hand, hummed happily as she rummaged through the wastepaper baskets. I sucked in a breath to avoid barking at her.

She loved discovering what she called her treasures, abandoned scraps of fabric. She had a point—students in the classes tossed away pieces big enough to be put in a quilt. Bottles and cans were just a recyclable bonus. I used to object, but Ina had told me I was ruining Gussie's fun. So I forced a smile when she greeted me, waving a treasured two-liter bottle.

Gussie bought all her clothes at the secondhand store—and only when they were running a sale. Consequently, her outfits tended to span fashion trends. Today she was wearing jeans with beaded pant legs and a seasonal sweatshirt with a leering scarecrow. A sparkly hair clip, the kind usually found on a playground, was holding back her brown-and-gray-streaked hair. Some people marched to a different drummer; Gussie jigged to a whole 'nother band.

I sidled up to Ina, who was trying to take down an unused table. The leg wouldn't budge. I kicked it expertly. "I'll do this. Go sew."

"We have to set up the quilt frame first. I'm sick of coming in and having to move things before I can find a place to do anything," Ina said. Nothing torqued her off more than a messy classroom.

"Hey," I defended. "You know we're getting ready for the sale this weekend. We're kind of busy."

Jenn looked at me for advice. She was still holding the pile of the QP Original sample quilts that were to be featured on Saturday. "Where can I put these?"

I shrugged. "They'll be hung up in the next day or so. Put them in the store, but keep an eye on them. We can't lose any. Or worse, have them stolen."

Jenn strode out of the room. Vangie followed her with a second pile.

I called after them, "And get the quilt frame out of Celeste's car."

Ina winced as I yelled in her ear. Ina was a member of the Stitch 'n' Bitch group *and* an employee. It wasn't good when she came to

25

the store to have fun and ended up working. I tried not to let that happen. I needed her around. Ina had been working at the store longer than anyone else, hired by my mother twenty years ago. I valued her not only for her institutional knowledge, but for her verve and energy.

She was looking around the room, mouth pursed, hands on hips. The whole vibe of this group was off today. Gussie and Celeste were not talking to each other. Ina was unusually cranky. "Where are we going to set up the quilting frame?" she said. "And I'm teaching that Advanced Beginning Quilting class in this room beginning at six."

"Of course I know. I'm in your class, remember? You could have picked a better week to start, but I'm coming anyway. I might be late."

"It's only six nights out of your life, Dewey. You can handle it."

It wasn't the remaining five weeks of the class, it was tonight that was causing the time crunch. I couldn't afford to take three hours out of my night and spend it in class. Especially now. But this class was only offered every six months and I needed to continue learning the basics of quilting. I'd finished the beginning section several weeks ago. After I took this class, Ina's description promised, I'd be able to sew any quilt block. I was still waiting to fall in love with quilting like my customers. So far I was only in "like."

Jenn and Vangie came in with the unwieldy box.

I said, "Will there be enough room for the class once the frame is set up?"

"There's plenty of room," Ina said.

She stiffened as voices flared from the middle of the room.

Celeste was standing, pointing her threaded needle at Gussie. "Get out of the garbage, Gussie."

Gussie reached farther under the table for a can that was scooting away from her. "Oh Celeste, leave me alone. I'm not hurting anyone."

Celeste said, "Pawing through another's trash is unseemly."

"Waste bothers me more than appearing unseemly," she mimicked Celeste perfectly. "You're the worst offender. I found a perfectly good foxglove plant in your trash yesterday."

Pearl said, "Oh that reminds me, Celeste. I planted those seeds you gave me…" She stopped because Celeste was focused on Gussie. She hadn't heard anything Pearl said.

"Dammit!" Celeste rose from her chair. "Stay away from my garbage."

Gussie was unbowed by her friend's ire. She pointed an empty water bottle at Celeste. "Separate your recyclables and I'll leave your garbage alone. I can't sleep at night knowing our landfills are full of your junk."

Celeste said, "Isn't it enough that I bring you my coffee grounds and vegetable trimmings for your compost pile?"

"You benefit from that compost, too," Gussie said.

Pearl said under her breath, "And you don't have to have the mess in your yard."

What was going on? Usually these two could have been the stars of Paula Abdul's "Opposites Attract" music video.

Ina intervened. "You two know better than to talk about the environment, ladies. Can we shelve it for now?" Ina said. "Let's get the quilt on the frame. We've got work to do."

She opened the box that contained the rods and rails for the quilt frame. I'd seen them assemble this years ago. It would take all four of them several hours to put the frame together and mount the quilt—the better part of the day.

Still clucking, Celeste joined her, laying out a wooden rail on the floor. Pearl took the quilt top to the ironing board and sprayed it with water. The iron came on with a click.

Gussie reluctantly put down the Diet Coke can she was holding, and swept her finds into her tote bag, which she stashed under the table. She started toward the group, but nearly tripped as a rail came rolling toward her.

"Watch what you're doing, Celeste," she said, steadying herself with a hand on a chair back.

"I want to get this finished."

"We've got all day."

"Perhaps you do, but I have many things to attend to. Tonight's the guild meeting and I've got to get home and feed Larry before that."

Today was all fits and starts that were hard for me to watch. It was like having your favorite grandmothers duking it out over stuffing recipes at Thanksgiving dinner.

I picked my way carefully to the whiteboard. I just needed to move Vangie's jobs to my list, then I could return to the sanctuary of my office before I was caught in the crossfire.

Things were quiet except for the hiss of the steam iron, and the sound of the wooden frame pieces banging together. Gussie took a rail from Celeste who was putting it in upside down.

"Let me do it," Gussie said.

Celeste hissed. "Gussie the hussy."

Pearl started to giggle, and I had to turn my head. Celeste's reaction was so over the top. The idea of a slutty Gussie just made me want to howl with laughter. Ina caught my eye.

Ina said, "Girls..."

Gussie got down on the floor to tighten a screw on the crosspiece. "Celeste thinks I'm trying to steal her boyfriend. She has it all wrong. Larry is just helping me with my finances."

"Drop it, Gussie," Celeste warned, her eyes narrowing, her long fingers trembling slightly.

Gussie either didn't see or chose to ignore Celeste's growing discomfort. "I'm not interested in Larry that way."

I'd heard bits and pieces about Larry, Celeste's boyfriend, but I'd never met him. She kept him under wraps. I knew Pearl's and Ina's husbands. Pearl sent Hiro to the shop at least once a week for something she forgot. Ina's husband, Dan, was like a member of the family, hosting the store's annual barbecue each summer.

Not so with Celeste. I knew she and Gussie were widows, and before now, I'd never considered their love lives. I'd just assumed they had none. But here they were fighting over the same man. Vangie loved to tease my dad that eligible men over age seventy were rarer than hen's teeth, but I'd never guessed that Celeste or Gussie were in the husband hunt.

I had to ease the tension. I realized I hadn't shared Lark's phone call. "Guess what?" I said as brightly as a child star on Letterman.

Ina picked up the thread. "What? Good news, I hope." Her voice was faux cheerful, like she used on her grandson when she wanted him to stop touching the threads out front.

"Great news," I said. "The Quilter Paradiso segment on *Wonderful World of Quilts* is going to air on Friday."

Pearl clapped her hands, nearly tipping the ironing board over. She caught the iron as it headed for the floor.

I continued, "The QP Original quilts were featured, so I bet one of your quilts will be on the air."

Gussie smiled. Celeste's face eased just a little. I guess the appeal of being on TV was universal.

"I don't know if it was Celeste's or Gussie's scrap quilt or one of Ina's, but Kym told me she talked about the QPO quilts in the piece."

"Dewey, I want you to see something." Vangie was in the doorway, beckoning me. She was wiggling her eyebrows, and held a finger to her lips, like she was some sort of spy. I followed her, glad to be out of that room.

I heard Ina and Gussie speculating about whose quilt would be on air. As I closed the door, Pearl was promising that Hiro would tape the show and make them all copies.

In our office, Vangie gestured to her monitor. "What do you think?"

The new Quilter Paradiso website filled her screen. Of course with Vangie in charge, the site had a sixties flair, but she'd managed to capture my style, too. Our logo, quilts hanging on a line strung between two palm trees, had been stylized. The palm fronds were lime green, and the tree trunks hot pink. The quilts were brightly colored, with paisleys and stripes and marimekko-style flowers predominating.

"Already?" I asked in amazement. "I love the look."

She shrugged. "I had this prototype ready to go."

I moved the mouse around the home page. "I like the QP Originals section."

"Click through. A picture of the quilt and then a picture of the corresponding kit comes up." Vangie cracked her knuckles as she stared at her computer screen. She wasn't as secure in her abilities as I thought she should be. "It's not live yet. You can't hurt anything."

"Awesome." I moved around the pages, enjoying the top labels she'd used and the background. Vangie knew that quilters used the Internet, but the levels of expertise varied widely. The site was clearly marked and easy to maneuver.

I said, "I'm glad there's nothing blinking."

"Yeah, well, I didn't want any of our older customers to have a stroke," Vangie said.

"It's cool. When will the site be up and running?"

"I'm shooting for Friday morning. Right after the show airs. Some viewers are going to go straight to their computer when it ends."

This was happening so fast. I felt the butterflies of undone tasks start up again. "We'll have orders as early as Friday?"

Vangie smiled. "We might."

I stuffed the panic rising in my throat. How would we handle virtual customers and real ones at the same time? "We could use more staff. I wish there was time to put an ad in the quilt guild newsletter looking for more help."

Vangie said, "You could post a note on their listserv. Not everyone in the guild uses it, but those who do will spread the word. Remember how fast we got fabric donations when we were making those charity quilts?"

"That's a good idea. Someone out there has to be willing to work for what I can afford to pay."

"Nothing, you mean?" Vangie said with a grin.

"I'll give them a great discount," I said.

Vangie smirked and we returned to our computers. We were good together, able to work in the same small place without disturbing each other. Our rule was no talking for at least fifty minutes each hour. Then we took a stretching break and chatted.

I glanced out at Jenn. I could keep an eye on what was going on in the store from the window in front of my desk. When this had been my grandfather Dewey's hardware store, it had been the accounts payable window. One of the glass panels slid in front of the other, and a narrow wooden ledge jutted out into the store. The carpenters could rest their elbows while paying their invoices. Now, it was just handy to make sure my customers were being taken care of.

Everything looked quiet. Jenn was scheduled by herself for the morning until Kym came in later.

Half an hour later, an e-mail came from Lark. She'd sent a video clip from the show.

"Vang, look at this."

Vangie grunted, a signal that she was in the middle of something I shouldn't interrupt.

The video clip was only about thirty seconds. It opened with a pan of the store. My mother would have been proud. The store looked just like it did when she was alive.

I watched Kym closely. I had to admit she looked good on TV. I grinned. Probably because of her big head.

An idea was forming. I replayed the clip to make sure. This was too good. I needed Vangie to get started on this right away.

I scooted my chair over to her, carrying the laptop. "Vangie!" I waved my fingers in front of her monitor. Her face darkened.

I pulled her iPod connection out of the computer. "I need you for a moment. Take a look at what Lark sent."

She sighed and hit the save button on her computer. She glanced at me and then at the laptop.

"Whoop-dee-do. Kym and Lark. I can wait 'til Friday."

I set the laptop in front of her. "You've got to watch this. It's just a short clip."

I played the video. Lark and Kym stood in front of our cutting table. The wall behind was a kaleidoscope of color.

Lark said, "We're here in San Jose at Quilter Paradiso, talking to the floor manager, Kym Pellicano."

Vangie snorted. "Gave herself a promotion, I see."

I said, "Sssh. Watch this bit."

On the screen, Kym was explaining her method of appliqué.

"There," I yelled, pointing. I stopped the playback and touched the screen. "Check out that cord she always has attached to her apron. She's got a pair of those fancy scissors hanging from it. The ones with the palm-tree handle."

"I don't know why that's not outlawed," Vangie said, unconsciously crossing her arms across her chest. "Hanging scissors on a cord pinned to your boob? The idea gives me the shivers."

"Focus. Wait until you see what she does with them."

I pressed the play button and Kym leaned over, still talking, and clipped a thread hanging from Lark's sleeve. Lark looked startled at being touched and then miffed. She moved a step away from Kym, nearly cutting her out of the frame.

Vangie said, "She did *not* just do that."

"Oh yes, she did. Kym, Super Scissor Girl. She's ready to cut any errant thread."

"You never know when there's a thread-hanging emergency." Vangie laughed. "Lark looks pissed."

"Probably because she couldn't reshoot. But the point is, everyone's going to see Kym trimming Lark's clothing with those very sharp, very small ... very expensive scissors."

Light came on in Vangie's eyes. "You're thinking our customers are going to want those scissors."

I nodded. "Bingo. It always happens. Lark demonstrates something on the show and we get calls." The best way to make a profit was to have merchandise come in and go out again quickly. The specialty scissors was the perfect scenario. The TV show would create the desire. The scissors were unique; no other store would have them in stock. All I needed was to outlay the cash to buy the inventory.

"I want to order us at least a hundred pair and sell them this weekend."

Vangie whistled. "They were expensive. We had a half dozen in stock last summer. Took us six months to get rid of them. If I remember, they retailed at seventy bucks apiece."

Vangie was protesting, but her fingers were moving around, pulling up a browser and searching. "I don't remember the name of the company that makes them. It was a small scissor company back East, wasn't it?"

I said, "I don't know. But here's a challenge for you. You find them, get me a gross here by Saturday, and I will buy you lunch for a month."

"Deal."

I stuffed down the thought that I didn't have time for this. Opportunity never came at a convenient time. Retail was all about having the right inventory in stock when the fickle customer wanted it. I was betting these scissors were going to be the hottest sellers this weekend.

I only hoped I was right.

FOUR

THE MORNING WENT BY quickly. I worked on checking in the new inventory. In the last month, Vangie and I had made a list of every tool and notion used in the QP Original quilts and maxed out the credit card ordering them. Now the items were here, but needed to be counted and priced. The sixteen-page invoice didn't match the items in the box, so I was struggling.

From my desk, I could see that there weren't many customers today, a fact I could live with, knowing that many were waiting for the sale day. We'd make up the lost revenue then.

Vangie worked on her computer, her headphones firmly in place. I could hear The Doors blasting through. I waved to get her attention, and she stopped her MP3 player.

I needed to vent. "We're going to have to get going to decorate the store on Thursday, Vang," I said.

"That's my bowling night."

"Sorry, but I don't see a break in the schedule all week. We've got to hang up all the QPO samples and make sure the merchandising's done right."

She groaned. "I can't miss. It's a tournament."

"It'll be fun. We'll crank up the music, and turn on all the lights and burn through. I bet it won't take us more than a couple of hours. I'll have you in and outta here by ten."

"Nine," she said.

I went back to my computer screen and Vangie returned to hers.

Vangie went to lunch around one, promising me a burrito when she returned. Soon after, I heard Jenn calling to me. I slid the window open.

Her ears were red, so I knew she was flustered. "Dewey, I'm alone on the floor and I need some help."

Crap. While I'd had my head down, the store had filled up. I left my desk in a hurry. Four women stood patiently at the cutting table, chatting amiably, even though they were most likely strangers. Quilters weren't shy. One was loudly expressing her frustration with sewing on flannel. The listener was offering hints on special needles and batting. The other two were perusing a book. I heard one of them mention Fibonacci numbers.

There was no sign of my sister-in-law. "Where's Kym?" I asked.

Jenn smiled at a customer, but I could see that she was upset. She unfurled fabric, the bolt clunking on the table as she flipped it roughly. "I checked the schedule. Kym should have been here at twelve-thirty," she said.

A red-haired customer called to me from the checkout counter, "You want my money or what?"

"Of course I'll take your money," I said, returning her grin and joining her at the cash register. I rang up her sale.

I didn't move for the next half-hour, just ringing up sales while Jenn cut fabric and grabbed notions. We finally cleared the store of all customers.

"Why does that always happen?" I asked. "There's either a crowd or nobody."

"Don't you know? They stand on the sidewalk until they see others entering, then everyone jumps in at once," Jenn said, illustrating her point with extravagant gestures. Away from Kym, I liked Jenn. "And once they're together, it's a feeding frenzy. People buy because others are buying—it's as simple as that."

I laughed. I stretched, pulling one arm over my head, then the other, working out the kinks.

There were at least twenty bolts of fabric sitting next to the cutting table, and the fat quarters were in complete disarray.

"Can you handle putting away the fabric?" I asked.

"I would, but I'm already late. The kids'll be home."

"Did you try Kym's cell?" I said. She was probably having lunch with Kevin. I didn't want to think what they might be up to. What Buster and I weren't up to.

Then I remembered. "Oh, I forgot. No cell phone." Kym was our resident Luddite.

"I know," Jenn said. "Even my eight-year-old has a cell."

I struggled to keep from expressing my opinion about third graders with cell phones. "I could try Kevin's," I said.

The bell on the front door chimed, and Kym entered from the street.

"You two just standing around gabbing?" she said. "Good thing the store's not busy."

Jenn and I looked at one another and burst out laughing.

"You just missed a major rush, Kymster," Jenn said. I laughed harder because I knew Kym hated it when Jenn called her 'Kymster.'

Kym frowned. Jenn waved goodbye and headed off for her purse.

Kym followed her into the kitchen to stow her own purse, and called back to me. "I've got to use the rest room, Dewey. Can you stay up front until I get back?"

What choice did I have? I didn't like to leave the floor unattended. Shoplifting quilters were rare, but I couldn't afford any missing inventory right now.

When I heard the bathroom door open, I yelled down the hall to Kym, "Check out the whiteboard in the classroom before you come back. I want you to pick some jobs to do."

I was putting away the last bolt of fabric when Gussie came out of the classroom, in a big hurry. Her hair was standing straight up, the way it did when she had been nervously running her fingers through it. She was carrying her tote bag full of scraps and recyclables. She didn't seem to see me, intent on something outside. I saw a yellow car waiting at the curb.

Gussie didn't see Celeste either, trailing her. She started when Celeste put a hand on her. Gussie looked out the door as though that was where she wanted to be.

I took a hand appliqué book off the shelf that was in the machine quilting section. I found others out of place, and stopped to straighten them. I took my time. I needed to make sure I didn't end up with a catfight in my store. With my luck, we'd have another rush, just as these two were heating up.

Celeste's eyes flicked to the car outside, and her mouth thinned. "Aren't you going to help us finish mounting the quilt?" Celeste asked. It seemed like quilting was the last thing on her mind.

"You don't want me around," Gussie said. Her voice was so sad, I was embarrassed to be a witness.

Celeste crossed her arms across her chest. Her tone of voice was harsh, as though Gussie were a recalcitrant child. "I'm trying to help you. You don't know Larry like I do."

Gussie found her voice. "You're selfish, Celeste. You've never wanted me to do well. As long as I could be the poor neighbor, the one who always needs help, you like me. But the minute I stand on my own two feet, you're threatened."

Celeste was unbowed by Gussie's accusations. "Larry is not the man to help you stand on your own, Gussie."

I felt tears well up in my eyes. These two had been friends for longer than I was alive. What was it like to have a friendship for that long and then have it fall apart over a man?

Gussie sighed heavily, her whole body shaking. She pushed past Celeste and, moving faster than I'd ever seen her, got into the passenger side of the yellow car at the curb.

Celeste stood on the street watching them leave, her mouth wide open in surprise.

I went to the door and opened it for Celeste.

"May they both rot in hell," she said. She walked past me, head held high. Her back was so tight, I could practically see her shoulder blades touching under her jacket. She ignored Kym as they passed each other in the hall.

"What's her deal?" Kym asked.

"Man trouble. Have you ever met Celeste's boyfriend?" I asked.

Kym shook her head. "I don't think Celeste has ever come in with anyone besides the Stitch 'n' Bitch group."

"I think he just picked up Gussie. Celeste was not happy," I said.

Kym shrugged. "I hope he's worth it."

When I got back to the desk, Vangie had returned from lunch with a burrito for me. I took it into the kitchen to get a Diet Coke and eat my lunch at the kitchen table. My desk was too cluttered.

Kevin came in while I was finishing.

"Hey, sis."

Kevin was a good-looking guy, blessed with thick hair and expressive brown eyes. Unlike Dad, who went to work every day in matching Dickies, Kevin dressed nothing like the construction worker he was, favoring suspenders and blue button-downs. If it weren't for the yellow carpenter's rule on his belt, an affectation he'd started when he was ten, he could easily have been mistaken for a money manager or corporate banker.

He dressed for the job his wife wanted him to have: CEO of Pellicano Construction.

Mom's death had affected both of our professional lives. For me, it gave me a new career that I was beginning to like. For him, it meant only delays. Dad had been on schedule to leave the construction business to Kevin in two years, but now Dad was so entrenched, it looked like he would never retire. Downtime held no allure for my father any more.

Kevin struck a casual pose, leaning against the refrigerator, but we both knew he didn't show up at my office casually. Not lately.

I said, "Kym didn't tell me you were here."

"She doesn't know. I dropped her off, but decided to come back after stopping at the hardware store. I wanted to make sure you weren't mad at her for being late."

I didn't want to let him, or her, off the hook. "It left me in a bit of a bind. This is a busy week, you know."

Kevin's eyes flicked to my face and away. "She's trying to do the right thing, Punk."

I lost patience with him. "What the heck does that mean?"

He shook his head. "Just let me say, whatever she does, she's always got the best interests of the shop at heart."

I didn't like the sound of this. I searched my brother's face, looking for the guy who would tell me anything.

It hurt to know we were so far apart.

When he'd met Kym, he'd confided in me in the first flush of love and laid out his plans for a life with Kym. I'd been happy for him. It took a few years of life with Kym before I realized that there wasn't much room for me in this marriage.

Kevin wasn't interested in doing the *New York Times* crossword, or playing Boggle, or catching the latest Harry Potter movie at the opening midnight show anymore. The only books he read had titles like *How to Manage the Unmanageable* and *The Millionaire Inside*. Kym's only hobby was quilting and Kevin indulged her, driving hundreds of miles each weekend to check out guild shows and quilt shops.

Maybe my first clue should have been when Kym nixed his suggestion that I be his best man.

Things got more complicated when I started dating Buster, who'd been his best man. The Kym-approved best man.

"You seen Buster lately?" I asked. Buster had mentioned they kept missing connections.

"He doesn't talk to me about you, if that's what you were worried about."

Where was that coming from?

I ignored his jibe. "Maybe you two just need to have a basketball night together," I said. "You and Buster, the hoop outside my place. What do you say?"

"I can't this week, I'm pretty busy."

Okay. At least I'd tried. We were talking around what he'd come to say. I couldn't wait for him to begin. "So why are you here?"

"Kym wanted me to talk to you about some of her ideas here at the store. You've been ignoring her."

I rubbed my eyes. I didn't want Kevin to see how angry I was. I pushed back out of my chair. Sitting down and having this conversation wasn't working. I stood and leaned my butt against the table. That helped to put me on a more equal footing.

I crossed my arms across my chest. "Kym should not involve you in the store."

"It's the family business, Dewey."

"I don't tell you how to run the construction business. Mom left the quilt shop to me." Were we going to fight about that again? "I'm sorry if that doesn't sit right with you ..."

"I'm perfectly fine with that. It's just Kym." He didn't look fine. He looked miserable. He mopped his face with his hand.

I pushed forward, ignoring the pain just behind my breastbone. "You and I know she's not happy here."

"She used to be," he said quietly.

"Quilter Paradiso is not being run the way it used to be, Kev," I said, spitting out the words. He winced. I tried to dial back the sarcasm. "I can't be competitive if I keep doing things the way Mom did. I've got a dozen quilt shops breathing down my neck."

My business practices were not his concern. He finally got to his reason for being there. "Why are you refusing to publish her pattern when you're doing everyone else's? Even people who are not employees?"

"Is that what she told you?" My face flushed with anger. "Kevin, she missed the deadline. By a mile. She never gave us her notes. It takes time to write the directions, edit them, and try them out."

He was silent.

I continued, "The others had their work in a month ago."

I let what I'd said sink in. In his work, he had to meet deadlines. He had people counting on him to be efficient and do what he said he was going to do. On time.

This wasn't really about the pattern. "Maybe she'd be better off somewhere else," I said.

He didn't look in my direction, keeping his eyes focused on the state workman's comp poster. The air between us was electric. I'd said the unsayable.

Finally he said, "You know she thought she'd be running this place someday."

That was the heart of the matter. Kym, queen of Quilter Paradiso.

I said, "Things change. You'd be doing her a favor if you let her know that."

FIVE

THE AFTERNOON WAS RUINED. I had a hard time concentrating on my work after my argument with Kevin. Vangie went to the quilt guild meeting around five-thirty to leave some flyers about the sale. The Santa Clara Valley Quilt Association met in a church several blocks away, once a month on Tuesdays.

I called Buster after she left.

"Hey, don't forget I'll be at the store until nine," I said. "It's your turn to make dinner."

Buster's voice boomed. "Only if you're counting yesterday's pizza as your contribution."

"Absolutely. I paid."

"I'm beginning to notice a pattern here," Buster said.

"If it has to do with my cooking nights always involving take-out, I'd say that's why you're the detective."

"More like the stooge," he laughed.

I wanted to tell him about Kevin but decided to do it in person. I didn't want him to feel like he had to take sides. I could tell a lot from his body language. "What are you going to do before I get home?"

"Laundry. If I can use your machine."

Most men who wore a dress shirt every day, like Buster did, would have their shirts professionally done, but not my man.

I said, "Didn't you just wash everything? I swear you get off on the smell of detergent."

"Some people wash their clothes every week. Hard to believe, I know, when your method of saving it all up for a month is so enticing."

I ignored his teasing. "So it'll be just you and your laundry."

"And then the iron and the Giants game."

"Wild man."

"You could come home and distract me," he said, his voice getting softer and deeper. "Only you can save me from a night of washing and ironing."

"I promise to be there at a quarter after nine," I said, hanging up and laughing.

I glanced at the clock. I was almost late for Ina's class. I rushed across the hall.

Within the first few minutes, I was in trouble. Ina'd started out by giving us an overview of the class, telling us we would learn to rotary cut accurately, and piece complex blocks. She'd asked for questions, and I'd obliged. One too many times.

Ina stood in the front of the room, behind the wooden podium that nearly dwarfed her. She'd changed into a flowing jacket she'd made herself from the rayon batiks Mom had brought back from Indonesia. The violet hues brightened her steel-gray hair. Ina packed a lot of authority in her compact figure. She had been a high school math teacher before taking up quilting.

"There are no stupid questions, Dewey," Ina said. Her expression said something else: *How about shutting up and getting to work, Dewey.*

I'd asked her a series of questions about quilting. But I wasn't finished. "Why don't we just use templates?"

"Rotary cutting is quicker and more accurate," Ina said with a finality meant to put an end to my stalling. "You can learn to cut any shape. Tonight we will be doing diamonds for our eight-pointed star."

Every table was filled except for one right in front of Ina. Eleven students, twelve if all showed up. I recognized some of them from the Beginning class. Mom had contended that the beginning class was the most important one, gaining the store new customers, but more importantly, to her, teaching a skill that could change lives. To her, quilting was more than a hobby. It was an art, and had the same healing powers that painting or sculpting did. Her mission had been to teach people to quilt.

I was trying to keep that mission going. In order to do that, I had to learn to quilt myself.

I was sitting at a table in the back of the room under the windows, farthest away from the door. My tablemate was shuffling her fabrics around, hands fluttering. Our instructions had been to bring two fabrics that coordinated. She'd paired a bright green polka dot on pink with a multicolored stripe. My eyes went out of focus looking at them. She'd confessed earlier that she was pretty sure she would never make anything as beautiful as the class samples hanging over Ina's head. I tried to reassure her, but I knew how she felt.

Ina asked the students to introduce themselves. The final introduction was interrupted when the door flew open. A man with a shock of red hair burst in. He looked myopically around the room, and then headed for the empty table. He was carrying a QP bag, a backpack, and a metal toolbox. We all watched in silence as he took out a folding carpenter's rule and a Swiss army knife. He squared the edge of a metal T-ruler on his table.

I perked up. This was my kind of quilter. He had tools I knew. A sewing machine had a cord and a motor but I didn't have the same affinity for it that I had for my router or band saw.

Women's work. The phrase passed through my brain as I looked at the female heads in front of me. Gray curls directly in front of me, middle-of-the-back, thin chestnut hair to the right, an expensively streaked-blonde bob to my left.

A man in the class changed the atmosphere. Some of the women sat up straighter. A few smoothed their outfits, and one grandmother took out a jewel-encrusted mirror and re-applied her lipstick.

Ina was not daunted. She looked expectantly at Kym, who'd escorted the man in.

"This is Tim Shore," Kym said. "He's just decided to take the class tonight." She smiled at him, totally enamored. "I'm off now," she said, unnecessarily. The class bade her goodbye as a group. I wondered how much Kevin would say to her about our talk.

"Welcome," Ina said. She let him introduce himself.

"I got the quilting bug from my grandmother," he said. "God rest her soul. I sleep under the quilt she made me every night."

He looked around the room. All eyes were on him now, his charms on display. The entire room sighed when he finished by saying he wanted to make a quilt in her memory. I saw one women wipe away a tear.

Ina started her lecture, flipping over her standing chart to show us the next step. "This week," she announced, "we are strip piecing."

"What time does the stripper arrive?" I shouted, getting a girly giggle from some of my classmates.

"Eight o'clock," Ina said without missing a beat.

She talked quickly, to forestall more wisecracking. "We will sew together long strips of fabric, and re-cut them to use in our blocks. That is the essence of strip piecing."

She held up the yellow-handled rotary cutter. "*This* is our friend."

She was talking to me. After finding a quilter dead from a cut inflicted by a blade like this six months ago, I'd avoided using the rotary cutter. But I needed to get comfortable with it in order to wait on my customers.

Ina rapped the podium for attention. "Now," she said, in her best Dr. Ruth imitation, "we are going to practice our stripping."

"Pick up your rotary cutter, and hold it like so." She was ignoring my silent pleas to stop channeling the German sex therapist. It was all part of her shtick. Poor Tim. Women's humor.

"You will notice the curve of the cutter," she said, moving her hand salaciously down the cutter. Everyone else laughed. I actually blushed. Tim's ears were turning red at the tips.

"Feel how nicely your hand fits. Now push the red button. You're ready for action."

The entire class picked up their cutters. After a nasty glance from Ina, I did, too. The plastic handle was cool, not at all sinister. I took a deep breath.

"Now lay your fabric out on the mat like this," Ina said, demonstrating.

I straightened my fabric, first creasing the fold and aligning the selvage edges. I smoothed and tugged, so the ends would meet. Out of the corner of my eye, I saw Ina stopping at each table, giving hints and reassurance. I picked up the ruler and laid it perpendicular to my fabric, lining up the edges with a line on the ruler.

Through the closed windows, I could hear voices in the alley. Must be Mrs. Unites' workers taking out the trash at the burrito shop.

"Are we supposed to cut a three-inch piece or two-and-one half?"

My tablemate was crowding my elbow, asking her question to me. Ina'd told us earlier that she wanted the students to address her with questions, not each other. According to her, that's how bad information got disseminated. But she was across the room showing Tim Shore the difference between his metal ruler and her plastic one. I checked the handout Ina had given us. I pointed at the line of text that called for two-and-one-half-inch strips.

"Thanks," she said. Moving away, she gave me space to cut. I waited until she was back at her own mat. I tried not to think about accidentally nicking her if she got close again. When I was sure she wasn't going to interrupt me again, I picked up my rotary cutter. I felt the heft in my hand and clicked open the safety catch several times. It snapped shut tightly. All I had to do was put the blade to the fabric and cut.

I took another deep breath.

The store phone rang. The ringer was off on the classroom extension, but I could hear the bell faintly through the wall of the classroom. I tried to find the two-and-one-half-inch mark on the ruler. The numbers swam in front of me. The phone rang again. And again. I couldn't find the right line. After the sixth ring, I left my table, leaving my fabric uncut on the mat. Ina caught my eye and shook her head. I ignored her and reached for the phone.

Ina got there first. She put her small fist over the receiver.

"Do *not* get that, Dewey."

"Vangie must be busy." The phone trilled. "Or not back from guild."

Ina rapped my forearm. "It's probably just another Halloween mom, looking for black and white striped spandex, so her precious nine-year-old can dress up as David Lee Roth."

I stifled a giggle. Ina's pale green eyes were flashing, so I knew laughing was not a good idea, but the image of a miniature David Lee Roth was a funny one.

"No phone call is that important. That's why I ban cell phones." She pointed to the basket that sat on a small table by the entrance to the room. Ina didn't trust people to just turn them off, she insisted people empty their pocketbooks. We almost always had a panicked phone call the next morning from a student who left hers behind. I'd stashed mine in my office, so as not to incur her unreasonable cell phone wrath.

The phone stopped ringing. I went back to my fabric and the dreaded cutter. Ina moved away to answer a question.

The door opened. I was surprised to see Vangie enter. Ina glanced up sharply from across the room. She had a strict closed-door policy when it came to her classes. Grim-faced, Vangie made a beeline to my table. She tilted her head, indicating I should come out into the hall. I didn't look at Ina as I followed her out of the classroom, but I felt her eyes on my back.

"Was the phone for me?" I asked.

Vangie look startled and shook her head "Um … I don't know. I didn't get to it in time."

I quickly saw why she looked so disturbed. A uniformed police officer was standing quietly in the hall near the back door. I recognized him as the neighborhood liaison officer. Wong. He had jet black hair cut so short, I could see his scalp. If it wasn't for the uniform, I would have thought he was still in high school. I guess that was a sign of being thirty. Everyone younger than you was of indeterminate age.

Vangie was overreacting, but I knew she didn't like the police. As a teen, she'd felt targeted because of her Mexican heritage, and she couldn't let go of the idea that most police officers had hidden agendas. She made a small exception for Buster.

I put out my hand. "Officer Wong? Is this about the Neighborhood Watch? I swear I'll make the meeting next week." I'd been ignoring the e-mail notices about October being Crime Prevention month.

I knew he wasn't here about that, but, as long as my mouth was busy, my mind would not acknowledge why a grim-faced policeman was standing in my store. I only hoped it wasn't as bad as I thought.

Vangie spoke before he did. "Mrs. Unites found a dead body in the alley, Dewey."

My stomach fell. I couldn't have heard her right. "Someone died in my alley?"

The alley between QP and the burrito place began in the small gravel parking lot behind the store and ended at the street. Not wide enough to drive a car through, it was home to the dumpster and recycling bins. The shortcut was popular with teenagers on their way to Starbucks. And the homeless.

"Is it Juan? Our homeless guy?" I said to Wong. "Maybe he's not dead. When he's asleep out there, sometimes I swear he looks like a bundle of rags. Usually if you talk to him, he'll move on." I looked at my watch. It was nearly seven PM. That was early—Juan usually waited for the store to close before he went down for the night. His was often the last face I saw when I left the store late at night.

That would be bad, but a homeless guy dying of natural causes was not the worst thing that could happen. Please, please, please, I repeated silently, like a kid hoping for the claw to grab the toy once and for all.

Wong said, "I know him, too. This is not Juan, and he is definitely not sleeping."

"Then who?" I asked.

Wong's lips were pressed tightly together. I wondered if this was his first body. If so, I was two up on him.

"I don't know at this time. The medical examiner will retrieve his wallet when he arrives. Until then, I'd like assistance with a visual identification," he said. "Would one of you be willing to come out and view the deceased?"

Vangie blanched and shook her head. She cracked her thumb knuckle, making my skin crawl. Right about now, she was probably wishing she'd never heard of Quilter Paradiso.

I had to be the one to go out there. My store. My alley. My body.

I glanced back at the closed door to the classroom. If the medical examiner was coming, the alley would soon be full of people, lights, and noise. There was no way to keep this from the students. I could only hope to prolong their time in class, so they'd be interested enough to come back next week.

Police investigations took as long as they took, and they were never quick. It was going to be a long night. The first order of business was to keep Vangie occupied.

"Can you make us some coffee, Vang?"

"Coffee?" Vangie's tone was disbelieving. She looked at Officer Wong, who was holding the back door open, waiting for me. "Okay," she said.

She disappeared into the kitchen. I heard the water run and the refrigerator door open and close.

I followed Officer Wong.

The air was cool, but the night was clear. The sun had set since I'd last been out, and the sky was navy blue. The back parking lot was brightly lit from the flood lamp at the end of the building. The lot was filled to capacity with eight cars pointing into the vine-covered fence. Vangie's bike was locked to the small metal railing that lined the concrete steps.

Everything looked normal. But that was only because I couldn't see into the alley from here.

We turned to our left. I saw the edge of the green dumpster. My heart was thumping wildly. I glanced up at the classroom windows that looked out over the alley. Luckily the windows were closed, and the curtains Mom had sewn were drawn tight. The last thing I

54

needed was for those people to know there was a dead body out here.

A pile of broken-down cardboard lay in front of the recycle bin. Mrs. Unites had obviously been getting rid of boxes when she came out here. She was standing near the back of her restaurant, talking to a female officer. I gave her a faint smile.

Three more steps, and I saw the man lying on the ground. He was sprawled on the concrete pad, between the blue recycle bin and the green metal dumpster. His jacket was a bit worn, but his pants and shirt looked clean. I had the silly thought that he must have been like Buster, fussy about his clothes. His hair was thin, the brown strands lank across his forehead. His nose was long and angular.

The dead man looked as though someone had tripped him, and he'd been too tired to get up. He'd rolled onto one side and was staring one-eyed at me. I shuddered. He didn't look like he'd died a serene death.

I was relieved. "I don't recognize him. How do you think he died?"

"See that grimace?" Wong said, pointing with his pen. "He was poisoned."

SIX

My worst fear. Not just a police investigation, but a murder investigation. I reached for my phone to call Buster, but I'd left it at my desk to comply with Ina's no cell rule. Damn.

Wong was watching me closely. I took a deep breath and sat on the steps.

A black sedan pulled up. Wong straightened his belt that carried his gun, radio, phone, and assorted other tools. A short man with black hair slicked back from his high forehead got out of the car. He conferred with a trench-coated woman with shoulder-length blonde hair who'd been driving. They split up, with the man heading toward me and the woman finding her way to Mrs. Unites.

He came at me smiling, his worn cowboy boots causing him to list slightly. He put out a hand. A gold bracelet encircling his wrist caught the light as it fell into the meat of his palm. I got up, and he introduced himself as Anton Zorn, looking deep into my eyes as though he was trying to read the writing on my soul. I was glad he was on the law enforcement side, because if he used his charms for evil, no woman would stand a chance.

Wong said, "This is Ms. Pellicano. She owns the fabric store."

"Quilt shop," I said automatically.

"I'm very sorry for your inconvenience, Ms. Pellicano," Zorn said. "How many people are inside?" Zorn asked, addressing Wong.

Wong looked at me for the answer. I counted on my fingers. "Vangie and Ina. Twelve people in the classroom. Minus me. Thirteen all together. My sister-in-law went home a little after six."

"We'll need to talk to everyone," Zorn said. "I'll need your sister-in-law's number." Even though I felt like I had his attention, his eyes never stopped moving. That was a neat trick. He was processing the scene in front of him. Me standing by the steps of my shop. Mrs. Unites with the other homicide detective standing near the back door of the burrito place. The dead man between us.

I said. "I'd be happy to give you that. Do you think my class will be able to continue?"

I knew as I said it, it wasn't possible. The noise level out here was getting louder as more police personnel arrived. The alley ran alongside the classroom. Even with the windows closed, pretty soon everyone would know what was going on. I would have to tell them.

He didn't answer me. "Who do these cars belong to?" Zorn pointed to the QP parking lot.

I took inventory. My car was out on the street in front of Ina's. Our policy was to leave the parking lot open. "The students. They park out here and come in through the back door. They're carrying a load—sewing machines and all their class supplies."

He was watching my face closely. The man never seemed to blink. "What time was that?"

"Class started at six."

"You're saying there was a lot of activity out here just before six?" he continued.

The shift in his tone of voice was subtle, but I knew the interrogation had begun. "Yes. No, wait, I don't really know. I stayed in my office until the last possible moment." I decided not to mention that I'd been talking to Buster. Cops were as territorial as those Discovery Channel meerkats. "I got to class just as it was starting. One student was late."

Officer Wong had his notebook out, and was writing down what I said, but Zorn was asking the questions. He seemed confident in his memory. "Who was late?"

"I think his name is Tim Shore. Would you like a copy of the class list?"

He nodded. "That would be helpful, with their contact information. In fact, why don't you give me that information for everyone who was here today, say, after three o'clock?"

Wong said, "There's no telling what people saw. We need to know if anyone saw him, and how he was behaving just before he died."

Zorn cast the eager-beaver Wong a look that shut him up.

"Why in my alley?" I swallowed hard. I hated playing the victim, but I really wanted to cry out pitifully, why me?

He narrowed his eyes at me. "That's right. Seems like a funny place to die, don't you think?"

I swallowed my self-pity. I knew better than to go there with a homicide detective. I ignored his attempt to engage me in speculation.

I put on a brisk tone, signaling the end to this casual chat. "There's coffee inside, and you're welcome to use my kitchen." I knew they would need a place to talk to witnesses.

Zorn nodded. "Officer Wong, go, set me up. I'll want to chat with everyone one at a time. Let's keep them from talking to each other." He walked over to his partner, who was questioning Mrs. Unites.

I headed back inside the store. Wong followed me. The smell of brewing coffee wafted out.

I'd only gotten a few feet inside when the classroom door slammed against the wall so hard it bounced. I jumped back, stepping on the policeman's heavy black shoe and throwing myself off balance. Wong steadied me until I got myself upright. Ina came out of the classroom, eyes flashing.

I got a glimpse of my fellow students, hunched over their fabric. Mine was forlornly sitting on my green cutting mat. The woman closest to the door could see the police uniform. I saw the question on her face.

I reached for the classroom door, smiling at the students in a way I hoped was reassuring. Tim Shore caught my eye and frowned.

I said, "No worries, folks. Keep working. Ina will be right back." I closed it. Wong could break the news to them in a few minutes. I wanted to keep things as normal as I could for as long as I could.

Ina was fuming. "What's so important out here, Dewey?" She inhaled, ready to give me her best shot for ditching her class. She stopped short when she saw Officer Wong. She looked to me for explanation. "What's going on?"

"It's nothing, Ina. Someone died in the alley."

"That's nothing?" Ina yelled. Ina sometimes thought she was my moral compass. She worried that I'd gotten cynical after finding that body last spring.

I laid a gentling hand on her. "I meant nothing to do with us."

The young police officer's eyes were darting between the two of us. He'd probably thought he'd gotten the easy job—go talk to the little old ladies in the quilt shop. He was getting far more than he bargained for.

I knew cops liked nothing better than potential witnesses to a crime arguing. Who knew what might slip out?

"You can use my office." I told him.

He peeked into the cluttered room. My desk chair and Vangie's were the only clear space. Both our desks were overflowing, and the floor was a morass of merchandise that needed to be put out for sale. He sighed slightly. The sight disheartened me, too.

He backed down the hall. "I'd prefer the kitchen," he said, poking his nose in. Someone had wiped down the room earlier, and the tabletop was gleaming like a TV ad. Vangie was gone but she'd set the table with the thermal carafe, paper cups, and sugar packets. The fake Irish Cream nondairy cream bottle sat in the middle, a punctuation mark. Even though she wasn't happy about making coffee, she still did her best. I was surprised she hadn't gotten out the cookies.

I let him assert himself. "The kitchen it is." He walked in. Vangie was not there.

I hung back with Ina while he checked out the space. "What do you think I did? Arrange to have someone drop dead in the alley just to avoid my quilting class?"

Ina's arms were crossed tightly against her ample chest, a tic in her cheek making her look like she was chewing tobacco. Her face was creased with frustration. She knew this disruption was enough to sink her class for the night.

"If you could have, you would've. Don't bother to deny it."

"Someone died out there, Ina."

"Don't you get all pious on me," she said. "I'm sorry some poor soul died out there, and I will pray he has a better life in the next life than he did in this one, but you have to learn to quilt."

Sweet. If I'd just learn to quilt, my whole life would fall into place. The store would earn enough to pay me a decent salary. Kym would morph into the cool sister I never had. And Buster would drop the celibacy act. Yeah, right.

"Listen, Ina, there's a homicide investigation going on. This guy is going in there to tell your class that a detective is going to want to interview each one of them. The class will be over for tonight. Who knows if they'll want to come back for the next session? I'm going to lose revenue." I took a breath. Ina didn't know how much financial trouble the shop was in.

She considered, watching my face closely. She could tell something was going on. She unwound her arms and softened her tone. "I'm sorry. It's not your fault. I thought you were just out here, goofing off." She tsked loudly. "A dead body," she said in wonder. "Oh, Dewey."

There was so much angst in those two little words.

Ina set her shoulders back, her resolute nature taking over. She was used to handling messy situations. "I'll check the class calendar. If nothing else is scheduled for that Wednesday, I'll extend the class a week."

"Thank you," I said.

She went on her way. I poured coffee for Wong. Zorn strode into the room, like a surgeon whose team had the patient all prepped. He settled in a chair facing the doorway, took the cup from Wong and sipped.

"Go stay in that room, Wong. I don't want any talking. Just tell them what has happened, and send them in here, one at a time."

He turned to me, "Didn't you say there was another employee here?"

"Vangie Estrada."

"Let me talk to her first."

I found Vangie out front, wrestling with fabric bolts. I sent her in, ignoring her obvious reluctance, and retreated to my office. I called Buster, but got only voice mail. I left him a message to call me, without filling him in. The wall between my office and the kitchen was thin. I didn't want Zorn to hear me talking about the murder.

I plopped myself in Vangie's chair. From here, I could see into the hall and watch who went from the class into the kitchen. I could also try to listen in on the interrogations.

I had a knack for eavesdropping. It started with having three brothers who didn't want their sister around. I'd learned at an early age that knowledge was power, and if that meant lurking in corners, I was okay with that.

Vangie finished with Zorn and stuck her head in. She looked surprised to see me at her desk, but didn't ask why. "I'm going to close the register. We'll be shutting down early, right?"

I nodded, then I remembered something. "Hey, did you take your brownies home?"

Vangie smiled. "Ate them," Vangie said.

I looked at her askance.

"I couldn't leave them lying around," she said. "There were only two. Small, and very mild."

"Do we need to talk about this?" I said.

"Under control, boss, always," she said. She disappeared from the doorway, humming "In-A-Gadda-Da-Vida." Smart ass.

I checked my phone to see if Buster had called back. Nothing. The laundry or the Giants game must be enthralling.

I could hear more police cars arrive in the parking lot. I could hear Vangie out front, dropping coins into the metal cash box. I could hear Ina talking about rotary cutters.

But I could hear only murmurings from the kitchen. Until it was Tim Shore's turn.

I felt the office shudder as he closed the kitchen door with a bang. I jumped out of my chair and leaned into the wall to hear him, his deep voice carrying easily.

"Officer, I want to know why you continue to hold us." He was unhappy.

I crept closer.

Zorn's voice rumbled. "I'm investigating a death, sir. I understand this is not how you expected to spend your night, but I can't really help that. Just answer a few questions, and you can be on your way."

The first question Zorn asked was why he'd arrived late. Shore's excuse was traffic, the one thing no one could dispute in Silicon Valley. He gave Zorn excruciating details of his drive over the hill from Santa Cruz. He'd left before four, but there was a fender bender at the summit, which slowed him down. He hated to be late and so was concentrating on nabbing the last spot in the parking lot and getting in to class. He'd been so distracted, he hadn't noticed anything in the alley.

A class he thought should continue tonight.

He pleaded with Zorn. "I paid my money, and I want to learn how to quilt."

I looked him up in the database on Vangie's computer while he talked. One of the joys of computerizing the store's files was that I had records of all the transactions going back several years.

I looked in the customer screens. Tim Shore, there he was. I moved over to his sales history. The class was his first purchase.

Zorn was slowly explaining to him the fine points of an investigation. I remembered I'd promised him a list of students. I clicked back to the class, and viewed the other names enrolled. Most of the beginning quilters were new to the store. Our future customers. Sure enough, I didn't recognize most of the names. I generated the report with names, addresses, and phone numbers.

A note on the class list caught my eye. Alice Quick was enrolled, but she hadn't paid. Damn. That was against store policy. Either you paid in advance, or you weren't put in the class. It just made sense. I couldn't have someone filling up a spot that a paying customer might have taken.

My stomach roiled. This was one of those new rules I'd established. In years past, classes hadn't filled up. My mother was okay with low enrollment, holding sessions with as few as two students. She'd never considered that she might be losing money. I'd done an analysis and found that the break-even point was six students. Unless I had more than six paid students in my classes, I wasn't making money.

One of my staff had signed up Alice without paying. Against the rules. I looked to see whose initials were on the sale. KP. Kym Pellicano. It figured.

I went out to where Vangie was closing the drawer. She'd counted the cash and was putting the credit card slips in order. "Do we have any open tabs?" I asked. With this computer system, we could keep an open sale and add to it until the customer was finished or until the end of the class. Maybe Alice had paid tonight.

Vangie looked at the cash register screen and shook her head.

I said, "There's an unpaid student in the class."

Vangie raised her thick eyebrows. "Who signed her up?"

"One guess."

Vangie made a disgusted sound. I let her stew for a moment. I knew she would do what needed to be done.

"Would you please go collect from her?" I asked.

Vangie frowned. "I *hate* having to ask for money after the student is already in the class. It's embarrassing. Most of the time the customer forgets they haven't paid and then I feel like a bill collector."

"I hear you. I'll go with you."

She paused on her way to the classroom, and hesitated. Her brown eyes clouded and she cracked a knuckle. "Did you see the body?" she said quietly.

"Yeah."

A heaviness filled the air between us.

"Anyone we know?"

I shook my head. "Just a random guy."

"Okay." Vangie turned and walked away, her shoulders looking lighter than they had a moment ago. She liked to pretend she was a tough street kid, but underneath she believed in unicorns. Or maybe Puff the Magic Dragon.

I followed her back down the hall. The kitchen door was closed. I couldn't hear Shore, so Zorn must have a different student in there—maybe the granny whose lipstick was pumpkin orange.

We entered the classroom, which was quieter than I'd expected. Once inside, I could see why. Officer Wong was standing in the corner watching the group, killing any conversation. Most of the students had already packed their gear. They were seated quietly at the tables, tote bags refilled, sewing machines covered, tools put away. Tim Shore had hauled out his backpack and was stuffing his fabric into it with angry movements.

Ina was trying her best to amuse the customers, telling tales about the peccadilloes of famous quilters she'd taken classes from, but most were paying her no attention.

"I can't tell you her name, she's too famous," she was saying. "She brought her Shitza-poo-poo everywhere, even putting him in a basket on the podium while she gave her lecture. He barked through the whole thing. She didn't even notice. After the first fifteen minutes, I had such a headache."

Vangie went over to a woman with a name tag that read "Alice" and whispered in her ear. The customer got red-faced and got out her credit card. Vangie left to ring up her class fees and complete the charge. Both she and Alice were feeling awkward, a situation Kym had created. I felt another wave of irritation.

I called for the class' attention. All heads turned to me expectantly. "I am sorry about the inconvenience," I said.

"You need to talk to the police. They're not letting us move our cars," my tablemate said.

I looked to Wong. He shrugged. Police investigations trumped comfort.

The lipsticked granny called out. "How are we supposed to get home?"

I had to do something. "Let me go ask Detective Zorn. Maybe he can tell me how long it's going to be."

I crossed to the kitchen. The door was open, and I waited for Zorn to finish talking. A curly-haired brunette had replaced Tim Shore. As soon as I realized more flirting than questioning was going on, I broached the room.

"Listen," I said. "Is there something I can do to move things along? I mean, my customers need to get home."

"I'll talk to them," he said, watching the student leave. It was amazing how long it takes to watch a pretty woman walk away— and with such concentration. I was just about to jump into his line of vision when he followed her to the door.

He paused in the doorway to let me go through first. "They can go once I've talked to them."

He took a stance alongside Ina at the podium, legs spread and hands on his hips. Superman pose.

"People, this is an official police investigation. I appreciate your cooperation. I'm sorry to put you out, but your cars are in the midst of a crime scene and will not be released until the investigation is complete. That could take several hours. You may want to secure alternate means to get home."

The group turned to me, standing in the doorway. I held up my hands helplessly. "I'm sorry. You can use the phone in here or in my office to call husbands or friends to come get you. Just dial nine for an outside line."

That satisfied most of the customers, and they spread out and began to make their calls. Two remembered their cells and retrieved them from Ina's basket. Tim Shore was the lone holdout. He was angry and not budging. Typical male. Even though there was nothing to be done, he wanted something done.

Tim opened his mouth to complain.

I tried to forestall his scene. "I will provide cab fare for anyone who can't get a ride home."

His face slowly creased into a smile, and he gave me a thumbs-up. He was quite handsome when he smiled.

Vangie came into the classroom to give Alice her credit slip, just in time to hear my offer. When she heard what I'd said, she nudged me hard and whispered, "Do you know how expensive cabs are? We've got exactly eighty bucks in petty cash."

"Can you drive anyone home?" I whispered.

"On my bike?" Vangie laughed, and started humming the music to *The Wizard of Oz*. "That would be a sight."

I had the last laugh. "Isn't your bike part of the crime scene?"

She stopped humming. "Damn."

Ten minutes later, I was out on the sidewalk in front of the store. Vangie and I had carried out sewing machines and schlepped bags and rulers. Most of the students had gotten rides home from family members. Ina was dropping off the remainder.

Only Tim Shore was taking me up on my offer of cab money. I held out the petty cash. Tim plucked a twenty from my fingers, like I'd told him to *Go Fish*.

"I live in Santa Cruz," he said.

After a moment's consideration, he pulled out one more.

I saw Vangie roll her eyes. This was money I could ill afford to give away. I bit back a retort when he came back for one more. My heart sank, but I gave Vangie a brave look.

He walked away, saying he would get closer to downtown to catch a cab.

Vangie and I didn't wait for him to get out of sight before we locked the front door. The store was quiet, serene even. It was hard to believe what was going on in the alley.

There was a loud rap. Vangie and I jumped. The rap came again, and I could see Buster standing in the front window, fist raised, college ring tapping on the window. I was so glad to see him, I covered the distance in a few steps and flung open the door.

"Are you okay?" Buster said, gathering me in his arms. I let myself rest there a moment. "Sorry, I just got your message. I had my cell off," he said, and greeted Vangie.

She acknowledged him with a nod and a grin. She was glad he was there, too.

"I can't compete with laundry, I know." I managed to stick to a teasing tone, but I was a little peeved. It had been only an hour since I'd called him, but it felt like forever.

"Do you know the vic?" he asked.

Vangie shook her head vehemently.

I said, "He looked sort of familiar, but you know how it is in this neighborhood. There are tons of people that I say hi to on the street, but I don't know them."

I moved Buster over to the cushy chair in our book section. A hand-me-down from my parent's den, it was a well-broken-in leather recliner. Buster sat, and I perched on the arm. Vangie leaned on the book rack.

Buster was dressed in a sky blue SJPD Pistol Range T-shirt and navy sweats. I looked down at his feet clad in leather moccasins. He *had* rushed out of the house. He was practically in his pajamas. For him, going out in public in sweats was akin to being naked.

"You know I'm in for a long night," I said to him. I'd been through this before. The police would take their time processing the scene outside. "I haven't given my statement."

"Are you okay with that?" he asked.

I shrugged. "I just want them to do what they need to do. I don't need a homicide investigation going on all week. How would it look like if my parking lot had crime scene tape roping if off on Saturday?"

Buster took my hand and kissed it. I slid into his lap. "They're not going to leave the tape up forever. As soon as the coroner takes the body away, they'll be done. You'll have your lot back by the morning. Mid-morning the latest."

Vangie said, "They'd better. The sale is only three days away."

"And you don't need to stay here the whole night. There's nothing you can do. Who's the detective in charge?"

"Zorn," I said. I was surprised when Buster pulled a face. He clearly didn't like the man. "What?" I asked.

"Ms. Pellicano?" We were interrupted as Zorn and the other homicide detective came in from the back hall. Buster stood abruptly, nearly dumping me out of his lap. The police department was as fanatical as a gang about showing respect. A gang or a family of baboons.

Buster walked toward the pair, hand out. "Zorn. Peters," he said, with a nod to both. He rubbed his hands on his sweatpants. I hid a smile. Not being dressed in his detective drag, a suit and tie, was killing him.

"The ME pulled the driver's license. We've got an ID," Zorn said. "Frank Bascomb."

Peters and Zorn watched for a reaction. I didn't know the guy. I looked at Vangie who shrugged, and studied the book in her hand. I made a mental note to check my database.

The other detective said, "The address is in Milpitas. I' going over to his place." She said her goodbyes and left.

"What are you doing here?" Zorn asked Buster.

"This is my girlfriend's store."

Zorn smirked. "Your girlfriend? How cute."

A muscle in Buster's cheek twitched. Buster was always teased about being the youngest homicide detective. Like most bullying, he chose to ignore it.

I was more concerned when I saw Vangie's back stiffen. Zorn's voice dripped with condescension. She didn't care for cops much and any one who put down Buster was doubly bad in her book. I shook my head at her, hoping to avoid a scene.

"Ms. Pellicano," Zorn said smoothly. "Thank you for your cooperation."

Vangie said, "Do you really think the guy was poisoned?"

Zorn looked her over, taking in the nearly faded gang tattoo on her finger and her Dickies jeans and hooded sweatshirt and Doc Martens. We both could see he was making judgments about her. She thrust out her chest. Buster put an arm around Vangie.

"We will be investigating," Zorn said. "He has a nasty bump on his head, but it was probably just a bad burrito."

Vangie snapped, "Those are the best burritos in town. Mrs. Unites' kitchen is spotless." Vangie's loyalty was fierce. She loved our neighbor.

Buster gave her a fond look, and said, "I'm taking this one home. She's already given her statement."

Zorn shrugged. I smiled at him. That was Buster, thoughtful. He knew he was doing me a favor by making sure Vangie got home okay.

"I'll take you up on that," she said.

"I can stay until you finish using my kitchen," I said to Zorn.

"That would be great. Though as homicide, we're used to being out in the cold, aren't we, Healy?"

Buster smiled and walked Vangie out to his truck. I followed them and gave him a kiss. "I can swing back for you," he said.

"No sense in both of us losing a night's sleep."

I wasn't sure I meant that.

I waited until the CSI van came, and made more coffee for everyone, which they accepted gratefully. They brought in large lights that illuminated my parking lot and alley. Neighbors came out of their houses down the street to see what was going on. The police talked to everyone. I waited until the investigation was well underway, and then made my way home.

I opened the door into my tiny galley kitchen. The nightlight over the stove was burning, meaning Buster had made himself a cup of tea. A mug sat on the kitchen counter with my favorite tea bag already in it. I turned on the now-cold electric teakettle. A grilled cheese sandwich was on a plate beside it. Leave it to Buster to use a plate. I swiped the plate with a paper towel and put it back in the cupboard. I took a bite of my sandwich and went to look for Buster. I called his name but there was no answer.

A quick glance in the bedroom showed me it was empty. My guitar was missing from the stand in the corner, though. My heart skipped a beat. I loved to hear him play. Mostly I liked watching his fingers manipulate the strings.

I didn't hear any playing, though. My stomach growled angrily. Standing over the sink, I shoved the sandwich into my mouth with two fingers. I poured my tea. Maybe Buster was waiting in the living room, ready to end our embargo. Anticipation swelled.

I tiptoed into the living room to maintain the mood. But there was no mood to break. I heard a gentle snore.

I'd stayed at the store for about forty minutes, which looked to be thirty-five minutes too long. Buster was laid out on the couch, half-empty cup of tea and guitar on the coffee table, sound asleep. His eyes fluttered when I shook his arm, but closed again. He was a heavy sleeper, I knew. He'd sleep here for a few hours, then go home to get ready for work.

I pulled the flannel rag quilt off the back of the couch and kissed his cheek. He reached up and grabbed my hand, pulling me into him. I tumbled onto his chest.

"You think you're going to get off that easy?" he said, nuzzling my hair.

"You're asleep."

"Wrong. I was asleep."

I laughed as he faded again, his long curly eyelashes fluttering. "You can't keep your eyes open. I can wait. At least until you're awake enough so we can both enjoy it."

He let go of my hand and was asleep in ten seconds. I sighed, the sigh of the sexually frustrated female.

SEVEN

"Over my dead body," Kym said with a hair toss that would snap the wrist of a lesser woman. Vangie, sitting next to her at the kitchen table that doubled as conference table, ducked to avoid being blinded.

I winced at Kym's words. I had yet to address the possibly murdered man in the alley at the staff meeting. I'd met Jenn's earlier questions about the story in the paper by promising to give everyone the full scoop at the end of the meeting. I had an agenda that we had to get through. I couldn't allow even a man dying in my alley to get in the way of this sale.

"I'm not wearing pajamas to work. That is tacky," Kym said.

I hadn't realized Kym objected to tacky. I didn't want to remind her that calling it The Butt Crack of Dawn sale had been her idea.

Vangie muttered, "I bet you have a pair of pink bunny slippers you're just dying to show off."

I was afraid that just the opposite was true. Kym's pajamas were probably all silk and lace. Red teddies. Black negligees. Since she was married to my brother, I struggled not to picture the possibilities.

At least the silly problem of what not to wear was enough to keep us off the subject of dead men.

I said, "Customers get a deeper discount if they show up in their pajamas. From six to seven, the discount is 30 percent to anyone wearing their pajamas, 25 percent until eight a.m. Then the discount goes to 20, and stays there the rest of the day. By eight o'clock, everyone will be in street clothes," I said. "I just thought it would be fun if we were dressed in our nightclothes, too. At the very least, wear your QP T-shirt."

Kym looked somewhat mollified. I knew she would bedazzle her store shirt and pair it with a fringed skirt. She liked to look fashionable. I didn't understand who she was dressing for at the quilt shop.

"Let's get back to the agenda. We need to work on..." I didn't get to finish my sentence.

"The favors," Kym interrupted. "Work on the favors."

I swallowed a reprimand. Kym saw no problem in blurting out her every thought as it arose. Decorum, rules of order, agendas were meaningless to her. Like many of the changes I'd instituted, she ignored the ones she didn't want to participate in.

Some of the changes had cost money. Money I hadn't quite made back yet. This sale could turn that around in a weekend.

It had to.

None of the people at this table, especially Kym, had a clue what this sale meant to Quilter Paradiso. My new accountant predicted we had about three months left unless we had a large infusion of cash.

I looked around the table for support. Ina smiled at me, giving me the resolve to stand my ground. "We're not handing out favors, Kym."

"Of course we are," Kym said. "Remember I told you about those adorable lapel pins that looked like palm trees. Just like our logo. I made six in under an hour, so I'm sure we could make plenty by the weekend."

I tried to appeal to her inherent laziness. "I'm expecting hundreds of people through those doors on Saturday. We'd go crazy trying to make enough favors for each person."

"I'll make them," Kym said.

"I'll help," Jenn said. She smiled at Kym as though the two were curing cancer.

"You don't have time." My jaw ached from holding back my anger.

Vangie tapped her pen on the paper in front of her impatiently.

"That's not for you to say, Dewey," Kym said. "We have time."

Not for me to say? If not me, than who? I was the owner of the store. My cheeks reddened as I realized I'd given Kym the upper hand again.

Fighting back the exhaustion I felt, I put more force behind my words. "You do not have time. It's Wednesday already. Did you even look at the whiteboard in the classroom?"

I ticked off on my fingers all the work that had to be done before Saturday.

"Number one, we've got to clean the store from top to bottom. Number two, package the QPO kits. Number three, more fat quarters need to get cut between now and then." I could hear my voice rising, but I couldn't stop myself. By the third to-do on the list, I was practically yelling.

I took in a deep breath, trying to hold myself together. I continued, "We've got a huge shipment of notions that will have to be put out. Displays have to be made. We have to hang all the QP Originals."

"We used to have favors," Kym said.

The lament of the left behind, "We used to." All I could think of were the things that wouldn't get done because Jenn and Kym were making silly pins that would end up in the bottom of our customers' junk drawers.

"I forgot," Kym said. "Things are being done differently now."

I winced as she mimicked one of my favorite catchphrases.

"Ina, your report, please," I said ignoring Kym's gibe.

I wasn't the only one getting mad at Kym. Vangie's brow was dangerously furrowed and she looked like she was about to blow. Vangie could stew for hours after a scene with Kym. I needed her focused and working.

I gave Ina a pleading look, and she took us back to the business at hand.

"The Old Maid's Puzzle quilt is being finished," Ina said. "The raffle tickets are printed. The Stitch 'n' Bitch group will be in the classroom, hand quilting it on Saturday. Of course, all the proceeds are going to Women First shelter."

"Great, thanks." I touched Vangie's hand. "Let's let Vangie tell us about the publicity."

Vangie gathered herself and stood to give her report. She had put on a few needed pounds in the last year. She had gained confidence, too, now able to speak in front of the group without mumbling. I smiled at her, but she didn't need my shoring up. All eyes were on her, except for Kym who was now flipping through the latest *Quiltmaker Magazine.*

Vangie chose to rise above Kym's insulting inattention. "A postcard about the anniversary sale went out to everyone in the database and an e-mail reminder will go out tomorrow. Now for the real exciting news."

Vangie reached under the table and brought up a rolled-up poster.

"Drum roll please," Vangie said. Jenn used her index fingers on the edge of the table, until she caught a glance from Kym. The drumming came to an abrupt stop.

"Ta-da. Here's the Quilter Paradiso Original Quilts poster."

I led the applause as we passed around the colorful sign. It was brilliant. Vangie had taken our logo, the palm trees with a clothesline strung between them, and substituted the QPO quilts for the more traditional quilts that usually hung on the line. There was Celeste's Garden next to Ina's Over Easy and Pearl's Coastal Landscape. Vangie's Starry Nights hung next to Jenn's Home for the Holidays.

Vangie continued, "Fabric is cut for kits for each of the quilts. The customer will be able to duplicate the quilt pretty closely with the kit. If someone wants to use their own fabric, we'll have the patterns available for sale as well."

Quilt kits were tricky. Some of my customers adored buying them. Loved that the fabric and pattern were included. Loved having all the decisions made for them. Loved the idea that the kit was ready whenever they had a chance to work on it, which for many, was the middle of the night.

On the other hand, a kit could retail for upwards of three hundred dollars, depending on the size of the finished quilt. Not only was the cost prohibitive for some of my customers, fabric in a kit was merchandise taken out of circulation. Unless the quilt kit sold, I didn't get back my investment. Profit was on hold until then. I couldn't afford to tie up too much of my inventory in kits in case they didn't sell.

It was a balancing act—have enough kits made to sell, but not too many. As this was the first time the QPO kits were available, I had no historical data to mine. Vangie and I had come up with a conservative estimate, with the idea that we could cut more kits if the demand was there.

Vangie said, "We cut enough fabric for five kits of each quilt. We still need to package those, in bags with the patterns attached and display them."

I waited for the chatter around the new quilt kits to die down. Kym went back to perusing the ads in the back of the magazine.

Vangie said, "Dewey and I'll be hanging the samples up after the store closes on Thursday, to maximize the surprise effect. No one knows about the Quilter Paradiso Originals Line, and we want the customers to be truly surprised."

"I noticed I'm not on the poster," Kym said, scowling.

I hid a smile. Vangie could, and would, exercise her own power.

Vangie said, "I never received the directions to your Joyous Hearts quilt, so I haven't been able to write up the instructions. No instructions, no QP Original Quilt."

Jenn asked Vangie a question, something about pictures. Vangie told her she'd talk to her later. I got the impression Vangie didn't want me to hear. I was intrigued. That was an unlikely pair of comrades.

I jumped in before Kym could give her excuses. I turned my laptop screen toward the group. I'd already pulled up the e-mail with Lark's clip on it.

"Two more things. Big things. One, is that the Quilter Paradiso segment is going to air on *Wonderful World of Quilts* on Friday morning," I said. "We have a preview." I pushed the button and let it play.

An excited buzz started around the table. Jenn put two fingers to her mouth and wolf-whistled. Ina high-fived her. Even Vangie smiled.

Kym tossed her hair back and struck a pose. "I look damned good on TV," she said.

Vangie leaned over to me, and said *sotto voce*, "You better hope she never discovers YouTube."

I laughed. "We need to spread the word. Kym, let everyone know you're going to be a star. I'm sure your parents will want to tape it. Vangie's going to put an announcement up on our website. I'll include it in the e-mail about the sale."

Ina said, "I can send a message to the guild list."

Jenn said, "I'll let my small quilt group know, and all the Yahoo lists I'm on."

Kym was beaming, the spotlight back on her. "Can you send that video to Kevin? On his e-mail thingy?"

"Yes," I said. "I can do that." I could have done it yesterday, but I'd wanted to surprise everyone at the meeting instead.

"This is our first nationwide exposure," I continued. "I'm sure it'll bring in plenty of new business. For sure, everyone will end up working really hard on Saturday. I'm recruiting extra help."

Kym had stopped listening. She said, "I've got to call Kevin." She started out of her seat.

"Hang on, "I said. "We're almost finished."

She reluctantly sat back down. "The other thing isn't quite as pleasant. A man was found dead in our alley last night."

Jenn said, "The paper said he might have been murdered."

Ina nodded. "The quilt guild listserv is full of speculation about that."

I made a mental note to monitor the chat on the group for the next couple of days. The last thing I needed was mass hysteria from my customers. The postings on that message board could heat up quickly.

"It's not clear how Mr. Bascomb died. Let's be a little more vigilant. No one stays alone in the shop. Use the buddy system to get to your car at night. I don't have any reason to think it's not safe in our parking lot, but it won't hurt to pay attention to your surroundings."

Ina nodded her approval. Jenn chewed on her fingernail. Kym looked like I'd brought up the dead man just to ruin her place in the limelight.

I glanced at the clock. It was five minutes after ten. The shop should have opened already. Not that I expected a lot of customers. Most would be saving their shopping until Saturday.

Jenn asked, "His name was Bascomb?"

I looked at her. Her lower lip was trembling. Did she know the guy? "Frank Bascomb, yes."

I waited for her to say more, but she just shook her head, so I continued.

"There is something else. Detective Zorn'll want to talk to each of you. I don't know when, maybe later on this afternoon."

"All of us?" Jenn said. "Even those of us who weren't here last night?"

I nodded. She'd gone even paler.

Kym opened her mouth, but I anticipated her question. "I will pay you for the time spent off the floor with the police. Just be sure to come and get me or Vangie to cover the floor while you're gone."

I drained my coffee cup. "Okay. It's time to open up. Jenn, you can get started on packaging the quilt kits. Do what you do best—make them pretty, impossible to resist."

She smiled at me. I hoped the work would distract her from whatever she was feeling. The group pushed away from the table.

I gathered up my notes. "Kym, I need to speak to you about something."

She lingered with as much enthusiasm as a kid called to the principal's office. "What? I've got to call Kev."

I ignored her urgency. "Last night, when we printed out a class roster, I discovered that one of the students in the class hadn't paid. Did you sign up someone without payment?" I'd spoken to her about this before. It was one of those bad habits left over from the way they used to do things around here.

Kym said calmly, "Oh yeah, well she wasn't sure if she could make it to the first class. She baby-sits her granddaughter, and ..."

I interrupted, "It doesn't matter why. I didn't know she wasn't paid, so I nearly didn't charge her last night. More importantly, I had people on the waiting list. What if she hadn't showed up? I'd have had an empty spot in the class that I could have filled with a paying customer. We can't afford to let that happen."

Kym was unmoved. "But Alice came, right? And she paid. What's the problem?"

I felt a throb in my head. Talking to Kym about proper procedure was a high-speed train to headache-land.

"Don't do it again. People do not go on the class list unless they've paid in advance. End of story."

She twisted her face in disgust. "Whatever."

She flounced away. I got the last word.

"Spit out your gum, Kym," I called after her. "You know you can't be on the store floor with gum in your mouth."

She stopped before exiting the kitchen. The garbage can lid swung open. She spit loudly. The victory was hollow for me.

I stepped to the sink to rinse out my coffee cup. Ina was still in the kitchen, putting away cups and wiping down the kitchen table.

"Yesterday was some day, wasn't it?" I said to her back.

"Today will be better," Ina said. "Things are definitely looking up."

I thought she was talking about her Stitch 'n' Bitch group, so I asked. "What was going on with Gussie and Celeste? Do you think they'll be okay?"

When there was no answer, I turned around. Ina was gone. Her friends' problems were not up for discussion.

I headed for my office, but was stuck out in the hall. Vangie had gotten there first and was blocking my way in. She was kneeling on the floor, arms in the safe that was positioned right behind the door, getting out the till money. I leaned on the doorjamb waiting for her to finish. The amount of stuff we had to do in three days was daunting. I stuffed down a worry about getting it all done.

The back door banged open. Coming toward me was a large box with two hands on the side edges. Dad's voice came out from behind it.

"Where do you want this?" Dad was his usual no-nonsense self. He wasn't big on hellos—or goodbyes, for that matter.

"What is it?" I said.

"How should I know?" he growled.

Kym came from the front of the store. She clapped her hands twice, like some kind of storybook princess. That was all she had to do around my brother and my father to have her wishes granted, a skill I'd never learned. "It's here. Thanks, Dad."

Even after three years of having Kym in the family, my stomach knotted when she called my father, Dad. I used to have the sole privilege of daughterly love, but now there was Kym. And for some reason unfathomable to me, he seemed to like her.

I could understand Kevin. At least he got to have sex with her. But Dad? Why did he like Kym so much? Did he really enjoy the fawning, the hanging on his every word of old stories. She laughed every time my father told her about dumping his Vespa in the old fountain in Cesar de Chavez Plaza. To me, it was another example of her short attention span and inability to retain anything.

"Hi, cutie," he said. He held still for her peck on the cheek. "Where do you want it?"

"I'm sorry, Dad. I thought Kevin would bring it over."

"Whaddya think? I can't handle it? What am I, a sick old man? I'm strong, like a bull. Watch this."

Vangie had heard my dad and was closing the safe, grinning. She loved to wind him up. Unless I wanted my father doing one-armed, Jack-Palance-style pushups in the hall like last time, I had to get him out of here. I didn't have the patience today. I gave Vangie a warning look, which she caught.

She twirled the dial on the safe and stood. She settled for an exchange of low-fives.

"Hi, Mr. P. What's in the box?" Vangie said.

Kym answered. "A custom rosewood light box."

"For you?" I asked, losing interest. If Kym wanted to buy one more thing she didn't need, it was none of my business. I scanned my desk, the throbbing red light on the answering machine drawing me in.

I'd only gotten two steps closer to the door when Kym's answer stilled me. "No, silly, for the store."

I felt the heat rise on my face. "What do I want with that?"

"It's just what the serious appliqué-er needs to trace her designs," Kym said. "It's beautifully constructed with an energy-efficient lightbulb. It's got a remote. The light panels move aside and an ironing surface appears. Come on, Dewey, wake up. It's the latest."

It was huge. "How much did it cost?"

"Three-hundred and fifty dollars," Kym said.

That was ridiculously expensive for a light box that the average quilter would use once a year. My heart was racing when I asked the next question. "How did you pay for it?"

Vangie gave me a worried look. She handed off the till money to Jenn, who'd appeared from the front and melted away. I heard Vangie get on the computer. I knew she was headed to the credit card site to check out balances.

Kym sighed. "I used the number that your mom gave me a long time ago. She told me to always be on the lookout for special products."

About once every six months, Kym used the store card for a special item she thought might sell. They usually didn't. This was my fault. I'd forgotten to take it away from her. I couldn't have her running up charges, especially now.

Kym said, "I went to that quilt show in Folsom last weekend. This darling man was there, selling his homemade wooden items. I couldn't remember the store address, so Kevin gave him Pellicano's construction's address and here it is. It's going to be perfect."

She sent it to the contracting shop's address so I couldn't refuse the shipment, which is what I would have done. And would do. "Send it back."

"I can't. It's a one of a kind."

Naturally. I knew that this purchase would put me over my credit limit. The bank would sting me with another penalty. Was Kym ever going to get out of way and let me succeed?

My frayed nerves snapped. "Give the invoice to Vangie and tell her to make a barcode. We'll try to sell it this weekend," I said.

Kym reared back in horror. "Sell it?"

"Yeah, Kym. That's what we do around here. Sell things. You'd better hope one of your appliqué goddesses is willing to shell out for this."

Kym left with an exasperated noise. "Why is everything always my fault?"

I stifled an urge to scream.

Dad was waiting by the back door. And watching. "Do you need to be so hard on her?"

"Please, Dad, you have no idea." I scrubbed at my eyes.

He was happy to change the subject. Battling women was not his thing. He'd much rather pretend Kym and I got along great. "What about your house? When do you want to start changing out your kitchen cabinets?"

"Have you forgotten? This weekend is the anniversary sale."

His leathery face shuttered. His eyes became hooded, and the lines under his eyes deepened. Years of working outdoors had made his face a roadmap of construction jobs. I felt like I could trace his career, from one job site to the next, just following the lines on his face.

The etching agent this time had been my mother's early death a year ago. Since then, the lines cut so deep, they looked painful.

I resisted the urge to stroke his face. He wouldn't know what to do with me if I did. There was no question he was still as strong as most men half his age, but his bandy legs seemed to carry an extra burden now. His shoulders were a little more stooped than before.

"Are you going to work the sale with us?" I asked.

In years past, he'd always worked the big sales. All of us kids had too, although what I used to do, bagging customer's purchases and putting away fabric bolts, had not prepared me for the job I had now.

I remembered being shocked by how my dad teased the customers. And they loved it. It was impossible to picture him flirting with anyone now.

His voice grew rough, the edges of his voice a little panicked. "I doubt it. Are you shorthanded? I can be here if you need me, but ..."

"Going fishing?" He'd been in the Sierras all through last year's quilt convention, when I really could have used his help.

"Dewey..."

I watched him leave. He had to mourn my mother in whatever way he could. Being in the store was hard, full of years of memories. For him, it was empty now without my mother. Emptier than I could imagine.

My job was to bring the store back to something he could be proud of. I only hoped I could do it.

EIGHT

Vangie was frowning, seated at her desk.

"How far over the limit are we?" I asked.

Vangie pointed at the screen. "Three hundred dollars."

Damn Kym.

"I did find those specialty scissors, but we don't have enough cash or credit to order them," Vangie said. She had several windows open on the computer. I could see our bank balance, the red bottom line visible.

"We're on a cash-only basis with both of the major distributors," she continued.

"Can't you find a minor one?" I said weakly. I knew the answer. It was a pipe dream to think I could afford to buy the scissors.

With Kym's using the credit card, any cushion I'd had was gone.

"I talked to the manufacturer, Felix Scissors Company. They'll overnight them if we get the money to them now. I thought I could talk them into net 30—but, no, they want to get paid up front."

There was one possible solution. "Do you really think we can sell them all? Tell me I'm not crazy," I said, seeking reassurance before stepping into this particular quagmire. I did have one untapped source of cash.

One I'd vowed never to touch.

Vangie said, "Are you kidding me? They'll fly out the door as soon as the show airs. Don't forget, I'll have the QP online store up and running, too. The customers don't even have to be in San Jose."

That did it. The online store would give us a huge pool of potential buyers. "Okay. How much do we need? Figure out what the exact cost will be."

Vangie looked at me worriedly. "What are you going to do—rob a bank?"

I scoffed. "Nah. Buster says bank robbers don't get much. There's hardly any cash at the teller's windows." I grinned at her.

There was really no reason why I couldn't use this money. The only thing holding me back was my own sense of loss.

Vangie gave me a sideways glance. "Dewey? I hope you're not selling your soul or something."

I said gaily, "I've already sold out to this place, don't you know?"

My flip answer didn't wipe the worry off her face, but I wasn't ready to share my idea yet. "Just tell me how much we need."

I watched the floor activity from my desk. Jenn and Kym were working together. Ina'd come out of the classroom, where she and Pearl were quilting the Old Maid's Puzzle quilt, and was buying thread.

Jenn had all the Celeste's Garden quilt kits spread out on our large cutting table. The kits featured twelve unique block patterns, covering a year in the garden. The quilter received the instructions and enough fabric to make each block. In this case, since Celeste's blocks were redwork, the kit consisted of Celeste's drawings and pieces of high-quality cotton to trace it on. Floss was included to stitch the design.

Jenn'd made piles of each, and was packing twelve of them into a pretty red bag. From where I sat, it looked like Kym's major contribution to the task was putting her index finger out so Jenn could tie a ribbon.

I checked the store's voice mail. Damn. Nothing but bad news. Zorn was coming later to talk to everyone. And at least one customer had heard about the murder.

"Vangie, listen to this." I played the tape for her. On it, the customer cancelled out of the Crazy Quilt class being held next week. She'd heard about the body in our alley and didn't feel safe around here at night. If we scheduled the class during the day or on a weekend, we should let her know. Of course, she would like a full refund of her class fees.

"I got a couple of e-mails like that, too," Vangie said. "It sucks."

My heart sank. Classes brought in a lot of money. There was the price of the class, plus the supplies—fabrics and notions—that we sold. Sales like the one on Saturdays were the race horses, the showy event that brought in a lot of cash. But classes were the workhorses, steadily adding to our bottom line. I couldn't afford to lose either.

"If customers don't feel comfortable coming here …" Vangie began.

I held up my hand. I didn't need her to verbalize how bad things could get if our customers got it in their heads that QP was not in a safe neighborhood. There were plenty of other quilt shops around.

"I get it. Oh man, I get it."

I crossed my hands across my stomach, trying to quell the ache that was starting there. My job was to keep things moving. "See if you can get that Crazy Quilt teacher to reschedule and let's keep track of who's bailing and make sure they know about the new class. That's all we can do for now."

Nothing to do but move forward. I picked up where I'd left off in the notion order and got to work.

An instant message from eBay came up on the laptop. Bidding had changed on a piece of pottery I'd been trying to buy. I clicked off it. There was no way I could afford that now.

My voice mail beeped. I hadn't heard the phone ring. The message was from Buster. He apologized for falling asleep last night and promised to make it up to me tonight. He was at his desk in SJPD, so his propositions were vague. He suggested I use my imagination. That sounded interesting. A smile crept across my face as I thought of all the ways he could put things right between us.

A rap came on the window in front of my desk, breaking me out of my reverie. Kym was gesturing for me to come out on the floor. A customer stood at the cash register, and another was at the cutting table, piling up bolts.

I went out to the store floor.

"Dewey, can you please help that dearie at the register? I've got Mrs. Lamb here," Kym said. "Jenn had to go to a parent-teacher conference. I told her it was okay."

I smiled at the customer through a tightly clenched jaw. If I'd known Jenn had to go, I would've told her it was okay, too, but it wasn't up to Kym to make that call.

I took the customer's money for the pack of needles. For such a small purchase, any other of my staff would have excused herself to ring up the sale, and then go back to helping Mrs. Lamb choose fabric. Not Kym.

I gave the customer her change.

She looked at what was in her hand. "I'm sorry," she said. "But you've shortchanged me. I gave you a hundred."

I tore my eyes away from Kym and looked at the cash register. It said I'd owed her $15.11 change. I'd punched in that she'd given me a twenty dollar bill.

"Are you sure? I thought it was a twenty."

"No, it was a hundred." She had pretty blue eyes that were puzzled, as though she was trying to reconstruct a conversation. "My husband left it for me this morning, and he always puts a little red heart in the corner of my mad money. I think if you look in your till, you'll find my hundred in there."

Sure enough, there was a hundred-dollar bill with a red heart on it. I apologized profusely, and handed her the rest of her change. She refused a bag and left with her needles. There were no other customers, so I started back to my desk.

Kym was leaning against the cutting table, still talking to Mrs. Lamb. The customer had picked out at least two dozen bolts of pink and brown fabrics. Kym was holding the rotary cutter in her hand, often using it for emphasizing a point, but there was no actual cutting going on.

Kym was notorious for chatting instead of working. Our customers were mostly women with plenty to say. It was a bit of an art to know how to keep listening and working at the same time. Ina was a master, and Jenn was learning from her. Kym, as usual, went her own way.

The customer was talking loudly and gesturing. "It's not like she can tell people not to shop here. Being guild president has totally gone to her head. She thinks her shit doesn't stink."

Ouch. Profanity in my store. That could not be tolerated.

"Kym?" I motioned for her to join me at the cash register. She laid the rotary cutter down with a huge sigh. Mrs. Lamb waved at me, and I acknowledged her with another forced smile.

I turned my back to the customer, and whispered to Kym, "Can you move this along a little? We've got so much to do…"

Kym sniffed and tossed her hair. "You really don't know anything about sales, Dewey. Service is what sets quilt shops apart. Mrs. Lamb's going to buy a lot of fabric. I've been helping her pick out what she needs for a baby quilt. She needs to talk it out. It's a girl, her first grandchild."

That explained all the pink. "Really? Her first grandchild is guild president?"

Kym made a disgusted face. "Customer relations, you ought to study it."

"Wrap it up. Now," I said to Kym's back. I stood in the doorway until I saw Kym pick up a bolt and cut. She threw me a snide glance and I went back to my office.

Half an hour later, Kym and the customer were finally headed toward the cash register. Kym saw I was looking, so held up the big pile of fabrics she'd cut. She was right, that was going to be a sizable sale. I relaxed a bit.

Vangie came in from getting lunch, and plopped down on her chair.

"How are the numbers today?" she said, pulling up the P.O.S. program. "Ugh," she said when she saw the dismal sales totals.

"It's about to get better," I said, pointing out my window to Kym. Vangie whistled appreciatively.

"I barked at Kym earlier because she was talking to that woman forever. Maybe I was wrong."

Vangie chuckled. "Never-ending job, this soothing of Kym's ruffled feathers."

"What can I say? Can't work with her, can't fire her. She's family."

Vangie smirked. I started out to the front. The customer's phone rang and she stepped out on the sidewalk to answer it. I took advantage of her absence and approached Kym.

Pride wasn't easy to swallow, but I think I managed to sound sincere. "Nice job, Kym. That is a great sale. It'll make our day today."

"Told you." She was concentrating on using the cash register, so the playground taunt was the best she could muster.

I couldn't resist sniping back. "I still think you should have ended the gossip earlier."

Kym just screwed her face up tighter, as she stared at the screen. I'd better leave her alone. I didn't have time to correct any mistakes she'd make if her attention got too fractured.

The customer came back in, waving her phone, and shouting. "She's got a penis!"

Kym and I looked at one another. Had this woman lost her marbles?

She shoved her cell phone under Kym's face. I got behind Kym and could see it was an e-mailed sonogram. The arc of wavy lines meant there was a baby in there. I couldn't see the penis that meant this was not the expected baby girl, but a boy.

A boy who most likely wouldn't be swaddled in pink.

Penises—so often more trouble than they're worth.

Mrs. Lamb shrieked, "I'm not having a granddaughter after all. I'm having a grandson. A baby boy! Jackson George."

Kym had rung up the sale but had yet to receive any money. To her credit, Kym looked as sick as I felt.

She tried. "Okay, Mrs. Lamb, that'll be four hundred and forty-eight dollars…"

She didn't get to finish. The customer waved her off. "Oh, no, this fabric will never do. I'm going to have to start all over. I saw some lovely blue and yellows over at Fabrics 'n' Fun that'll be just perfect."

Her cell rang again, and she went out the front door without another word.

Kym slumped over the counter. I took the pile of fabric out of the bag. There were some yard cuts, lots of half yards, and one big piece that was probably meant for the back of the quilt, at least four yards. Kym had sold this woman a lot of fabric. More than she'd needed for one baby quilt. Kym must have convinced her to make the kid a new pink quilt for the next five birthdays. She'd even recommended several books, and got the woman to add on thread and a ten-pack of new rotary blades.

"That was a good sale," I admitted. I looked over the receipt. I'd have to over-ring the sale so the drawer would balance tonight.

"Was," Kym said.

I had no time to cry over spilt fabric. "Take the biggest piece and wind it back on the bolts. The smaller pieces will have to be cut into fat quarters. I'll need to change the inventory." More make-work. Just what I needed.

Back in the office, Vangie handed me the purchase order for the scissors. The bottom line was over four-thousand dollars. If we sold them all, we'd make that much again in profit. I felt like a gambler in front of a roulette wheel. I was about to spin the wheel and let it ride. I had to take the chance.

I said, "I'm going to go to the bank."

"Go git 'em," Vangie said.

I stood at attention. "I shall return with a cashier's check in the amount of four-thousand, six-hundred and twenty-three dollars."

"And eighty-eight cents."

I saluted her. The company was asking for a cashier's check, which meant I had to visit the bank in person, not do my usual online transactions. The bank was several blocks away. The short walk would do me good.

Vangie said, "If you get the check to the post office by three, you can mail it without having to pay extra Express mail charges."

I checked the clock. It was almost one. "Will do."

"Do you want me to address an envelope for you to take with you?" Vangie offered.

"Nah, I'm going to walk to the bank, and the post office is in the other direction. I have to pass right by here anyhow."

"Okay, then," Vangie said. She'd already plugged her headphones back in.

One step out the back door, and I was reminded of Frank Bascomb's ugly death. The cops had been gone before I got to work this morning. The only sign that anything untoward had happened was a scrap of yellow tape that clung to the vines across the back fence. I pulled the piece off and stuffed it in my pocket.

How did the dead man get here? I looked at the gravel. If he'd been dragged, there would be marks on the ground. The police had preserved the scene until early this morning, so I looked. I didn't see anything. The area around the dumpster was pretty messed up. Mrs. Unites had been out here when she found the body, so it'd be impossible to figure out if she scuffed the gravel or if a dead body had been dragged back here.

There were hedges along the back wall. I looked to see if any branches were broken. I could see nothing. No way to tell how Frank Bascomb ended up dead in my alley.

My parking lot was still full. Most of the night class customers had day jobs and hadn't been able to get here to get their cars before work. Today's customers would have to park somewhere else. Lots of inconvenience to go around, as Zorn said.

Taking up a spot, plus half of another, was an old Econoline van. I hated it when people hogged spots.

To my surprise, the driver's door opened. Tim Shore got out. "Ms. Pellicano, I'm glad I caught you. Someone hit my car while it was parked in your lot."

I followed him as he moved around the car.

"Look here." He pointed at the passenger side door panel. I had to bend closer to see anything. There was a small indentation about midway up on the back door.

"Really?" I tried to keep the skepticism out of my voice, but it was hard. How did that happen? He'd been the last person to arrive last night. "I'm so sorry. Did they leave a note?"

He shook his head. It used to be that I'd have called my dad and let him handle something like this. The insurance agent was an old friend of his, having written polices for my family for years. I didn't want to bring him into this. I wanted to stand on my own two feet. And that meant dealing with customers who were not happy.

I straightened. I walked around the car. "I don't understand how that happened. I mean, no one could park right here. Do you think it was a door?"

I could play sweet and naïve.

"Maybe," he said.

His evasiveness made me angry. "Mr. Shore, no one else has parked here. In fact, the way you're parked, there's barely room for another car."

He said, "Maybe it was a key instead. What do you care? You're insured for this kind of stuff."

I looked at him. He was messing with the wrong girl today. "I've got business to attend to, Mr. Shore. If you file a claim with your insurance company, I'm sure they'll contact me."

I walked away, trying to inject plenty of attitude in my stride. First the taxi fare, and now this. This guy was turning out to be more trouble than he was worth.

I tried to shake off my concerns about the store, Tim Shore, and Frank Bascomb and just enjoy my time outside. It was a typical October day in San Jose, sunny and cool. The morning fog had burned off, and the sun shone brightly. Wind whipped up the Alameda, bending the branches of the newer trees and knocking down the leaves of the older ones. My footsteps were audible, crunching on the brittle leaves.

I welcomed the cooler weather and the rainy season that was coming. Fall meant clouds racing across the sky, giving the bland blue sky character. Summer weather was like an overly matched bedroom suite from Ethan Allan. I preferred my furniture with a few scratches and dents.

Just like I preferred Buster with a five o'clock shadow.

My neighborhood was great. Everything I needed was in a three-block radius. The Alameda was a mix of old buildings and new, chain stores and mom and pops. Right next door to QP was the burrito shop, beyond that a pawnshop. Across the street new condos were going up, with a Starbucks on the ground level. We already had a Peets a few doors down. The old Towne theatre now showed Bollywood movies with their brightly attired actresses on posters out front.

The bank was the old-fashioned kind, built when marble and gilt were meant to give the impression that hard-earned money would be safe here. Once the twelve-foot doors closed behind me, the sounds of the street were immediately muted. The ceiling was trimmed by graceful cove molding painted in light and dark shades of cerulean blue, giving the space a cathedral air. The marble floor was yellowed, but age had been good to the woodwork, leaving it soft and mellow.

The elevated teller windows were to the left. Years agod, the bank tellers had sat behind ornate brass scrollwork, but there was no sign of that now. Instead, each window was decorated for Halloween with faux spider webs criss-crossing the space.

A huge golden bank vault took up much of the back wall. It was open, the intricate workings of the lock visible. As a kid, I'd been afraid to get too close. Afraid that the heavy door would close behind me, and I'd be locked in for hours until the bank manager, then a dour woman with helmet-like hair, would let me out. Kevin, on the other hand, had been fascinated by the door, begging each time we'd banked to be allowed to turn the wheel. He loved to watch the levers move.

The bank was crowded, with a line snaking around the lobby. The commercial teller was closed, naturally. No point in having a teller dedicated strictly to businesses if she was going to be open all the time. I swallowed my resentment.

I settled behind a sun-burnished man in well-worn jeans and a cowboy hat. As soon as I took my eye off the beautiful architecture, the list of things I had to do back at the store began running through my brain, like the annoying scroll across the bottom of the TV. I'd covered the bottom part of my screen with sticky notes to block out the intrusive news. I tried to do the same now, mentally covering up the trailing thoughts with virtual post-its, but I failed.

In the cavernous lobby space, voices carried. I realized that the same little old lady in a stretched-out Irish cable knit sweater had been standing in front of Teller Window Four since I'd come in. The woman's voice rose and fell. "It's my money, and I demand access to it. This is the second day in a row you've been difficult with me."

That voice. I took a step out of line to get a better look.

The college-aged boy with straight black hair and a maroon knit tie was getting flustered. He spoke louder. "I'm just following procedure, ma'am. You need to see the manager. As soon as she's finished with her customer, she will be with you."

The woman's gray hair was inexpertly dyed the same color as her brown polyester pants, and her shoes were broken down at the heel. She was carrying a tote bag with three-dimensional rabbit ears that read, "You're no bunny until some bunny loves you."

I knew that tote bag. Yesterday, it had been full of water bottles and fabric scraps. It belonged to Gussie Johnston, from the Stitch 'n' Bitch group. What had she done to her hair? No wonder I'd hadn't recognized her. It looked like she'd found a bottle of do-it-yourself hair dye at the Goodwill.

Gussie drew herself up on her tiptoes in an effort to get level with the counter. She rapped on the wood, oblivious to the black plastic spider that tumbled out its web and onto her foot.

"Young man, I am not stupid or incompetent. Does the sight of an older woman set you off so much that you think I am incapable of handling my affairs? I've been trusted with the disposal of my money since before you were born. Since before your mother was born for that matter."

I'd never seen her angry before. I approached her, stopping just behind her shoulder.

"Gussie?"

Gussie didn't acknowledge me, her attention focused on a dressed-for-success woman making her way through the hidden door behind the other teller stations.

The woman stopped alongside the young man and addressed Gussie.

"Ma'am, please lower your voice," the manager pleaded. She checked the customers in line, smiled so that no one thought she was abusing this frail old woman. "We are required by law to ensure that you are not being swindled. There are procedures. Forms. You have requested a large sum of money."

The manager said that last sentence in a whisper. She was trying to be discreet. I looked around. Everyone was staring. Gussie didn't seem to care.

"To some people, perhaps." Gussie was channeling her inner Celeste, putting on her haughtiest voice.

I stifled a laugh, nudging her side.

She finally noticed me. "Dewey. Good, you're here. Tell them I'm in my right mind. I only want to withdraw funds from my account. I don't know why that should be such a big deal."

"And who is this?" the manager asked.

Gussie pulled me forward with her liver-spotted and gnarled hands. "This is my granddaughter."

Her granddaughter? I could only stare at her, amazed at how easily the lie came tripping off her tongue.

The teller and manager exchanged a look. The manager nodded silently with the air of someone who'd just been let off a legal hook.

"Is your grandmother okay?" the teller asked earnestly. The manager was watching me closely, so I put my arm around Gussie.

I thought about it. My living grandmother, Nona Pellicano, lived in Carmichael in a retirement community. If throwing devil horns at errant golf carts and spitting on the sidewalk and talking back to soap opera characters is okay, my grandmother qualified.

Gussie pinched my arm, hard. Startled, I looked at her. She was begging me to go along. This was more than a bureaucratic snafu. She needed this money. Badly.

"Of course she is. She's gray-haired, not harebrained."

I was pretty proud of my turn of phrase, and Gussie smiled triumphantly and patted her thinning hair.

The manager made a decision. "Go to the vault, Paul. I will help Mrs. Johnston with the paperwork at my desk. Follow me."

Gussie pinched me again, this time gentler. "Thank you," she whispered. She was excited, two red spots high on her cheeks. She'd attempted lipstick, but it had worn off except for a thick pile in the corner of her mouth. Going to the bank was a special occasion for her, too.

"I came in yesterday," Gussie said, as we left the teller window. "They wouldn't give me my money. Said they didn't have enough cash on hand, if you can believe that."

"How much money are you trying to withdraw?"

Gussie said, "Twenty-nine thousand."

My eyes widened, and I suppressed a gasp. I didn't know Gussie had that kind of money. She was always pinching pennies. This had to represent her entire savings.

The manager shot me a look over her glasses. I remembered my role as dutiful granddaughter and clamped my mouth shut.

Halfway between the teller windows and the manager's area, I stopped Gussie.

The line had disappeared, the customers waited on and out the door. No one was within earshot.

"Why so much cash?"

She leaned in. "You can't tell anyone. My grandson, Donna's son, Jeremy, is buying a house. Jeremy told the bank he had thirty thousand in cash for a down payment."

Her voice got quieter still, and I had to move closer to get it all. Her fingers closed on my arm, one ragged nail scratching me. "He lied."

She continued. "He needs my money to make up the difference. There's some problem—if I gave him a check, they would trace it back to me, and then there's tax implications. I don't get it all. All I know is he needs my help, so here I am."

The teller walked past with a package, smaller than I thought nearly thirty thousand dollars should be. He handed the money to the manager, ignoring Gussie's outstretched hand.

"Please sit," the manager said to us. "Federal banking regulations require that we fill out this form."

Before she sat down, Gussie glanced out the large plate window that overlooked the parking lot. She pulled me close, turning her head away from the manager, and talking behind her hand.

"Do me a favor. Go and see if there's a yellow Taurus in the parking lot."

I'd already lost my place in line, and I still needed to get my cashier's check. "I can't."

Gussie pleaded, "I've been in here longer than I thought I would be. My ride should be here by now. I don't want him to leave."

I couldn't stop playing the dutiful granddaughter now. It would only take me a minute to look out the window for the car, then I could get my cashier's check.

But a line was forming again. I hesitated.

"Go," Gussie hissed at me. "I'll be out as soon as I can, but I don't want to miss Larry."

Larry? Celeste's Larry? Oh-oh. Maybe there was something going on between them after all.

I crossed to the big window. The parking lot was half-full, but no yellow Taurus. I went back to the desk. The bank manager had her head down, and Gussie was admonishing her for being slow.

"There's no car like that out there, Gussie," I said quietly.

She looked up, startled. "Well, he has to be somewhere. He's waiting to take the money…" She stopped, when the manager raised her head quickly.

Gussie changed tack. "He's waiting to take *me* to Redding."

"What's in Redding?" I asked.

The manager was listening intently, her eyes flitting from me to Gussie and back again.

Gussie sat up tall in the chair. Only her fingers gave away her uncertainty. She held them low in her lap so the bank manager couldn't see how they fluttered.

"Your cousin, dear. You remember. Jeremy."

"Of course, that cousin." I nodded as though she'd refreshed my memory. The bank manager relaxed in her seat, and returned to filling in the form.

My own work had to get done. "Gussie, wait for me. I need to get a cashier's check. I won't be long. I want to talk to Larry before you take off." I needed to make sure he knew what he was getting into, squiring Gussie around, with thirty thousand dollars in her tote bag.

Gussie returned to harassing the manager. I got back in a line that was now ten people long. Two tellers had shut down. I hopped from one foot to the other, anxious to get the line moving, but knowing I looked like a little kid who had to pee.

Out of the corner of my eye, I saw Gussie walk toward the door, her bunny tote bag stuck under her arm. I called to her, but she ignored me. I was sixth in line now. I'd made some progress and wanted to maintain it. I craned my neck, twisted my body, keeping one foot in line and could see Gussie had settled on a bench outside the bank door to wait for Larry. I could just barely see the top of her head.

I looked at my watch. It was nearly two. I had to get the cashier's check and get to the post office by three. I had to stay in line.

My neck developed a crick as I tried to watch Gussie and the tellers at the same time. She stayed on the bench. People came and went without so much as glancing at her. She might be a sitting duck with all that cash, but the good news was that no one would think anyone who looked like Gussie would have that kind of money on her.

There were three people ahead of me. I'd moved forward to a point where I couldn't see Gussie anymore. I strained to see her, looking around the plus-size woman behind me.

"Would you hold my place in line?" I asked her.

She sighed, but agreed. Her purse was the size of a carry-on bag. A small dog poked its head out and yapped as I passed, causing my heart to trip hammer.

I took a couple of steps and could see Gussie still sitting on the bench. She seemed to be talking to herself. That was okay, acting a little nuts could be the key to keeping her safe.

I squirmed around again. The lady in back of me gave a noisy tsking sounds. "My grandmother," I explained. She rolled her eyes.

The logjam broke when two tellers returned from lunch. I stepped up and asked for the cashier's check.

Gussie had completely distracted me from the task at hand. I had to empty a bank account in order to buy these scissors. Money that I'd banked a year ago. Money that I'd vowed never to touch. Money that I wished I'd never come to possess.

Five thousand dollars, proceeds from my mother's life insurance policy.

NINE

I PAID FOR THE check and got out of the bank as fast as I could, but Gussie was no longer on the bench. Larry must have come for her.

Okay, one problem solved. At least she wasn't wandering the streets with all that money.

I stopped to fold the check neatly and put it in my back pocket. This check represented all the money I had. I was gambling, but the profit I could make from this was enough to give the store some breathing room.

I did a last quick glance around the parking lot for the yellow Taurus. There was one man at the ATM machine. Oh, crap. Tim Shore. The last person I wanted to run in to.

I turned away from the ATM, hunching my shoulders and moving quickly. Just seeing him made me angry all over again.

When I reached the street, I saw Gussie was on the sidewalk, walking away from the bank. Shit. She was going in the opposite direction from Quilter Paradiso. I couldn't let her walk the streets by herself. I sighed, and took off after her. She moved slowly and I caught up to her just past the pet store. A cat stretched in the window, pretending to ignore us.

"No sign of Larry?" I asked. "Where are you going?"

"I'll wait for him at home," Gussie said without breaking stride.

I swallowed a bit of annoyance. What about me? She could have waited for me. There was a fine line between independence and downright orneriness. Gussie was being ornery now.

Unless there was another explanation. "Maybe you were supposed to meet somewhere else?" I asked gently. My older customers were notorious for getting their signals crossed. Just last week, I had a woman in the store who was sure she was meeting her girlfriends at QP before lunch. When the friends showed up an hour later, full of split pea soup, it turned out they'd been waiting for her at the diner across the street.

Gussie considered. "No."

"Why don't we call Larry and see?" I tracked the cars that passed us. No yellow cars. I had visions of Larry waiting in the bank parking lot, her sitting at home. This could be a nightmare of missed opportunities.

We were walking past the post office. Vangie's offer of the envelope came back to me. Damn. That would have made this so simple. The sign on the post office said all Express Mail had to be out by 3:00 p.m. in order to be guaranteed for the next day. My trip to the bank was supposed to take only a few minutes. I sighed. First the run-in with Tim Shore in my parking lot, and now Gussie had cost me precious time.

"Let's call Larry," I said, pulling out my phone.

"I don't have his number, dear," Gussie said.

She didn't have his number? I knew what that meant. Men who didn't give out their number were usually married. Larry wasn't exactly married, but he was involved with Celeste. That rat was playing the women against each other. I'd have thought women in their eighties would be safe from fast men. Guess a guy was never too old to want to have his cake and eat it, too.

I held my phone in my hand. "How do you get in touch with him?"

"He calls me or stops by," Gussie said.

"Okay, let's check your message machine and see if he's had a change of plans."

Gussie looked at me like I was demented. "I don't have one of those."

Oh great, I thought. Was the Goodwill out of answering machines the day she went? How did anyone live without one? I chastised myself for having such a mean thought, but I had to get back to work. I couldn't let Gussie wander around with that much cash.

Maybe I could enlist one of her friends to take over for me. Ina was babysitting her grandson and I didn't have Pearl in my cell directory. Thumbing through, I saw I had one number we could use. I tried to be delicate. "Shall we call Celeste?"

Gussie growled, "Not a good idea. She doesn't know that Larry is doing this favor for me."

I gave up. I was walking her home. "Where do you live?"

"On Monroe."

Well, at least that wasn't far.

We turned into my parents' neighborhood, the Rose Garden. The homes here were a lovely mix of small apartment buildings, bungalows and large family homes. The neighborhood was an eclectic array of California architecture—Craftsman, Spanish, Tudor, Prairie. The steady hum of leaf blowers greeted us as we walked on the uneven sidewalks.

Halloween decorations were up here, too. A tree was decorated with hanging ghosts. In one upstairs window, a pair of stuffed legs hung out, as though the person had gotten stuck climbing out.

Gussie went up the walk of a pink stucco bungalow that seemed to lean toward its much larger neighbor. Her car sat in the driveway that was split with weedy grass. Scraggly geraniums in mismatched pots lined the concrete porch steps. A plant, maybe even the foxglove that Celeste had thrown out, sat on the top of a metal milk bottle container, next to a bright green ceramic frog. I was no gardener, but I could see why Celeste had pitched it. The main spine was broken, surrounded by little sprouts of new growth. I guessed, to Gussie, it wasn't ugly enough to throw out.

From the front door, we stepped right into a trashed living room. Panic hit me. She'd been robbed already.

A large pile of magazines had toppled out of their basket, leaving a slippery hazard. Beyond, I could see an overturned TV tray table that Gussie had been using as a surface to collect small quilt blocks she was piecing. Her tomato pincushion was full of threaded needles and a pair of silver folding scissors lay nearby.

"Should we call the police?" I asked, picking up the box cover to a thousand-piece puzzle.

She looked at me like I was nuts. "Why?"

I looked around the room and then at her. She was not upset, and picked her way through the clear path on the crowded floor. I realized with a gulp that this was the way she lived. "No, it's just that..." I stuttered.

Gussie laughed. "My creative clutter? Don't worry, you're not the first person to think my house has been ransacked."

I laid the puzzle lid on a card table to keep her from seeing my flaming cheeks. The half-finished puzzle looked like it would be a covered bridge scene when finished. I resisted the urge to linger and fill in a piece of fall foliage.

"I figure heaven will be nice and orderly," she said. "I'll probably hate it."

She moved aside a stack of quilt books that blocked the egress to the kitchen at the back of the house. "I'm a very visual person," she explained. "The minute I put something away, I lose it. So I keep my projects in sight. Believe it or not, I know where everything is."

I made agreeing noises, but inside I was flipping out. Every surface was covered. Quilted wall hangings fought for wall space with souvenir plates. Next to the window was a framed picture of two black silhouettes surrounded by a heart-shaped mat. The side views of a man and a woman, it was dated September 6, 1947, Niagara Falls, NY. No doubt from Gussie's honeymoon.

A dusty philodendron looped around the curtain rod. A sun-bleached sand art in a terrarium shared a space with several African violets blooming in cracked tea cups.

Two cats tussled in the corner. They were fighting over a skein of purple yarn. I could see now that they were the reason for the toppled TV tray. The same yarn was twisted around the legs.

The smaller cat broke away and ran over my feet to beat Gussie into the kitchen.

I took in a deep breath. There was no question a woman lived alone here. There was no couch, only a threadbare recliner next to the TV table. A spindly dining room set was visible through the arch. No longer used for family dinners, the top was covered with fabric scraps like the ones she'd picked out of the garbage cans at the store.

Was this what I had to look forward to if I never married? Could my collection of pottery morph into this mishmash of old lady stuff? If I continued to haunt the online auction sites, it just might.

Looking closer, I was surprised to see that the fabric scraps had been sorted by color and size. A piece of paper on each gave the approximate dimension. Some of the fabrics had been cut into triangles, with the long corners nubbed, ready to be sewn. Maybe there was a method here after all.

Gussie moved quickly through the clutter, knowing just where to put her feet. I followed her.

The kitchen was better. The pale green countertops were worn and faded, but gleaming. Clean dishes were laid neatly in a rack next to the sink. Fresh oranges and a ripening tomato were in a bowl under the kitchen window.

Time was passing. I wasn't going to make it to the post office unless I got going. Maybe I should have Vangie meet me at the post office with the purchase order and the addressed envelope.

Nah. That was overkill. I did the calculations. Five more minutes here with Gussie. Her house was only a few minutes walk from the store, and then I had a few minutes walk to the post office. The whole trip shouldn't take more than fifteen minutes. I was okay.

Gussie laid the tote bag on the counter next to an antique blender.

My phone beeped with a text message from Vangie. "WHR R U?" Where was I? "Coming, Mother," I typed back.

"What are you going to do about the money?" I asked.

"Nothing I can do until Larry comes by for it. He'll be along soon." She washed her hands. The window over the sink looked out into the backyard.

"He'd better be. With that afternoon commute traffic, he'll never make it to Redding today."

"I'm not worried. Larry and Jeremy have talked and figured out the timing. Jeremy's lucky. Larry's got connections at the title company, and he promised to take care of any problems."

She was very calm for a woman who'd just set down a tote bag containing nearly thirty thousand dollars. I couldn't keep my eyes off it, but I wanted to know more about this guy she was giving her money to.

"What's Larry's deal?"

"What do you mean, his deal?"

"What does he do for a living?" I nearly groaned when I heard myself ask that. My father had asked that same question about every boyfriend I ever had, starting when I was fourteen. *Paper boy, Dad.* Duh.

"He's retired mostly. He sells some things on the Internet." She took out a worn tea towel from a drawer, dried her hands and laid it over her shoulder. "Come out to the garden. I meant to bring this zucchini to the store yesterday but I forgot. It'll only take a moment."

Before I could stop her, she upended the tote bag. Bundles of money spilled out onto the counter and the floor. I bent down and picked them up. I had to fetch one pack from under the refrigerator. By the time I'd wiped off the dust and turned back around, Gussie was outside. She'd grabbed a broken-down straw hat from a hook by the back door, and was walking resolutely down a stone path.

I followed her with a backward glance at the pile of money on the counter. I tried to remember if she'd locked the front door.

Gussie was still talking about Larry. "He took five of my old quilts and got a couple hundred dollars for them. He's always after me to give him my old toy sewing machines."

I'd seen the shelf running around the top of the kitchen where pink and blue mini-sized sewing machines were on display.

"He says he could get thousands for the five of them."

I must have looked skeptical because Gussie patted my hand. "You're not to worry. He knows what he's doing. Celeste trusts him. I trust him."

Looking at her, trying to read her expression, I tripped over a watering can laying on its side. Gussie's garden was like the inside of her living room. No sense of order. Plants growing without boundaries. Pumpkins surrounded by hydrangea. Marigolds mixed with mint. Raspberries and roses.

Next to the fence that separated her yard from the house next door, there was a pile of weeds. The plants had been pulled out and tossed in a heap. The leaves were large and serrated with seed pods that looked like spiky helmets.

Next to the weed pile, I saw several three-leaved plants that looked suspiciously like something my college roommate had grown in a closet. Did Gussie know what she had there? Was this what Pearl was baking into Vangie's brownies?

I moved closer. "Umm, Gussie? What's this?"

She looked at me. She was holding a piece of mint in her fingers, breathing in its fragrance.

"Oh, that's Celeste. She's been over here pulling weeds again." She laughed. "You can imagine how much my garden annoys her. She's in here all the time, trying to restore order."

I let it go. It wasn't my business.

I looked to where she pointed, the large Craftsman home next door. "That's Celeste's place? I didn't realize you lived right next to each other."

Celeste's yard was quite different. Plants were grown in raised beds, with formal brick walks in between.

Gussie stopped pulling the squash off the vine. Her eyes got cloudy and unfocused. "I wish Celeste would stop trying to take care of me. She's all wrong about Larry, you know. He really loves her. He and I are just friends. But she can't see it. She's so sure he's going to leave her. She won't be happy until she drives him away."

I started to get uncomfortable again. All this talk about senior love reminded me that one day my father might be experiencing these same pangs. That I did not want to think about.

Gussie saw me shifting my feet. "You've got things to do, I know you do," she said. "Go on back to the store. I'll be fine." She handed me the bunny tote bag of zucchini. It was full and weighed a ton.

I hesitated. "I'd like to stay with you until he gets here, but I can't. I don't like leaving you here with all this cash."

"This is the safest place there is. Who's going to think this crummy old house has tons of money in it?"

118

That was true. The old hide-in-plain-sight gambit. Except that the money was all over the kitchen counter.

I pointed inside. "Only if you put that pile somewhere more secure."

"I promise."

I wanted to be sure. "Let's do it right now."

I opened the flimsy screen door, and she followed me. She pulled an old stainless steel bread box off the top of the refrigerator. It was hard to hang on to, and she nearly dropped it. I grabbed one end and helped her settle it on the counter. All this was taking time. I glanced nervously at the bird clock over the kitchen sink. Just past two-twenty. I was okay, time wise. I checked my pocket. The cashier's check was still there.

"Where can we put this? Something with a lock?"

Gussie thought, fingers on her chin. "There's an old footlocker in the shed. I had a padlock on it when I used to have pesticides."

"Okay, perfect."

We went back outside. The shed was rusty with holes in the roof, but the footlocker looked intact. I doubted anyone would think to look here. We put the money in the footlocker and Gussie put on the padlock. I waited until she had twisted the lock.

"All right, I'm going back to work," I said.

Gussie laid a hand on my arm and handed me the tote bag I'd laid down. "Dewey, don't forget the zucchini." She didn't take her hand away. She looked over at the neat garden next door. "Larry might be at Celeste's. I can't go look. Will you?" Gussie said. "It's on your way back to the store."

I couldn't say no.

119

"There's even a short cut," Gussie said. "This is how we get to each other's houses. Or at least we did, when we were still speaking."

She opened a gate in the white picket fence that separated their yards. A bare dirt path on Gussie's side gave way to a herringbone brick walk.

A fountain trickled in the middle of Celeste's backyard. I was willing to bet it was in the exact center of the space. Everything in the garden was symmetrical. Nothing out of place.

I'd just put my hand up to knock when the back door opened. "Don't just stand out there like a Jehovah's Witness. Come in, Dewey," Celeste said.

She led me into her kitchen. It was cool and quiet. The cherry cabinets had intricate geometric inlays of lighter wood. The slate on the counters changed colors from blues to pinks and back to purple.

"I've never been in here," I said, using the hushed tones usually reserved for museums.

"Of course you have," Celeste said. "You helped serve at my husband's funeral."

I remembered now. Mom had dragged us along to the funeral and back here. Kevin had disappeared outside and I'd been stuck, alone, delivering plate after plate of mini quiches.

At that time, I had no interest in Craftsman style. It had taken a freshman college course in Architecture to light that particular fire.

I spotted a ceramic cup on the counter. My heart rate jumped. I felt like Lovejoy near a real Louis XVI Porter chair. "Is that an Ohr?"

I pointed to the cup, which I knew was a mortar and pestle. It had the fluid lines that the famous Arts and Crafts potter was known for. It was unglazed, so it had to be one of his later pieces. Kind of ugly, if one didn't know the value.

"I didn't know he made mortars," I said, reverently.

The lines of the piece were so inviting. Without thinking, I picked it up. Celeste stiffened. I would never have had the nerve to touch it if I'd thought about it. I promised not to drop it.

Rubbing my fingers along the curvy top, I could see a few seeds inside. "You use this?" I said in amazement. One Ohr piece could sell for thousands of dollars.

Celeste gently released my grip and took the mortar from me. She pulled up a corner of the apron she was wearing and wiped out the inside of the cup and the pestle. "Everything I own has a function and purpose. That's the Craftsman credo."

That was true. "I have an Ohr mug," I said, trying to imagine putting coffee in it. "My parents got it for me as a graduation gift."

"I know," Celeste said, with a slight smile on her face.

"Did you ... help Mom find it? I wondered where she suddenly got the expertise."

Celeste nodded, placing the mortar and pestle back on the counter. "It was one of my pieces. I have an extensive collection."

I half-remembered a built-in cabinet filled with pottery that I'd thought was ugly when I was fifteen. Now I'd love to see it. "Can I see the rest?"

A shadow crossed her face. "Another time perhaps."

She pointed to the tote bag full of zucchini. "I see you came from Gussie's. Are you here to broker a peace?"

"Not exactly," I said.

She led me into a redwood-paneled living room. It was like stepping into a picture from one of my architecture books. The sideboard looked to be Royersford. The stately grandfather clock was Stickley.

"Is that an Ali Baba bench?" I asked, my voice cracking at the sight of the rare piece.

Celeste was amused. "You look like you've seen a ghost."

A ghost? A dream, maybe. This was my house, all grown-up. "I live in a small Craftsman," I said. "Of course it's nothing compared to what you have."

"I should think not. This is a Maybeck."

My knees buckled. This was the real thing. "I didn't know he did houses in San Jose."

She was quiet, waiting for me to get to the point of my visit. Arms crossed, she stood in front of her fireplace. Family photos lined the mantel in matching silver frames. To the left was a book-lined inglenook. I wanted to build one of those cozy reading areas in my house.

I shook myself. "I was looking for Larry. He was supposed to meet Gussie. An hour or so ago."

Pain shot across her face. "Larry's gone."

"Gone? Gone where?" I asked.

Celeste's back sagged before she caught herself and straightened. "Gone for good. He packed his things and left me."

This was bad. "I'm sorry." Was Gussie the reason Larry left? Did she know? She couldn't have; she'd sent me over here.

"When?" I asked.

"Yesterday evening," she said.

Yesterday, I'd seen Larry and Gussie pull away from the store. He obviously had never told Gussie his plans to leave. Gussie was expecting him today.

She walked past me and opened the oak-carved front door. "You won't mind if I don't want to talk about this. This is my private life. Not for public consumption. I apologize for the scene in your store yesterday. That will never happen again."

Gussie was waiting for him. "Where did he go?" Maybe Larry had yet another woman stashed somewhere else.

Celeste just compressed her lips into tiny white lines. She held the door open.

I said, "He told Gussie he was going to help her." Was he going to keep his word and help Gussie get the money to her grandson?

"If I were you, Dewey Pellicano, I wouldn't worry about Gussie. She's been taking care of herself for as long as you have. Longer. She's perfectly capable of handling her life."

"But ..."

"I don't know how you know about Gussie and Larry's plans, but it's really none of your business. We are independent women, taking care of our own affairs. Tell me, did you give any thought to what your mother was doing most days?"

That hurt. That was not fair. My mother's life was cut short. She would never get to be an old woman like Celeste. My mouth twisted painfully as I tried not to cry.

"I thought not. We don't ask for your help, Dewey. We don't need it. I will tell Gussie that Larry is no longer available, and that will be the end of it."

I had no choice but to go through the door.

She nodded. "Larry is not a part of my life anymore. Or hers."

The wonderful grandfather clock chimed three times. I'd missed the post office. What an idiot I was. Of course Gussie's clock wouldn't keep the correct time.

TEN

I walked back to the store, the bunny tote bag conspicuously full of squash. It was too heavy to tuck under my arm, so I had no choice but to carry it by the handles. Thankfully, I saw no one I knew.

Celeste's words had hurt. Was I substituting Gussie's problems for my own? I was ignoring everything I had to do.

I went through my mental checklist of the chores I'd neglected for the last couple of hours. Top of the list was the scissors. I was the one who'd messed up getting the cashier check in on time, I'd be the one to fix it. I'd call the company first thing in the morning, and beg.

I should be able to finish checking in the notions before my date with Buster tonight. Once I got those entered into the inventory, I would have Jenn or Kym tag them and put them out for sale. I wanted to be sure that the customers could easily find what they needed during the sale.

My step got lighter as I got closer to the store. I'd had an idea that might earn me a few brownie points with my newest customers.

I walked in through the back door. Vangie was in the hall, breaking down boxes and bundling the cardboard cores that fabric came wound on. Each one represented a bolt of fabric sold, and that was a good thing, but it also meant a never-ending recycling battle.

I checked the classroom. Pearl and Ina were working on the Old Maid's Puzzle quilt. The quilt frame was up and the two women sat on either side of it, hand quilting. They looked a little lost as the frame was big enough to seat at least six people, and they were the only two there. I'd look in on them in a minute.

I handed Vangie a piece of cardboard that had fallen. "Need help?"

Vangie shook her head. "Last load. Did you get the cashier's check?"

I patted my back pocket, then held up the bag of zucchini. "But I ran into Gussie at the bank, and, long story short, I missed the deadline to mail it at the post office."

She glanced at the clock. "It's too late to call them now. Too bad, these New Yorkers already think all Californians are weirdos. Now we go and flake on them. I told them I'd have the check to them by eleven tomorrow."

This wasn't Vangie's fault. It was on me. I held my hands up. I laid the bag on her desk. She made a great ratatouille. "I'm sorry. I know I screwed up. I'll make it right."

I took the check out of my pocket and put it in the safe.

Vangie said, "Zorn's here." She motioned with her head toward the kitchen. "He's in there. Mrs. Unites nabbed him on the way in."

126

She bumped the back door open with her hip and headed for the dumpster.

Pearl called to me from inside the classroom. "Dewey, come here."

I poked my head in and told her I'd be right back. "I've got to do this one thing."

I gathered a dozen fat quarters, those cute little bundles of fabric that quilters loved, picking the latest fabrics in an array of colors. Kym watched me carefully. There were no customers in the store, and she was busily inspecting her fingernails for chipped polish.

"What are you doing?" she asked.

"Customer relations. I'm giving a free fat quarter to everyone whose car got stuck here overnight."

She tossed her hair back. "Aren't they all locked?"

"I assume so, which is why I'm going to stick them under a windshield wiper."

Kym watched as I pulled the barcodes off and stuck them on a spare piece of paper. I'd have to write these off as promotions, and I needed the barcodes to do that. I gathered some business cards and tossed her the feather duster from the hook behind the cash register.

"As long as you're not doing anything..." I said. She caught the bright pink thing like it was a tadpole and reluctantly flicked it over the nearest shelf.

Outside, I tucked a fat quarter on each windshield in the back parking lot. I wasn't even sure they were all from the class last night but it couldn't hurt. I attached a Quilter Paradiso card and hoped it would be enough to waylay any hard feelings.

The big van was last. There was no sign of Tim Shore. I didn't really want to leave him a gift, but I couldn't skip him. Good customer service didn't get talked about, but bad always did.

His windshield wiper was out of my reach. I stepped on the black rubber step by the driver's door and grabbed the door handle to hoist myself up. The door swung open, nearly dumping me on the ground.

I brushed myself off and laid the fabric on the front seat, then thought better of it. He might just sit on it, without noticing my goodwill gesture. I decided to move it to the console. A stack of coffee-stained mail was sitting there. The van smelled as though someone lived in it. I looked around. The back seat had been taken out and the back equipped with a bed. The Shore family obviously liked to camp.

I dropped the fat quarter, knocking over the pile of mail. The entire stack fell next to the passenger seat. I had to climb farther in to reach them. I felt ridiculous, half in and half out of the van. If Shore saw me or worse, Zorn, I'd be mortified.

Straightening out the pile of bills, I noticed the address on the PG&E bill. It had been sent to an address in Milpitas.

That asshole. He'd taken enough taxi money from me last night to get him the twenty-five miles to Santa Cruz, when he really lived less than five miles away in Milpitas. My face flamed. He had sixty dollars of mine. I hoped I was around when he came back for his van, so I could give him a piece of my mind. For free.

Zorn was still monopolizing the kitchen when I went back in.

I went into the classroom where Pearl and Ina were quilting at the frame. I'd promised Gussie not to tell her friends about her huge withdrawal. As for Celeste's breakup with Larry, that was her news to tell, not mine. She would never forgive me if word got out before she was ready.

But I was concerned about Gussie. Maybe I could leave the money out of the discussion, but still find out if Gussie's house looked like a train wreck normally.

"I ran into Gussie," I said as an opening gambit after greeting Pearl and Ina. "She took me home with her. The place was such a mess, I was thinking of asking Officer Wong to check on her."

Pearl was aghast. "You would call the pigs on Gussie?" Pearl was a veteran protester.

"Come on, Pearl. Have you seen her house?"

Pearl and Ina glanced at each other, and laughed.

"That's what set you off?" Ina said. "How did it look? Piles of magazines? Fabric and yarn everywhere?"

I nodded.

Ina took off her red reading glasses and waved a dismissive hand. "That's Gussie in the middle of a project. She hates to pick up after herself—thinks it interferes with her creativity."

"It would be ridiculous to report her to the police, Dewey," Pearl said. "They would assign her a social worker, who might decide she's not capable of being on her own. Once you put someone in the system, it's impossible to get out."

I didn't mean to open such a can of worms. "Never mind, I won't tell him then. I'm sorry. I was a little worried. I thought she'd been robbed."

They laughed again. I wanted to ask them if she was growing pot, but I wasn't going to risk being humiliated again.

"What about Larry? Have you seen him today? Gussie was looking for him," I said.

Pearl said, "Leave the old ladies be, Dewey. We're perfectly capable of taking care of ourselves."

Ina said, in her best school teacher voice, "This is a great time for you to catch up on last night's lesson."

I headed for the door. "No way. I've got a million things to do."

Pearl stopped me, and twirled me around. She said, "Oh, but look. It's right there on the whiteboard."

Sure enough, someone had written on the bottom of the To-do list: #26. Quilting lesson. It was underlined in red and followed by several exclamation points.

I looked from one to the other. They were very pleased with themselves. "Very funny."

Ina giggled, and Pearl laughed. "Come on, Dewey. I've already set up the sewing machine."

My grandmother's shiny black Featherweight sewing machine with the ornate scrollwork was plugged in and ready to go. They'd gotten out my fabric and cut several pieces from last night's lesson.

"Mark a line at a quarter-inch on all the pieces, Dewey," Ina said. "You're going to sew only to that mark, and then stop and pivot."

I wasn't sure I could do that. I whined, "Pivoting sounds hard."

Ina shot me a look. "You're making it harder."

I said to Pearl, "Do you know how to do this, sew these fancy seams?"

"I do," she said. "I choose not to. I make art now, not quilts. Seam allowances and mitered corners are meaningless."

"Why can't I do it like that?" I said to Ina, piteously.

"You've got to learn the rules to break the rules," she said. She bent to break a thread with her teeth. Taking advantage of Ina being out of sight, Pearl shook her head and mouthed, "no you don't." I laughed and ducked my head down so Ina wouldn't see.

But Ina knew something was up. She had teacher radar that told her when someone was goofing off in class. And she wasn't happy. She pointed a thimbled finger at me. "Listen, you asked me to teach you how to quilt. That's what I'm teaching you. If you want to learn something else, then stop wasting my time."

"Okay, okay," I said. I hated to have her mad at me. Now there was no way I could get back to the work waiting for me in my office without spending a few minutes sewing, just to appease Ina.

I carefully lined up the two pieces of fabric and put them under the needle. I lowered the presser foot. The unfamiliar action made me nervous. It wasn't that I didn't like quilting, I just felt like a real klutz. I was always sure I was going to sew over my finger.

Pearl and Ina were quilting quietly. After a few minutes, I realized this was a good opportunity to find out more about Gussie's grandson. Having his contact information might not be a bad thing. If Larry wasn't going to take the money to Jeremy, the kid would have to come and get it.

"Whatever happened to Gussie's daughter, Donna? I remember when she dropped out of high school to have a baby."

Ina looked up, surprised. "You do? But she's what—five, six years older than you?"

"Yeah, I was in middle school, but it was a big deal. It was the first time I'd heard about someone getting a GED."

I took my foot off the power pedal and turned the big flywheel so the needle stayed in the fabric. I said, "I remember, because I thought a GED was a venereal disease."

Pearl guffawed. Ina joined in.

"Oh, the elastic mind of an eleven-year-old," Pearl said.

"She had the baby, right?" I asked.

Pearl said, "That's Gussie's grandson, Jeremy. He was trouble right from the get-go."

Ina said, "Donna's started a new life for herself. She has two baby girls and a new husband and lives in the Central Valley somewhere. Last I heard, Jeremy's in college."

Vangie stuck her head in the classroom. "Dewey? Quick question." She talked over the noise of my sewing machine, so I kept sewing, slowly. "One of the students from Ina's class last night is here to get her car. She wants to drop out and get a refund."

Ina and I exchanged a look. I'd hoped that by the time Ina's class met again next week, this would have all blown over. There were eleven people in that class. If I offered a refund to one, I'd have to offer it to all.

Ina said, "Want me to talk to her?"

I shrugged. "Would you please?"

"I know you can persuade her to stay on," I said sweetly. "If you can talk me into quilting instead of doing my real work, you can talk anyone into anything."

Ina frowned, "Don't shine me on."

"I'm not ignoring you, Ina," I said, ducking my head.

When she got to the door that Vangie held open, Ina turned back and said. "Don't iron until I come back. I want to show you the correct way."

"YEE-Ouch," Pearl said painfully. She laid down her needle and pulled her other hand out from under the quilt top. I saw a drop of blood. She sucked on the tip of her middle finger. "This is why I hate hand quilting. It hurts."

"How come?" I asked. I moved my hands farther away from the bed of the sewing machine.

"You have to use your bottom hand to know when to push the needle back up," Pearl said. She demonstrated, poking the tiny needle into the quilt top, and slipping the injured hand underneath. "If the needle doesn't go through all three layers, you're not quilting. But if you let the needle go too far down, your stitches get big and unseemly. The only way to know if the needle has pierced all layers is to feel it with your finger."

"We carry a tape. It's padded, I think, and it's supposed to avoid that problem."

Pearl shook her head. "I've got to be able to feel the tip."

I looked at my own fingers. "So you let the needle cut your fingertip? Over and over again? Seems like a silly way to do things. You're always hurting yourself."

"It's the only way I know how," Pearl said. "You've got to feel the pain to know where you're at."

She took some more stitches, and I sewed on the machine. I stopped and rolled my arms, trying to work out the stiffness that was building.

Pearl poked her needle in the quilt top. She got up and came behind me, kneading my shoulders. "It's easy to get tense sewing," she said. "You have to make sure to take breaks."

I stopped sewing. "Thanks," I said, wriggling my back. "A little to the left, please."

She laughed, but complied. We were quiet, while she got rid of the knots in my neck. She had me in a tight grip when she said, "Why all the questions about Donna? You pregnant?"

I pulled myself out of her grasp and twisted around to see her face. She looked so disingenuous, I laughed. "That would have to be a miraculous birth," I said.

Pearl's hands flew up to her face. "Oh, sorry, I just assumed." She was flustered, a rare sight. "You and Buster have been dating, and you're not…?"

I shook my head quickly before she could finish the rude gesture to illustrate her point. I held her hands in mine.

She pulled up the chair next to mine and leaned in, looking at me closely. "Is there something wrong with him? I mean, you know…"

I put my hands over my eyes. "Omigod, no. He just wants to take it slow."

Pearl frowned. "Slow? More like glacial. Is it a religious thing? Did you take some kind of oath?"

I started sewing, as much to drown out Pearl's question as to get finished. I watched the fabric fed into the sewing machine, feeling my ears go red. "Not exactly an oath. More like a bet. I've been trying to get him to move the deadline up, but we're having a little trouble with that."

"You *are* having a rough week," she said sympathetically.

Tears welled in my eyes. "It's not just Buster. It's the store. I need this sale to go well, and everything I do turns to shit. This afternoon, I blew a good opportunity to make cash. And if I don't get the e-mail notices out soon, no one will come to the sale."

"You'll get it all done. You always do," Pearl said. She gave my back a series of quick pats. "This, too, shall pass."

"Hard to remember," I said.

"That's for sure, but just remember it's all minutiae, when it comes to your real mission on this earth."

I laughed bitterly. "Like I know what *that* is."

She frowned. "What happened? You were so clear last spring. You wanted to run the shop."

Her words felt like the x-ray apron at the dentist. Heavy and dense. I wanted to throw them off.

I thought I knew what I wanted last spring. "I guess the reality is different than what I'd imagined."

"Always is, kiddo, always is. But you've got to keep in mind what you're passionate about." Pearl turned my chair to face her. She looked into my eyes.

I tried to take in what Pearl was saying. Why *did* I want to run the shop? In fact, I had more reasons now than I'd had last spring.

There were so many things I hadn't known then. Like how many beautiful, unique finished projects the customers would bring in to show me. How proud I'd feel knowing that they used QP fabrics. I didn't know yet how many stories I'd hear about the babies who carried their quilts with them all the time, or the teenage boys who went to sleepovers with their quilts, or the fathers in nursing homes with lap quilts that warmed their bodies and souls.

I'd had a chance firsthand to see what quilting meant to people. I'd gone to the homeless shelter and handed out quilts to kids without families. I'd gathered Pink Ribbon blocks that were made into quilts and auctioned off to raise money for breast cancer research. I'd shipped quilts to Katrina victims. I'd really grown to love my customers and my workers. And quilts.

There was plenty that touched my soul. But there was also more trouble.

Pearl touched my hand, bringing me back. "What's the one thing you can do to make this store better? More like the place you envisioned?"

"Get rid of Kym." As soon as the words were out of my mouth, I felt guilty, but then noticed an easing in my gut. It felt good to say the truth aloud. Even if I could never act on it. "We really don't belong working together, but what can I do? She's my sister-in-law."

Pearl crossed her arms and leaned back. "Did you ever consider she might not like working for you any better than you like being her boss?"

I turned back to the machine, sewing another three inches, concentrating on stopping the needle right on the yellow chalk dot I'd marked. "She loves it here."

Pearl lowered her voice. "No, she *loved* it here."

I couldn't have this discussion now. "I've got to get through Saturday," I said. Pearl gave me a sad smile and scooted back closer to the frame and started quilting again. In and out, over and over again.

The trouble with quilting was that it gave you time to think.

I pivoted, turning the fabric under the needle and sewing down the next seam line. It wasn't as hard as I thought.

Ina came back in the room. "One satisfied customer. She said thanks for the fat quarter, by the way. She found it on her car?" She looked at me questioningly. I just shrugged.

"Anyhow, she's looking forward to the sale and spending lots of money."

"Great job." I pulled out the fabric from under the needle and cut the thread. The seam was tight with no signs of puckering. I felt a flash of pride. I'd done a good job.

"How does my block look?"

Ina picked it out of my palm and frowned. She prodded at the seams I'd sewn, and pushed down the middle with her fingers. "Pretty good. Go iron."

Ina kept up her quilt talk. I tried to follow what she was saying, but it wasn't easy. "Be careful," she said. The edges of your diamonds are bias, so you have to be very careful of the way you iron them ..."

"Iron? You didn't tell me there was ironing in quilting. Come on, I'm the one who irons wrinkles *into* my clothes. I'm a great folder."

Pearl was grinning.

I continued, "Trust me, if you're a good enough folder, you don't need to iron."

Ina said. "I'm sure that philosophy suits you well for life, but in quilting you must iron." She pointed to where the ironing board leaned up against the wall.

Pearl said, "Don't worry, it's far more fun pressing quilt blocks than khakis. Go on. Set up the ironing board."

I was shaking my head as I pulled the ironing board away from the wall. The legs made a terrible screeching noise as I put them down. I tried not to think of it as my own screams.

One glimpse of the ironing board's new cover told me why the two women were grinning.

The entire top of the new cover was a photo of a nearly nude fireman, abs rippling, red suspenders defining his pecs. His fire pants rode low on his hips, showing just the beginning of the hairy line that led from his navel and disappeared.

"Oh my," I said.

Pearl and Ina roared with laughter, Ina snorting and Pearl throwing her head back so hard she nearly tipped her chair over.

Pearl said, "Like him? We're calling him Petey."

"Or Major Johnson."

"How about King Leer?" Ina and Pearl were both sputtering now.

I giggled. This was a first, being pranked by these senior citizens. "You two are crazy."

"You should have seen your face," Pearl said, giggling.

The door opened with a bang. Mrs. Unites came into the classroom, her eyes wild.

"The dead man is speaking to me," she said.

ELEVEN

"Looking for me?" I stood in front of the ironing board, practically covering it with my body. Pearl and Ina were beginning to laugh harder.

"That policeman is not listening to me." Her voice was high and reedy. She was breathing hard. "He keeps making jokes about bad burritos. You know my food is always fresh."

I did know this about her. She was fanatical. "He doesn't really think you poisoned him. He just doesn't want to reveal too much," I said.

"I'm telling you, like I told him. DDT."

She looked around to see if we were tracking what she was saying. We must have looked a little nuts ourselves, caught in the silliness of the ironing board trick.

She sounded desperate. Her usually flawless English became heavy with the Mexican cadences of her parents. "I know this. I know what it looks like. My parents were migrant workers. When a girl found herself in a family way that was not anticipated, a little DDT would take care of the problem."

She stopped. "Too much, and she'd end up with the same face as that man the other night."

"Frank Bascomb?" I asked.

Mrs. Unites smacked the table. "Exactly like that."

Ina was rolling her eyes, and Pearl was about to make the crazy sign by her temple. Mrs. Unites caught them and shook a finger at the pair.

"You'll see I'm right." She left the room in a huff.

"What was that?" Ina asked.

Pearl giggled. "She needs to chill. She could have used a little glimpse of Colonel Weiner."

I wasn't sure. Her ranting set my teeth on edge. "I don't know, you guys, she's usually very together. This murder investigation has her way off track."

"All of us are a little loony," Ina said. "Now close that board up and get Vangie in here. She's next."

I dutifully went to the office. I could get back to my work now.

"Ina and Pearl would like to see you," I said to Vangie.

"Where've you been? Your cell has been ringing. Buster's ring. Isn't it about time you went home to get ready for date night?" Vangie asked.

I reached in the box of notions to count the red floss I'd ordered. I glanced at the clock. It was going on four. "Soon. I should leave by five-thirty to have enough time to wash my hair, and shave my legs."

"Shaved legs, huh?" She leered at me.

I ignored her innuendo. "Did you talk to Zorn? What did he ask you about?" I wondered what he'd thought about Mrs. Unites' theories.

"He asked a lot of questions about my trip over to the guild meeting. Did I see anyone walking funny? Like that."

"Did you?"

Vangie shook her head. "Not me. But the guild e-mail group is full of people who thought they saw a drunk walking in the neighborhood."

One more thing I'd forgotten to do. I'd fallen down on the job of watching that listserv. I pulled up my e-mail. Usually, I kept up with what the five hundred quilters who made up the local guild were doing and talking about, by going to their meetings once a month and subscribing to their list. A digested version of their messages came in my inbox once or twice a day, depending on the volume. Sometimes days went by with only one or two messages. There was always a flurry right before their monthly meetings.

And there was a storm now. I scrolled through.

The guild meeting had started at six on Tuesday. According to someone called quiltingsassy, she'd called 911 just before the meeting because there was a drunk wandering in the street nearby. Someone else had gotten to the meeting late and saw him closer to the street that QP was on. There was plenty of speculation about who he was.

I closed the e-mail.

My cell rang. It was Buster.

Vangie recognized his ring, too. "Told you," she said. "That boy is eager."

"Go," I said with a shooing notion. "Ina, Pearl, remember?"

"All right," she said and pushed away from her computer. I took a peek. She'd been working on the online store website. She'd scanned fabrics and was grouping them in batches that would make them easy to find on the Internet. I felt a jolt of excitement at the prospect of having customers in New Zealand or Germany.

I answered my phone.

"How's everyone doing over there?" Buster asked.

I brought one leg up under me and got comfortable in my chair. Out the window, I could see a customer wandering through the fabric. Probably planning her assault on the store early Saturday morning, when the discount was highest. I wrote myself a note to check the usual hiding places. I had one or two customers who liked to stash bolts where only they knew where to find them.

I heard gales of laughter coming from the classroom. Vangie had met Petey.

I got back to Buster. He was talking about me meeting him at my house.

"I'm going home early. I need to go to Los Angeles in the morning," he said. This voice, the low one meant just for me, set off bottle rockets in my stomach. "Can you get home soon? Like in ten minutes? I'd like to start Date Night early."

My insides were getting even warmer as I tried to figure out if I could get out of here. I had piles of work to do. Then again, I could always come back here after our date and catch up. I was warming to the idea. I might even be able to get more work done after hours.

Date night had started as Buster's effort to court me and, like so many things we did, it had turned into a contest. We took turns planning our Wednesday nights, trying to outdo one another. So far we'd been to the shooting range (my idea), to the Demon roller coaster at Great America (his) and plenty of restaurants and bars.

They'd all been fun, but last week had been the best one yet. And not because of where we went.

We'd stopped at Gayle's Bakery in Capitola for take-out and took the pasta salad and sandwiches to the beach at dusk. The night air was soft and balmy. We'd spread out an old quilt on the sand and ate. Someone had lit a bonfire down the beach.

Bay Area weather was contrary. October nights were warmer than July ones. The sun set and the fog had lifted, revealing a canopy of twinkling stars. I was loving being right where I was. With Buster, under the stars, on a quilt made long ago by my mother. My heart swelled and I leaned in and gave him a kiss.

"What was that for?" he asked, gathering me close to him.

"I'm having fun," I said. Silly as it sounded, I was. There was no place I'd rather be.

"This is your idea of a perfect date, huh?" Buster asked. He propped himself up on one elbow and was watching me. He moved a stray hair from my cheek. I could barely tell the difference between his touch and the soft breeze.

"Not quite perfect," I said, just to see his worried look. The eyebrows came together and the two lines at the bridge of his nose got very deep.

"All I need..." I paused for great effect. "...is to see a shooting star."

His forehead didn't unfurrow as I'd expected. Instead he said the sexiest thing I'd ever heard.

"I want you to have what you want," he said and turned his face upward as if he could force a star to start hurtling toward the earth.

I waited to see if there was more to come, but Buster stayed quiet, his breath going in and out of his chest. I let his words sink into me. So simple, but so profound. Was there anyone else who wanted that and only that? Whatever I wanted? The notion that what I wanted was so important to this man stopped me.

No shooting star that night, but it didn't matter. I had what I wanted. A guy who got me, who knew what was important to me, and would help me get it.

Now he was saying that again. He wanted me to have what I wanted. I had to be sure we were talking about the same thing.

"Are you suggesting that we might meet at my house and have sex?" I said. "Before the official Date Night?"

"Yes," he said.

This was getting interesting. "Full-on, mind-blowing, head-board-slamming sex?"

"You don't have a headboard, but yes. But we can't be late for our reservation, so you better get here soon."

"You're there already?" I said, jumping out of my chair. I'd tell Zorn he could talk to me tomorrow.

"I called from the car," Buster said, and hung up.

I had to get out of here. The thought of Buster in my house, ready to break our agreement, without me, was killing me. I headed back to the kitchen to talk to Zorn.

Zorn wasn't there. I pulled open the back door to see if he'd gone outside. Instead I found Jenn standing in the parking lot, staring back at the green dumpster. She was smoking.

"Jenn?" I'd never known her to smoke. The sight brought me up short. "I thought you'd gone home hours ago."

She put the cigarette behind her back. "Officer Zorn asked me to come back."

I saw with satisfaction that some of the cars were gone from the lot. No fat quarters were on the ground, so the customers must have found them under their wipers. Shore's van was still here. The hood of the van was open and a ratty mat was underneath. Shore himself was not around.

There was no sign of Zorn, either. Jenn blew smoke out of the side of her mouth and waved her hand around. "Sorry. I found an old pack of Kym's in the kitchen. It's really stale."

She took another drag and coughed.

"Why are you smoking? I know it's upsetting having the police around."

"It's not that."

"What?" I was beginning to see how worried she was. She'd bitten her trim nails down to where the nail beds were bleeding. Her usually perky ponytail was limp.

I laid my hand on her shoulder, and moved her back to the porch so we could sit down without seeing the dumpster with its fine dusting of fingerprint powder. Enough staring at the place where the body was found.

I remembered her trembling earlier. "This morning, it sounded like you might have known Frank Bascomb."

Her pale blue eyes widened. She nodded. I waited. Jenn needed to talk this out. I was the one to hear it.

A motorcycle roared by, and she jumped. She threw her cigarette on the ground and rubbed it out. She picked up the butt before I could.

She crossed her arms across her chest and rocked forward. Her voice was high and tight, like she wasn't taking in enough oxygen. "I never thought I would hear that name again."

"You knew Frank Bascomb?"

She nodded. "Unfortunately. Met him when I was in college. The sorority house was in bad shape, and we never had enough money to fix it up. He'd do odd jobs. Clean the gutters, paint the porch, fix the screen door. I just thought he was this weird guy who thought of us as his granddaughters and wanted to help us."

She looked off in the distance. Her pretty face tight with worry. "Man, was I wrong."

She had the matchbook in her hand and looked at the cigarette butt as though she was thinking of relighting it, but settled for gnawing on a fingernail. I fought the urge to pluck her finger from her mouth.

She said, "When he said he could help me pay back money I'd borrowed, I listened. My family didn't have the money to send me to school, so I went through on student loans and credit cards. I thought he was talking about loan consolidation. Stupid, stupid, stupid."

This was not going to end well. "What happened?"

I didn't have to wait long. After taking another glance toward the dumpster, she looked at the closed back door and finished her story in a torrent of words.

"He had me give him my next grant check. In a week, I got that money back plus more. We did that a couple of times. I thought I was going to end with up with enough money to pay off my student loans. But after awhile, the returns stopped coming in, and I had to borrow more money just to finish school. I wound up with loans for nearly twice what I owed. Seventy-six-thousand dollars. I never saw Frank again."

Ouch. I tried to imagine myself with such a huge debt right out of college. I wouldn't have been able to buy my house or run the business.

I was out of words. "Wow."

She nodded miserably. "I was dating Brad at the time. When he found out, he was livid. My husband has always said if he ever got his hands on Frank, he'd kill him. But Frank disappeared. I never figured he'd be back in San Jose again."

"You sure it's the same guy?" I pictured the prone body. "Was your Frank Bascomb about six feet tall?"

She shrugged. "I guess."

"Kind of thinning, sandy-colored hair?"

"He had a full head of hair back then. This was nearly fifteen years ago."

I said. "Officer Zorn is going to want to talk to you."

I wanted to wait for Jenn and make sure she was okay after she talked to the police. This was a big step for her. Buster, and my sex life, was going to have to wait.

I headed for my office to call him. I heard more laughter from the classroom. Vangie was getting a real kick out of Petey.

As I turned into in the office, the sight of Kym using Vangie's computer stopped me in my tracks.

"Kym! What are you doing?" I shouted, grabbing the mouse out of her hand. The day's frustrations caused a dam to burst inside of me.

She let go with a jerk and a squeak. "Hey," she said.

I tried to modulate my voice a little. "Geez, you know better than to use Vangie's computer."

There was no sign of remorse in her eyes. She pounded a few more keys. "I can't open my file," she said. "Or whatever you call it."

Kym's hatred of technology usually translated to her breaking programs irretrievably. Vangie had banned her from our office more than once. The computer program that ran the point-of-sale system was meant for the average person. Not so our office computers.

"Move over," I said, bumping her off the chair and sitting down. "What file? You don't have any files on here."

She was clutching a note that was in my brother's handwriting and thrust it in my direction.

"Kevin sent over a file with the directions for the Joyous Hearts quilt. He told me how to get it open," she said, brandishing the paper like it was a hall pass. A pass that allowed her to go places she wouldn't ordinarily go.

I looked at the screen, praying she hadn't done too much moving around. Somehow she'd gotten to a folder that needed a password. How had she managed to navigate here? A thousand monkeys, or one Kym, was all it took.

I minimized that file. That was not where the e-mail was.

Kym was whining. "Vangie can't say I didn't get the instructions to her. Kevin sent them, they're in there someplace."

I moved over to the store e-mail. There was Kevin's e-mail with an attachment, called JoyousHearts.doc, unopened.

"Are you kidding me?" I cried. "I told you this morning, it's too late. The patterns are finished. We don't have time to make a new one."

Kym stuck out her lower lip in a pout and crossed her arms. "Vangie said if I wrote up the directions…"

"That was six weeks ago. You can't expect her to be able to finish it in one day."

"It won't take that long," Kym persisted.

I sighed. She had no idea how long it would take. She expected the computer to do everything quickly and seemingly without human intervention. I tried to explain to her that Vangie would have to format the files and add our logo and the other graphics that would make it a part of our QP Originals. That it would take time to do it right. She wasn't having any of it. She left the office in a huff.

I clicked off the e-mail. The file she'd stumbled on came back up. It wasn't like Vangie to password-protect a file. I tried the store password, but it didn't open. I typed in an old one. Nothing. The title of the file was 20something. Maybe it was one of her music files.

I closed the file and shut down the e-mail. I could only hope Kym hadn't gotten into anything else. She could be as destructive as a computer virus.

I put my call into Buster, promising to get home as soon as I could. As long as I was stuck here, I continued working on my box of notions. I printed out barcodes and took the items out to the front for Kym to price and put out for sale. She took the box from me without a word.

Walking back to my office, I passed the kitchen. It was empty except for Zorn, making notes. I rushed to the back door, but Jenn was already pulling out of the parking lot.

I was sorry I'd missed her. I'd really wanted to make sure she wasn't too upset. I wondered if she would tell her husband.

I went back to the kitchen. "Is Jenn's guy the same Frank Bascomb?" I asked Zorn.

Zorn leaned against the door frame. "Probably. The guy in your alley had a criminal record. Small-time, but that could mean he just never got caught. Those kinds of cons rarely get reported. Case in point, your Ms. Carroll never told anyone."

"So was he a con man?" I asked.

Zorn shrugged. "Most likely."

"Does he have other victims?" I asked. So many of my customers were women. Vulnerable women.

"None that I've met so far," he said.

"Anyone see him before he died?"

Zorn nodded. "He was seen in the general vicinity that day."

"What about his family?" I asked. Somebody must be worried about this guy.

"Nothing so far. There is no missing persons report that fits his description. We put his picture up on Crimestopppers, and we placed an ad in the paper looking for relatives."

"What if no one claims him?"

"After sixty days, he's cremated and his remains are stored," he said.

"Stored?" I didn't like the idea that this man, even if he was a crook, would be stashed away without anyone knowing who he was.

"Yes, ma'am. We keep the remains in a storeroom on the premises."

Ugh. Stuck in a box in the police station for an eternity. I couldn't think of anything worse.

I said, "What about a picture? Do you take a picture of him?"

"Of course," he said.

"Okay, I'll put it up on the bulletin board at the store. Someone on my staff might know him. Or one of my customers. Someone's bound to recognize him, if he's local."

"You do realize he was dead when the picture was taken?" he asked.

I remembered the awful expression on the dead man's face. "Never mind."

TWELVE

BUSTER'S BIG BLUE TRUCK was parked in front of my house, dwarfing the elm tree that struggled to grow in the grassy median between the road and the sidewalk. I pulled into my driveway, jumped out of my car and flung open my kitchen door.

I hollered, even though I knew I'd left the store too late. But what were dinner reservations in the face of breaking our celibacy? "Okay, dude, you'd better be naked …"

"You're too late."

I followed his sing-songy delivery. He was in my spare room. The closet door was open, and I could see a row of freshly pressed shirts in a color-coordinated line. Yesterday's laundry that had been interrupted by the murder in my alley.

He was pressing his black jeans, wearing only red plaid boxers, a white sleeveless undershirt and black socks. A bright yellow shirt was hanging on the doorknob waiting its turn.

He smiled at me and went back to focusing on the crease in his jeans.

"Good thing you carry a gun," I said, peeling off my sweater, and dropping my backpack. "Otherwise this obsession with perfectly pressed clothes would make me worry about your manhood."

He ignored my sexist remark. Ironing put him in a totally mellow zone that was impossible to break.

"Everything go okay with Jenn?" he said. His voice filled my small house. I went back into the kitchen.

I didn't want to talk about the murder investigation. "Took way too long, and then she went home. I never saw her after she told Zorn she knew Frank." I grabbed two water bottles from the fridg. Drinking from one, I walked back to the spare room and placed the other on the end of the ironing board for him.

"Am I really too late?" I said, trying to sound as plaintive as I could.

He smiled his thanks. "We've got a half-hour to get to our reservations. It'll take us ten minutes to drive to Santana Row."

Santana Row? That was intriguing. Not our usual choice for dinner. It was always crowded with high-gloss people. Our age, but not our crowd. We were more burger and fries than Asian Fusion. That did explain the need to dress up.

Buster was still doing his countdown to departure time. "That leaves you twenty minutes to get ready. Reservations are impossible to get, even mid-week."

"We don't have to be on time," I said. "We don't even have to go there."

Buster looked up and frowned. "This is my date night. Next week, we can go to St. John's Tavern and play trivia. Again."

I'd been counting on something a little more grown up. Like a bubble bath for two. I gave up.

"How was your day?" I asked.

He shrugged. "Another exciting day at the computer. I'm looking at security footage. The pictures aren't the best quality, so I have to stare at them. The only danger I'm in is of getting eye strain."

His not being in danger was okay with me, but Buster found safe boring and not why he joined the force.

I took a pull on my water bottle. "Are you getting closer to solving the case?"

"Maybe," he said. "I'll feel better once I see the guy in L.A. myself."

I loved this part of our relationship. Catching up at the end of the day. I found his work to be endlessly fascinating and he really cared about Quilter Paradiso. It was sweet to have someone to talk things over with.

He checked the time, taking in my rumpled appearance. "Shouldn't you be getting ready?"

"It won't take me that long. I like watching you do that. It's sexy to see a man iron his clothes."

"What's so sexy about it?" He put the iron down flat on the board. Tiny feet jutted out of the bottom, raising the hot metal off the surface. That new-fangled iron had been a gift from me to him. When I saw it introduced at a trade show, I knew he had to have one. He loved hearing the little woosh the iron made when it raised up.

"You look so competent," I said, as he pulled on his pants. He moved the shirt onto the ironing board and picked up the iron again.

I kept going. "Your forehead gets all wrinkly. You practically stick your tongue out when you go around each little button."

Buster shot a burst of steam in my direction.

I was well out of range, and I laughed. "Hey, if word ever got out that you iron, wash dishes, *and* put the toilet seat down, you'd be swamped with marriage proposals."

"That's the real reason I carry a gun," he said, without looking up. "To fend off desperate women."

"Of course the celibacy doesn't really work in your favor."

"Get out of here and let me finish."

"Got to work on the chastity thing," I teased, as I backed into the hall.

"Later," he promised.

My heart did a two-step. A promise was a promise.

The bathroom was misty. Buster had showered in here recently. The smell of his aftershave was acrid and tangy. Like nothing at the quilt shop. I breathed in, savoring the maleness of the scent.

After my quick shower, I ducked into my bedroom wrapped in a towel. A glance in the spare room told me that the ironing board was put away, no doubt in the spare room closet where Buster had installed a specialized holder. I could hear him in the kitchen, humming a Maroon 5 song he was trying to learn to play on the guitar.

I toweled off, putting on my only set of Victoria Secret matching bra and panties and pulled my dress over my head. The silky fabric snaked easily over the fullest part of my hips and settled around my knees. I glanced in the mirror over my grandmother's dresser. If I backed up to the bed and turned just right, I could get an almost full view.

I twirled a little, feeling a freedom that my usual khakis didn't impart. I liked this wrap dress I'd bought last year. Probably out of style by now, but the brown and black print looked good on me. The colors brought out the highlights in my hair.

I moved again, adjusting the diagonal front that cut over my breasts, making them look full. It was sexy but not trashy. The tie belt nipped in my waist, and the high cut hem meant my legs peeked in and out as I walked. I pictured myself sitting across from Buster at the table, letting him catch glimpses of skin as we ate dinner.

It was fine that we were waiting until after dinner for our love-making. Going out and prolonging our wait for just a few more hours would be fun, now that I knew there would be a payoff at the end of the evening.

We would have a bottle of wine with dinner, and flirt. Buster was a great tease. His blue eyes were expressive, and his lips always looked kissable. I'd kick off my shoes under the table and rub my bare foot on his leg.

I returned to my bathroom to put on lipstick and brush a layer of mascara on my lashes. I was humming along with his playing.

The strumming stopped. "Need some help in there?"

"Stay where you are," I commanded.

I wanted to make an entrance. Buster didn't hear the click click of my heels on the hardwood floor, as he was in the middle of a riff on the guitar. I watched him, sitting on the couch with his right leg crossed over the left. I felt my knees weaken a little as his fingers moved quickly across the graceful neck.

The yellow shirt looked surprisingly good on him, complementing his black hair and fair skin and blue eyes. His shirt was open at the neck. He wore a tie most days on his job as homicide detective. I liked him tieless. The splayed shirt collar gave me a peek at the black hair on his chest.

He saw me then, and looked up with a quick smile that quickly spread into a large grin. His eyes widened.

"You clean up good, Pellicano." He laid down the guitar.

"Back at you," I said.

"No, really. You look real good."

I felt a blush coming on. "Why, thank you," I said, doing a little dip at the knees. Dressing up was a bigger stretch for me than him.

He stood and came up slowly. "This really is a new beginning for us, Dewey. Nothing is going to be the same after this dinner tonight."

He ran one hand over my hip, lingering over the silky smoothness of the dress. I had to admit it felt good, the way his hand slid over the sleek fabric. I felt my motor start to purr. But it would be several hours before we got back here.

"Don't be getting all mushy on me, Healy, just because I'm wearing a dress. I can still kick your ass in air hockey."

He laughed. "And I can still admire your legs in those sandals."

———

The restaurant was packed, even though it was a work night. Silicon Valley worked hard, and played hard. I saw more than a few BlackBerries lit up as we made our way through the noisy bar.

Halloween decorations were up, and the hostess wore spider web earrings.

"Table for four. Healy," Buster said to her.

"Four?" I turned to him for an explanation. The warm feeling in my belly that had been building turned suddenly cool.

He put a hand on the small of my back and whispered, "My night. My choice. It's going to be fun."

"Your party is already seated," the hostess said, moving quickly, her heels, at least three inches higher than mine, made even louder clacking noises on the highly polished marble black floor. That was a contest I'd lose.

We turned a corner, and I stopped. I felt Buster's feet do a stutter step as he tried to avoid stepping on my heel. I turned and gave him a dirty look.

Under a large plant with twinkle lights in the branches, Kevin and Kym were seated at a table. There were two empty places opposite them.

I stopped, looked at Buster. "That's not our table," I said, the words spitting out of my mouth. His face changed expression. One second he was proud of himself, then he realized he'd made a big mistake.

"I thought—Kevin said—you've been missing him," he stuttered.

I closed my eyes. I could see he meant well. I had complained that I didn't see enough of my brother.

My fantasy of the sweet intimate dinner we'd be having, with me flirting and him appreciating the view across the table was dashed. Instead, I'd be making polite conversation with my brother and Kym. By the time we got home tonight, I doubted I'd be in the mood for the sexy climax I'd been envisioning.

The hostess moved on without us, cradling the large menus, gold tassels dangling. Now she was at the table, smiling expectantly. I wanted to run, but Buster kept his hand in the small of my back.

Kevin caught sight and waved us over. I couldn't walk away from my brother. He looked so happy to see us.

"We'll talk later about how wrong this is," I muttered to Buster. I sat in the chair opposite Kevin that the hostess pulled out. Buster waited for me to get seated and then sat down next to me. I felt him watching me, but I didn't want to look at him right now. The hostess handed us the menus, said our waiter would be Zach and disappeared.

"Glad you two could make it," Buster said. He and Kevin exchanged fist bumps. Kym leaned over to kiss Buster's cheek and kissed the air next to mine. So this is how it was going to be, we were going to act civilized. That must be why such a fancy restaurant.

Buster straightened the silverware in front of him, scooting his water glass over a millimeter. He fussed with his collar and shot his cuffs. I laid a hand over his, before he could adjust his belt buckle. His need to fuss was getting on my nerves. He hadn't earned the right to be nervous. He'd set this up, now he needed to live with the consequences.

Kym was smiling. Her face took on that glow it always had around Kevin. For as much grief as she caused me, I knew that she loved my brother and he loved her. But I didn't have to sit across the table and watch it all night.

Kevin looked from my face to Buster's. "I can see that you haven't figured out my big sister hates surprises."

I fake-smiled at Kevin. "The man still has a few things to learn about me."

"I'm sure you'll teach him, Punk," Kevin said.

The childhood nickname was not endearing him to me.

Buster put his napkin in his lap, not looking at either one of us. He knew he'd screwed up. I took a deep breath, trying to fight the rising anger. Tonight Buster thought he'd known what I wanted, but he was far off the mark.

Kym was ignoring us, studying the menu. Her fake fingernail followed the line of print. She fit right into the sophisticated vibe of the place. Her blonde hair was perfect, her makeup flawlessly applied, if a bit too heavy. I'd always maintained she'd look prettier with a lot less eyeliner. She'd come right from the store, and was dressed in the white batiste blouse with puffed sleeves and blue skirt she'd been wearing earlier.

In my year-old dress, I was feeling frumpier by the moment.

A waiter took our drink order. Kevin and Kym already had matching mojitos in front of them.

"What wine would you like, Buster?" I asked, just as he asked the waiter what kind of beer they had on tap. He froze as Zach rattled off the tap and bottled choices.

"I assumed we were getting a bottle of wine," I said.

"Oh, I thought I'd get a beer, but if you want wine..." he said.

"No, it's okay." So much for the romance of sharing some vino.

"Order the bottle. I'll have some with you," Buster insisted.

"Never mind," I said, getting pissed off. "A dirty martini," I said to the server.

Kevin and Kym were watching us like two cats watching the Nature Channel. We were creatures they'd never seen before.

Buster looked miserable when the waiter came back with our drinks a few minutes later.

"So, Buster," Kym said. "What can you tell us about Dewey's dead body?"

A pained expression crossed Kevin's face quickly. His arm twitched under the table, and I saw Kym flinch in surprise.

"No shop talk, please," Kevin said brightly as though he wasn't squeezing his wife's knee.

Buster put in, "Really. Because you know the next thing is that Kevin will be boring us with gripping stories of fixtures that didn't arrive on time, or plumbers on crack, or the depth of the water table in Santa Clara County."

"Hey," Kevin said. "Sure beats talking about facial recognition software or deteriorated DNA and the difference between mummification and ordinary decay."

Buster said, with a grin. "You're just jealous."

"Oh yeah, jealous of digging up dead bodies."

I knew these two were doing exactly the jobs they'd always wanted and they did too.

"Dewey just likes to talk about computers," Kym complained. "Bit maps or something. Bit naps?"

I ignored her and watched my brother and his best friend. Kevin laughed at Kym's bon mot. I was struck by how much he looked like my mother when he smiled. My heart swelled.

Being mad at Kevin for being married to Kym was ridiculous. It wasn't an all or nothing situation. I didn't have to love her. He did and that was enough. I did love him. He was my brother.

I nudged Buster under the table with my knee and grabbed his hand and squeezed. He met my eyes and smiled slowly. His smiles were a revelation, changing the landscape of his face so entirely. This one came from deep within. I knew he'd planned this dinner to make me happy, not to torment me.

I leaned into him, my voice husky with desire. "Stay over tonight?"

"If you'll have me," he whispered, kissing my hair.

The waiter came to take our orders.

"How about them Giants?" Buster said, finding a topic we could all relate to. The San Francisco Giants were in the playoffs for the first time in years, and baseball was a second language for all of us. Even Kym knew her earned run average from her RBIs.

"Did you hear about the Stitch 'n' Pitch night?" Kym asked. "Knitters take their projects with them to the game. My Appliqué Girlz group is going to protest. We're going to bring our sewing."

The rest of the night went by quickly as I told stories about my brother and Buster as kids. Kym never tired of hearing their antics, and as long as the topic was Kevin, I had her full attention.

"How about the shop being on that TV show," Kevin said. "Pretty cool, huh?"

"What's this?" Buster said, leaning back in his chair. His shirt gapped at the neck, giving me a nice view. He looked from Kevin to me, eyes questioning.

"I didn't tell you?" I said, hand to my mouth as I realized I'd never given him the good news. "I didn't tell you that QP is going to be on national television on Friday morning?"

"You never told me," Buster said. He looked hurt. "Is it a big deal?"

He said that almost wistfully. Like if it wasn't a big deal, it was no biggie that I forget to tell him.

"It's huge," I said sheepishly. "A spot on *Wonderful World of Quilts* could make QP a destination shop." At his blank look, I explained. "A shop that quilters travel to, just to say they'd been there."

"Congratulations," he said.

"Kym's the star of the show," Kevin said. He had his arm around her and was smiling proudly. Kym agreed.

I couldn't argue with that.

Kym said, "Come to the store to watch it, Buster. Friday morning at ten-thirty. Kevin's bringing in the big TV. I've invited a bunch of people. My parents, my quilting bee. It's going to be a party."

I hadn't heard any of these plans. Buster wasn't the last one to know. I was.

THIRTEEN

"Before you say anything, let me just say, Kym picked the restaurant."

"No kidding," I said. I let him off the hook. "It was okay."

"Are you ready for a stellar end to an awesome evening?" Buster asked as we waited for the valet to bring the truck around. We'd hung around after Kym and Kevin had left, listening to jazz, the Wally Schnalle Quartet, playing in the courtyard. The music helped me recapture the sexy mood I'd been in earlier.

"Awesome?" I said. "I don't know if I'd call it that."

He swung around, puzzled.

I said, "After all, there was *Kym*." I smiled at him to let him know I wasn't really mad at him. It wasn't his fault that Kym and Kevin came as a set.

Buster opened the passenger door and helped me in. He tipped the valet and climbed in the driver's seat. He checked his mirror and pulled out. "Yeah, but you and Kevin…"

I needed to put an end to this. I didn't want a lifetime of double dates. "Look Buster, I admit that I didn't realize until tonight how much I missed just hanging out with Kevin."

He nodded eagerly. "He told me he misses that, too."

I can't do it with Kym. "Next time let's invite Kevin to come with us to the batting cages. I see enough of Kym at work. It's like me forcing you to spend more time with Sanchez."

He laughed warily. His partner was not the most fun guy.

I said, "Or worse, Anton Zorn." I said his name like Zorn did, with all capital letters. "What is it with you two, anyway?"

Buster signaled and made a right turn on Hedding. His eyes were on the road ahead, and I couldn't see them. Dating a homicide detective meant I'd become more aware of body language and facial expressions. But being a detective, Buster knew how to hide his feelings.

His voice was neutral, as though what Zorn thought didn't mean much to him, but his words told me different. "He thinks I'm a green know-it-all who relies on the computer too much."

"How long has he been in homicide?"

"I don't know—thirty, forty years. Since the last Ice Age. To him, finding a murderer is all gut and experience. Since I have very little of that, he's suspicious."

"And because he's an unevolved human being, that comes out as petty jealousy," I said.

"Something like that." Buster smiled at me and touched the back of my hand reassuringly. "He's not the only guy on homicide that didn't want to see me become a detective. I'm younger than everyone else. Proving myself is just part of the job. No big deal."

I hadn't realized things had been so tough for him. I waited for him to say more, but nothing came. He was finished talking about work.

I patted his knee. "I think you're pretty special."

We were stopped for a light. Buster broke his thoughtfulness and moved in for a kiss, smiling. I happily raised my face to his. I loved the smell of him.

He put an arm around me. "Have I told you lately how much I like having you in my life?"

"You said you had the perfect end for this evening?" I purred, moving closer to him on the bench seat. We'd been in this truck a zillion times since our lunchtime tryst six months ago, but right now, I was feeling the good vibrations we'd left behind.

"I believe I used the term stellar," he said.

"Sex, Buster. That's what I want. Full on, mind-blowing, total body contact, your naked body next to mine. So close I can't tell where you begin and I end." There. I said it. I asked for it.

"Whoa," Buster said, revving the engine, loud. The young driver in the car next to us looked frightened. Horny couples were probably not covered in Driver's Ed.

He drummed his hands on the steering wheel, looking up at the signal. He pressed the accelerator and pretended to run the red light. "Is anyone looking?"

I laughed. "If you get a ticket, that'll just slow us down more. Get us home without police intervention."

He cruised through the green light. I leaned against him, looking at the stars out the windshield. It was a clear night. My belly thrummed in anticipation of the rest of the evening. It was only eleven, so we had plenty of time for sex and a good's night sleep. I would salvage this night. I sighed happily, rubbing his arm. I didn't want to move away from him. His body was so solid next to mine.

My cell rang in my purse, jarring me. Who was calling me? I glanced at the readout and saw it was the alarm company that QP used. My heart sank.

I sat up straight and answered. "Dewey Pellicano," I said briskly. Maybe it was just a sales call, trying to sign me up for more services. I would cut the operator right off.

"You're the contact for the Quilter Paradiso?" the voice said. "Your alarm is going off. We've notified the police. Thank you," he said, hanging up abruptly.

Buster looked over, eyebrows raised in question.

I ended the call, holding the phone out for emphasis. "The alarm is going off at the store," I said. "I can't believe this. Not now. This has never happened before."

"Probably just a squirrel or a crossed wire," Buster said.

I liked those scenarios. "Or the wind. That back door, if it's not closed just right, the wind can open it up."

Buster did an illegal U-turn to head us back toward the store. Breaking traffic rules now, for such a pedestrian reason.

He said, "When I was on patrol, we got these calls all the time. Usually it's nothing. I'll have you back to your place in no time."

"You'd better," I muttered.

Officer Wong was standing outside the shop in the back parking lot, on his cell phone when we arrived. He nodded at us and continued talking, "Yes, Detective Zorn, I'll let you know if there is anything here that relates to Bascomb. Right now, it looks like a routine break-in."

Break-in? My gut tightened, and I saw worry crease Buster's face. I knew he was reflecting the look on my face.

Wong was standing between me and the back door. I tried to go around him, but he held his hand up. He closed his phone and nodded at Buster, who nodded back.

"What's going on?" I said, while the two of them did their cop-dance exchange of expressions. Meaningful to them, I was sure. Buster was low on the homicide food chain, but he still had more prestige than Wong, even though they were about the same age. The police hierarchy was as complicated as a bee hive.

Wong said, "The call came in. When I got here, the back door was ajar. I've searched inside and found no one," he said to me.

"Does it look like someone forced their way in?" Buster said. A cold clammy sensation set up in my stomach. Buster was examining the lock and the door jamb, touching nothing, his eyes narrowed and brow tightened.

Officer Wong shook his head. "No sign of that." To me, he said, "I'd like you to go in and see if anything is missing."

I crossed the threshold tentatively and turned the alarm off. Most days I was the first one in the store, often before first light, but now the normal shapes looked sinister. I turned on the light that illuminated the hall. Buster was right behind me. I could feel his breath on my neck. I reached back and squeezed his hand, grateful for his presence.

We went through all the rooms, slowly and methodically. Buster asked me questions about where things had been. As far as I could see, nothing looked out of place.

Buster and I stood in my office. I checked the safe. The door was closed and securely locked. Buster looked for scratches on the surface to see if it might have been opened, but it was impossible to tell if they were new ones, or old, the result of me fumbling with the key lock on it.

I opened the safe using the key on my chain and checked the contents.

"Who locked up tonight?" Buster said, after I'd determined nothing was missing. "Is it possible that they just forgot? Then the wind caught the door and set off the alarm."

"It's possible," I said. "This is a crazy week. We're all really busy. Everyone's a bit absent-minded." I called Vangie. She picked up on the first ring. I knew she'd be waiting for Letterman to come on.

I said, "Sorry, I know it's late, but did you lock the back door?"

Vangie sounded like she was eating popcorn. She chewed noisily in my ear. "I left the store before Kym did. She was supposed to lock up. I bet she forgot. You know her, she's always in such a hurry."

Last month Kym had closed up and left a customer still in the bathroom. I'd gotten a frantic cell-phone call. "Damn. She must have gone out the front without double-checking the back. Sorry to bother you. I'll see you in the morning."

I hung up. Wong had joined us. I said to him, "It doesn't look like anyone was in here. I think the door just got left unlocked. One of my employees is a little lax."

Officer Wong looked grim. "Can you please follow me? I want to show you something."

I looked at Buster in a panic. My knees weakened. What had Wong found? Oh, please, not another body. I didn't want to move. Buster applied gentle pressure to the small of my back, and kissed my hair.

Wong was waiting in the kitchen, legs spread wide apart, arms akimbo. He looked stern. "Do you usually leave the keys on these hooks?" He pointed to the metal key rack that my mother had brought back from a buying trip back East. There were six metal houses, each one painted with a different quilt design. All of our keys hang from the hooks on the front doors during the day. Two store keys hung there now.

"When people come to work, they put their purses in the cubbies and put their keys on the hooks. It's convenient," I said. I finished weakly. "People around here lose their keys. A lot."

"Most of your employees have keys to the store?" Wong said. "And the keys hang here all day, with people in and out?"

I was getting the picture. "None have gone missing," I said defensively.

Wong said, "I'm saying, it wouldn't be difficult for someone to come in while the store was open, make a duplicate, and put the key back without your knowledge."

"And it's just foolish to leave this key here." He handed me the key clearly marked "safe."

I pocketed the safe key and accepted defeat. "I'll take the rack down tomorrow," I said.

Buster said, "You need to change the door locks."

That would cost hundreds of dollars. "I can't afford that right now."

Buster wasn't letting it go. "How many people have keys to the store, Dewey?"

I tried to count. When I realized all my mother's old employees might have keys, I stopped at a dozen.

"Everyone who has a key is trustworthy. My mother never had any trouble," I said.

Buster and Wong shared a look. To them, it was a cruel world, full of people ready to take advantage. "I believe you that your employees are nice people," Buster said. "But they have sons or boyfriends or nephews or nieces who might find the key a handy way to get in and help themselves to your stuff."

Wong said, "Happens all the time."

Buster and Wong were double-teaming me. I protested, "There is no way it's one of my employees."

Buster shrugged. "Chances are we'll never know. All I'm saying is you should think about changing the locks."

Sure, right after paying off my credit cards.

We rechecked the front door. It was secure. I walked with Wong and Buster out the back, reset the alarm and locked the door.

We started to say goodbye to Wong, when we heard raised voices. They were coming from the back of the parking lot, along the fence. Most of the cars were gone, only that hulking van remained behind. A second patrol car was parked on the street.

Tim Shore was talking with a policewoman.

"What's he doing here?" I asked, still ticked off at Shore for trying to pin the damage to his van on me earlier.

Wong said, "He was in his van when I got here. The noise of the alarm woke him up."

My scalp tingled. "He's sleeping in my parking lot?" I was incensed. "Where does he get off? Did you cite him?"

Wong shrugged. "He said the vehicle won't start, and he was afraid to leave it alone. Said it already got damaged once here."

I didn't care if Shore heard me. I raised my voice. "That guy is a scam artist."

Buster and Wong exchanged another look. I was getting mad that they weren't taking me seriously. I got louder. "He tried to tell me that that dent on his side panel was fresh. It's practically rusted. Not to mention someone would have to be a contortionist to hit his door the way the van is parked."

I clenched my fists. He really had my blood boiling. Where did he get off sleeping in my parking lot? "What if his van is still there the morning of the sale? My customers are getting here very early. I can't have him here. Can I have him towed out?"

"If you want to pay," Wong said.

More money. I shook my head in disgust.

Tim Shore made his way over. "Sorry about the break-in, Ms. Pellicano. Good thing I was here. I woke up when the alarm was going off, and came out to see what was going on. I think I scared him off."

His Eddie Haskell routine was too much to endure. He was trying to palm himself off as a one-man Neighborhood Watch. I didn't want to encourage him, so I ignored his comments about the break-in. "Look, you can't sleep in my parking lot. You need to get this van out of here."

He shrugged, his apologetic tone so different from the way he'd treated me this afternoon without the presence of Buster and Wong. "Sorry. I should be able to get a new starter tomorrow and get it out of your hair."

"Fine, but sleeping out here is not an option."

"I'll be out as soon as…"

Buster stepped forward. "Okay, buddy, it's time to move on. I'll take you over to the Flamingo Motel."

That was the local fleabag by-the-hour place. Buster winked at me and hustled Tim into his truck.

"I'll be back for you," he said, rubbing my upper arms.

Wong had paperwork I needed to fill out. "I'll have Wong drop me off. Meet me at my house."

This day could not end on just a sour note. After all this, I was more determined than ever to end this night with a bang.

It was just after midnight when I got home. Buster had started a fire in the living room. He was sitting on the couch when I came in, so I joined him, stretching out and putting my head in his lap.

"Everything go okay?" he said quietly.

I nodded. "I don't want to think about the store anymore. I don't want to think about anything."

"Okay," he said. His fingers circled my temples, and I felt myself begin to relax. I sunk a little deeper into his lap. Buster shifted slightly. I realized my head was causing him growing discomfort. I liked the feeling.

The fireplace crackled, making us both jump. I laughed and sat up. I wriggled my butt against his lap, feeling the anticipated stiffness. I settled back on his chest, letting my body rise and fall with his breathing. He tightened his grip on me, pulling me even closer.

I sank into Buster's strong body, suddenly feeling heat rise in me that wasn't coming from the fireplace. I twisted and caught his mouth full on.

His eyes opened wide as he felt the intent in my kiss. He opened his arms and laid down on the couch. I stretched out next to him, so we were lying face to face, our bodies taut. I kissed him again, lingering, feeding myself from his mouth. I felt everything else drop away. The busy store, Kym, Kevin, the break-in, one by one leaving my psyche. The more we kissed, the more the world disappeared.

His hips twitched. I felt a burst of energy and tugged his shirt out of his pants. He pulled the shirt and his undershirt off in one motion. I laid my head down on his bare chest and heard his heart beating wildly.

I pushed myself up on my arms and looked in his eyes. As blue as the sky and as open and trusting. There was nothing behind them but compassion and sweetness. His eyes flashed, and I saw something else. Passion. Desire. Love?

A shift occurred, and we both felt it. The time was right. No more teasing.

I dragged my fingers along his pant leg, and felt him surge toward me. He closed his eyes and sighed.

His phone rang. His eyes flew open and to the coffee table where he'd laid it.

"It's Sanchez," he said. He looked like he wanted to answer it. The phone rang again, and I sat up. He ruffled his hands through his hair. He looked so handsome, with his blues eyes flashing.

He picked up the phone and walked into the kitchen with it, adjusting his pants. I heard a few grunts of acquiescence. I went to the refrigerator and poured myself a glass of wine. I could tell by his voice, my evening fun was over. I felt like crap, like I'd been drinking too much. I went and put on my pajamas, a T-shirt and cotton pants.

When he hung up, he held the phone in his hand, running his other hand over the countertop between us. I could hardly see him. Only the night light on the stove was on, and little light came in from outside. I could hear crickets in my backyard talking to each other.

Buster folded his phone. "I have to go to Los Angeles."

"Now?" I said.

Buster nodded unhappily. "We've got to see this inmate at L.A. County Jail first thing in the morning. It'll take us five hours to get there." *no, it won't!*

I drank my wine, trying to feign a cool sophistication I didn't feel. I would be okay with this, just another in a series of interruptions, but right now it felt shitty. I tried to remember where I'd put that Costco-sized bag of M&Ms. I was going to need it.

Buster was apologetic. "The guy has a court date tomorrow, and if we don't see him before that, we'll never get in to see him. Depending how his case goes, he might be transferred..." Buster started.

"It's okay," I said. "It's your job. I understand. We just spent two hours dealing with my job, didn't we? That's how it goes." I sounded more understanding than I felt, but I knew the score.

Buster said, "The good news is my laundry is still in my truck, so I have a change of clothes to take with me. I don't need to go home first and pack."

"Okay," I said tentatively, not knowing where this was going.

Buster moved closer. "I have to pick up Sanchez in a half-hour. So I've got twenty minutes or so before I have to leave."

He took my wine glass and set it on the counter.

"Great," I said tentatively.

"I know just what you need," he said, sliding a hand under my waistband.

175

"What are you doing?" I said, startled. I was trapped between Buster and the counter.

"I might have to leave, but that doesn't mean I can't leave you nice and relaxed," he said, nuzzling my neck. His hand was snaking down my pants.

I jerked away abruptly, his head and mine crashing painfully. "What? Another one of your one-way tickets to the funhouse?"

I moved away from him.

"Whoa, what's wrong?" A frown crossed his face, his forehead creased like a boy learning table manners.

I grabbed my wine glass and moved into the living room. I stood in front of the fire, watching the sparks fly. "I *told* you I don't like being on the receiving end all the time," I said.

He followed me, putting his arms around my waist from behind. "You're tired, Dewey, come on. And you're mad because I have to leave."

I turned on him, breaking his embrace. "Do *not* diminish what I'm saying. Yes, I'm tired, yes, I'm upset that you have to leave, but I know how I feel. I feel like a geisha, performing for your amusement."

"Well, sorry," Buster's voice grew petulant. "Here I thought I was being a good guy."

Where was the guy I'd thought knew me so well? I felt a wave of despair. Was I making all that up? Did he know me at all? Did he know what I wanted enough to give it to me? Right now, it didn't seem like it.

Buster walked to the door. I took a deep breath.

I said, "Don't leave yet. We need to talk this out."

He looked at his watch, but came back and sat on the couch. I stood in front of him.

"Look, it's not that I don't love what you do to me," I said. "You know I do. But the one-sided stuff has got to stop."

He wasn't looking at me. "You've enjoyed it. I've seen you. I've *heard* you."

I ground my teeth. Why was he so obtuse?

I tried an explanation. "Didn't you ever have a friend who insisted on picking up the check every time you went out? Never let you buy dinner or a drink?"

He shook his head.

Darn. "Well, at first, it's kind of nice, but after awhile, you don't want to hang out with them. You drop that friend."

"Are you going to drop me?" His voice was low and full of self-pity.

I clenched my fist. It would be so much easier to pop him one like I used to do with Kevin when he wasn't listening. But we were grownups now, and I'd been told since preschool to use my words. I'd like to take the words, one by one, and drop them on his thick skull.

I took in a breath and flexed my fingers. I was in danger of snapping the stem of my wine glass.

I said, "It makes me feel like I have nothing to offer you. And that makes me feel like shit."

He stared at his hands clasped in front of his knees. "That's not how I intended it."

My mantel clock chimed twelve thirty. Buster pushed himself up from the couch. "I've got to go."

I burst out, "Are you scared, Healy? Is that it? Afraid that all this foreplay will amount to nothing?"

I knew as soon as the words were out of my mouth that I'd gone too far. No guy could withstand a direct hit to his manhood.

He left without another word.

FOURTEEN

I ROLLED OVER IN bed for the hundredth time, punching my pillow and pulling the quilt over my head. My mattress felt like a field of rocks, and my special quilt felt as scratchy and rough as if it was filled with straw instead of wool batting.

The night was never-ending. At two, I was practicing blasting Kym for leaving the store unlocked. At three, I was wishing I'd let Buster have his way. In between, worries about Frank Bascomb being murdered and Tim Shore sleeping in my parking lot wound around the anxieties about Gussie having all that money in her house. By five, I was in a cold sweat, because I couldn't afford the penalty that the alarm company would charge us. That led to an all-out panic attack about the sale on Saturday and an obsessive recalculation of how much money I needed to make. I had to clear at least ten thousand dollars on Saturday.

I had to take action. At six, I got up and called the Felix Scissors Company in New York. Their day began well before mine. Once I got squared away with them, maybe I could sleep.

"This is Dewey Pellicano, from Quilter Paradiso. I wanted to let you know I didn't get the cashier's check for our purchase order into the Express mail yesterday as I'd hoped."

The woman on the other end said cheerily, "No problem. We'll ship as soon as we receive it."

I had to be assertive. "That won't work for me. I need the scissors here tomorrow."

"Sorry," she said, in a fading voice that told me she was ready to hang up.

I had one card to play. "Wait. The scissors are going to be on national TV the day after tomorrow. Can I talk to your supervisor?"

Without even a "Hold on," an instrumental heavy-on-the-strings version of "Let It Be" played in my ear. I hit the speaker phone function, and started a pot of coffee. It was finished brewing before I heard someone pick up on the other end.

A raspy man's voice came on, "What's this about my product being on TV?"

"Hello, is this Mr. Felix?"

"Just Felix," he groused. "Mr. Felix sounds like a gay hairdresser."

I didn't want to ask him what his problem with that was.

"One of my employees is appearing on tomorrow's airing of the show, *Wonderful World of Quilts* and she's shown using your palm-tree-handled appliqué scissors."

"Those are my most popular item." His Brooklyn accent was thick. *Dos are mouy most paupular idems.*

Uh-oh. Meaning he didn't need any help selling them. I'd have to up the ante. "In the preview Lark Gordon sent, I saw the scissors featured prominently."

It wasn't the scissors placement that caught his attention. "You know Lark Gordon?"

"I do."

"Listen, kid. Here's how business works. You wash my back, I'll scratch yours. You call that Lark character, tell her I want to give her scissors to use on the show."

"I can do that..." I agreed tentatively.

"I've been trying to get my products on her show for years. Just put in a word. Paulie..." he yelled. "Ship that order to California. Now. Overnight. And throw in a half dozen of the new ergonomic dressmaking shears too."

"Thank you, Felix."

"Forget about it. I'm sure you and me will be doing lots of business."

Me and yous, I thought. I went back to sleep with a smile on my face.

I slept for several hours, then woke up, heart racing. I was late for work. The store had opened an hour ago. I took a pounding shower, using all my hot water, trying to restore my energy. The day before—dealing with Gussie, eating with Kym, the break-in, the fight with Buster—had completely drained me.

Today was going to be a long day. I was so far behind. I'd have to stay really late tonight. I needed to get the e-mail out, finish checking in and shelving the notions, make sure the store's supply of coins was filled up.

I called Vangie and told her I'd woken up late. She said cheerfully that I should take my time.

I drove to work, even though it was a short walk, mentally arguing with my inner environmentalist that today was different. I needed to get there now.

I put my car on the side street and came in through the parking lot.

Tim Shore's van was still here. I kicked his tire, releasing some of the pique I was feeling. I hoped his motel mattress was full of fleas. If he didn't get this heap of junk out of here by this afternoon, I'd have Dad come over with his Suburban and tow it out.

Stewing about Shore, it wasn't until I was in the store, almost to my office, that I noticed something looked different.

Out of the corner of my eye, I saw my mother's smiling face. The hall, usually a dim space that led from the back door to the front of the store, was transformed. Pictures of all shapes and sizes were hanging on the wall. Overnight, the hall had become the Portrait Gallery of Quilter Paradiso.

It was hard to believe this was the same space where Wong, Buster, and I had stood twelve hours ago. The usually blank wall was covered in photographs. Lights, stuck on the ceiling, cast a glow.

I gasped to see a picture of my mother, wearing a newspaper hat, mugging for the camera with a much younger Ina at her side. Pearl grinned in the background. Next to that was a picture of Mom and Kym with a grinning Kevin throwing up rabbit ears behind both their heads. I touched a photo of elves for the Christmas in July sale and witches for the Halloween Monster Mash.

The history of the store was here, in photos.

"How? Who?" I said, my voice cracking. Vangie came out of the office at the sound of my voice. She was grinning, and I knew who was responsible.

"You did this?" I put my hand over my heart and patted it. Words were suddenly too difficult to form.

"I came in wicked early this morning. I didn't think I'd get done in time. It's a good thing you were late."

Her face was flushed prettily. Her dimples were so deep, I could have planted dimes in them. I hugged her tight.

"This is what you've been working on so secretly?"

Vangie said, "I wanted it to be a surprise."

Kym came out of the kitchen, blowing on a mug of hot chocolate. "She certainly didn't ask me," Kym said. "I think you're wasting valuable space with the photos. Space we could have used for merchandising."

"No, it's perfect," I said. "Our customers are a big part of the store. They'll love seeing themselves on the wall."

"Well, that one's crooked," Kym said, pointing to a frame as she walked into the store. She shouldn't be taking a beverage out there, but I was too happy to call her on it.

"There's pictures from every year of the twenty years," Vangie said.

I couldn't stop looking. All the troubles of last night melted away, as my eyes flitted around the wall, catching sight of another familiar face. My three brothers were represented, wearing red-gingham aprons at one sale, jousting with packages of batting. In an old picture, the quilting frame was set up in the loft and a group of six quilters were seated at it, smiling into the camera. Celeste,

Gussie, Pearl, Ina, and two others I didn't know. The original Stitch 'n' Bitch group.

I paced the hall, having trouble forming a coherent thought. I squeezed Vangie's arm as I walked by her. She grinned broadly, her eyes rimmed with tears.

"It's nice to see you so happy," she said.

I felt like I had a fever. I was sure my cheeks were flaming red.

"You must have been working on this forever," I said.

She nodded. "Your dad helped, giving me the old photos. I stored the images in the computer and printed them out, when you weren't around. It was all very 007. I even gave it a code name—Project 20something."

That was the name of the file I couldn't open yesterday. I was so glad now that I hadn't been able to get it open and spoil the surprise.

I scanned the wall. My eyes filled with tears again, and I swallowed a sob.

The best thing was, in all the pictures my mother was smiling. Every single one.

I wanted to stay here all day, but work awaited. I tore myself away. I grabbed Vangie again and hugged her hard. "Thank you."

"Back to work," she said, shooing me into the office.

My phone had been ringing, and I'd let it go to voice mail. I checked for messages when I got to my desk. There were two. One, from Buster. He was in L.A. The prisoner wasn't available this morning after all, so he'd be staying there until late tonight. His message was short, with no mention of the way Date Night had ended.

I swallowed my disappointment. I hated the way we'd left things last night, but I knew I wasn't wrong. I didn't want to take back what I'd said.

The other message was much more welcome. Felix Scissors had shipped. I should have the scissors Friday morning.

"Yessss!"

Vangie looked up.

I gave her a thumbs-up. "I did it!" I said. "The scissors will be here in the morning." It felt so good to get something right.

"How'd you pull that off?" Vangie said. She held her hand up for a virtual across the room high five.

"I called the scissors place from my bed as soon as they opened."

"Buster didn't mind?" Vangie said.

"He went to L.A. early," I said. Vangie looked askance, but I ignored her and moved on to a safer topic. "*Wonderful World of Quilts* airs at ten thirty our time, and the shipment is guaranteed to be here by eleven."

"Perfect," Vangie opened up a screen on her computer. "I'll make the barcodes and print them out, so as soon as the scissors get here tomorrow, we can start selling them."

"Good deal." At least something was working out okay. One item off my to-do list. "I'll mail the check."

Now I needed to confront Kym about leaving the back door open last night. I went up front. She was bent over something and drawing.

I stopped. There were store things that needed to be done. She could vacuum the floor while there were no customers. The book rack needed restocking yesterday like I'd asked. The fat quarter shelves were low on inventory.

"What are you doing?" I asked.

She looked up. "Kevin put the light box together last night, so I'm setting up a display for the sale on Saturday." She showed me the applique design she was tracing.

I took a measured breath. The light box was so big, Kevin could have run his toy trains on it. "We don't have room for that."

I wasn't taking up valuable floor space to have her sit and draw all day. "No, final answer. Take it down."

This wasn't why I came out here. "Last night, Kym, I got a call that the alarm was going off. You didn't lock the back door."

"I thought you wanted to move forward," she said. "This is the future."

"The door, Kym?"

"It was locked," she said.

I let out a breath. "You couldn't have. The door came open, and the alarm went off. The cops were here and everything."

"Ask your brother," she said. "You know how anal he is. He went around and tried all the doors before we left for dinner."

That was just like Kevin. I knew my brother would not have left a door unlocked. Still, the alarm had gone off. "Are you sure that wasn't another night?"

Kym's hands flipped back her hair, first the right side, then the left. "Why are you always picking on me, Dewey?" Kym said. "I told your brother I can't do anything right in your book. You live to tear apart every little thing I do."

I gave up. Maybe Wong was right. Someone had made a key and broken in. That wasn't good. "Take down the light table," I said, leaving her. I felt her shooting daggers at my back.

When I came back in the office, Vangie was mumbling. She had the receipts from the day before in front of her.

"What's up?" I asked, alarmed by the look on her face. I could see Kym pull out a bolt of batik fabric and cut a yard of fabric for fat quarters. Finally, she was doing something useful.

"I'm balancing the drawer, and the cash is off." Vangie was chewing on the end of her pencil. I resisted the urge to knock it out of her mouth. I always avoided her pencil cup, not liking the feeling of teeth marks under my fingers.

"Let me see." I scooted my chair over to where she was going over yesterday's receipts.

She said, "It's weird. Eighty dollars even. I've looked through all the cash sales on the computer. The amounts received and the change match up."

I shifted gears, thinking about the sales yesterday. The store hadn't been very busy.

"It's as if someone gave back eighty dollars too much change," Vangie continued. "What kind of idiot would do that?"

My first thought was Kym, then my heart sank. It was me.

"Uh-oh. I had a customer who accused me of shortchanging her." I flipped through the open screens until I found the sale. "See. I entered that she had given me a twenty-dollar bill, but when I gave her her change, she insisted that she'd given me a hundred."

"And you fell for it?" Vangie's eyebrow peaked.

"Wait, I remember, she proved it was hers. The bill had a special mark on it."

Vangie had taken back the mouse, and was paging through the sale screens backward in time.

"Her husband had given it to her for her birthday, and he'd decorated it with a heart," I said.

"Look," Vangie said, pointing at an earlier sale. "Jenn took in a hundred earlier in the day. I'd bet you anything that was your sweetheart hundred."

Vangie looked up at me. "They must have been con men. Con women."

My heart sank. "But she seemed so nice," I lamented.

Vangie shook her head. "Face it. You were scammed."

Oh, man. Eighty dollars. That was a lot of money. Especially now. I was bleeding money left and right. I rubbed my upper arms, feeling a sudden chill.

"Should I tell the police?" I asked. "This is the kind of thing the Community Watch group is trying to prevent."

Vangie shrugged. "Up to you," she said. "I wouldn't. They're not going to catch them anyway."

I decided to tell Wong next time I saw him and went to work on the database. Vangie left to bank the deposit and get more coins and small bills for the till. I worked steadily until I heard Ina hooting and hollering in the back hall. "Look at us. Oh, my goodness, was I ever that young?"

I joined Ina. She'd set down her purse and gotten out her reading glasses. She perched the red glasses on the end of her nose, and leaned in.

"Can you believe it?" I said. "Vangie got these old pictures from Dad, scanned them and printed them out."

Ina's eyes glittered with tears. "It's really fabulous."

I warned, "Don't start. You'll make me cry. Again."

Ina sniffed. Her voice was thin. "It's almost too much to take in. I mean, these are the last twenty years of my life."

"There's the proof that it was good times."

Ina clapped her hands. "Look, there's Margie, and Patsy. I loved them. They're gone now."

"Dead?" I asked quietly.

Ina looked at me askance. "No. Moved to Mesa, Arizona."

Whew. I looked for the shot I'd seen earlier. "Isn't that the Stitch 'n' Bitch group?" I had a quick sense of a buried memory of these women teaching me to thread a needle.

"That's us. That was the first raffle quilt we did for the shelter."

They had a lot to show for their time together. At least twenty raffle quilts, and thousands of dollars donated to the shelter.

In this picture, the group looked happy, arms slung around each other. Dressed in matching Hawaiian shirts and straw hats, it was hard to tell them apart. Gussie and Celeste were hand-in-hand. Even in the picture, it was easy to see how close they were. Or used to be.

Ina tapped on another picture. "There's the sidewalk sale last July."

That had been my favorite weekend of the past year. The local business association had decided on a neighborhood-wide side-walk sale. It was the first event I'd planned at Quilter Paradiso from start to finish. We'd dragged tables outside and set up last-chance displays. I'd marked down fabrics and notions and patterns. We'd handed out yardsticks with our logo to every passerby. The day had not been a big money-maker, but it had been great community relations, and I'd gotten rid of a lot of old stock. Plus, I'd had a blast.

The shot was a candid one of the crowd. Parked just past the store, in front of the burrito place, was a yellow Taurus. The car that Gussie had been waiting for at the bank. Celeste's Larry.

"Was Celeste's boyfriend at the sale?" I asked. I'd like to get a look at the man who had dumped her so completely.

"Hmm?" Ina said, moving down the row. "Larry? I don't remember." She'd moved on to another picture and was smiling at some private memory. I looked for the Taurus. There were no more shots of the sidewalk sale.

After a few minutes, Ina shook herself and clapped her hands. "Enough already! I've got to get back to working on the raffle quilt. Pearl will be here soon."

"What about Celeste and Gussie? Are they coming?" I asked.

She nodded. "They should be here. We could use their help."

I wondered if Larry had shown up after all, or if Gussie had found another way to get the money to Jeremy in Redding. I was curious about Larry and wondered if there was a better picture of him in our photos. Vangie'd taken a lot of pictures at the sidewalk sale. They were all on her computer.

Vangie wasn't back yet, so I turned on her computer, looking for her pictures folder. I saw the password protected folder that had baffled me before. Now the name made sense. 20something. Not her age or peer group as I'd thought yesterday, but twenty years of pictures from QP.

Without the password, I'd have to wait for her to see if more pictures from the sidewalk sale were in there.

I was too impatient. I tried her birth date. The file wouldn't open. I tried the store password. No go. I decided to call her. I dialed her cell number. To my surprise, I heard it ring nearby. I found her phone on the corner of the desk next to the stack of CDs from Pearl. The CDs gave me a new idea. I tried Janis67. Sure enough, the file opened.

Bless Vangie and her organizational skills. All the pictures she'd taken in the last year were in folders named by the event and date. There were a hundred and twelve from the sidewalk sale. I skipped the shots of the setup. Vangie kept those as a record of how we'd decorated. About twenty thumbnails in, the people pictures started. I hit the arrow button again and again.

There. In a shot framing the shop taken from the corner, the yellow Taurus drove by. A few pictures later Celeste appeared. Her distinctive hair style was captured.

I didn't see her again for a few shots. Then Vangie had taken a picture of Celeste paying. I could see part of an arm. I opened the next thumbnail. There! A man stood next to her. I zoomed in for a closer look.

He'd been caught face front, with his arm extended, handing her a twenty-dollar bill. Smartly over-dressed in a three-button casual silk shirt tucked into dress pants with a shiny black belt, he was a bit taller than Celeste. He had concrete-colored hair, blonde grown grey, styled to take advantage of its thinning texture. He looked like the kind of guy who would date Celeste. Polished, sophisticated.

He also looked like Frank Bascomb, the dead guy in the alley.

The bank bag, filled with coins, landed with a thump on the desk in front of me. I jumped, knocking over Vangie's Virgin of Guadalupe statue. Vangie liked to believe that flowers could spring up without notice anywhere.

Vangie was in the doorway, hand over her mouth in horror. "Sorry," she said, "I didn't see you there. What are you looking for on my computer?"

"Don't sneak up on me," I said. My heart was pounding. "I was just looking at the rest of the pictures you'd taken."

She looked at me. "If you're interested, I bought a loaf of Greenlee's cinnamon bread, and I'm going to make a fresh pot of coffee," Vangie said and disappeared into the kitchen. Greenlee's bread was the usual cure-all around here, but not what I needed right about now.

I went back to her computer and looked at the picture again. I couldn't be sure it was the same guy. I tried to conjure up the picture of the dead man. I saved the jpeg of Larry in a new file on the desktop, so I could access it from my laptop, and printed a copy.

While it printed, I thought about what this meant. Larry had been at the sidewalk sale. He'd been to the store before. If the body was Larry, maybe his trip to my alley hadn't been random.

I needed a picture of Frank Bascomb to compare to this picture of Larry. Zorn had had one when he was here yesterday. He'd showed it to me and to the others. But I hadn't seen it since then.

I called Officer Wong. He was the neighborhood community liaison officer. I was hoping he would be less intense than Zorn. If I told Zorn I wanted the photo, he'd want to know why. I didn't want to tip my hand just yet. Celeste and Gussie were going to be devastated by this news. If I was wrong, if nothing panned out, no harm was done.

"Hi, Officer Wong. This is Dewey Pellicano, from the quilt shop."

The scribblings I noted while Vangie and I'd talked about the missing money from yesterday's sale were in front of me on my desk. I could start with that. "I had a customer rip me off yesterday."

"Tell me."

I explained to him about the hundred-dollar bill.

He said, "I'm not surprised. There have been reports in your neighborhood over the last couple of days. The women always work in pairs. Just like what happened to you, one goes in and pays for something with a large bill, then the other comes in later and describes the bill exactly, and so gets it back. The pet store was hit and the deli."

I got excited. Maybe he could recoup my losses. "Did you catch them?"

"No," he said. "They've moved on by now. Could be in Salinas or Grass Valley by now."

Well, that sucked. I was out a lot of money. "Do I need to file a police report?"

"You should, but chances are slim you'll get anything back," he said. "You can do it online."

He gave me the url and I web surfed over to the San Jose Police Department's website.

"One more thing. Can you send me over a picture of Frank Bascomb?"

"Sure," he said, waiting for me to say more. "E-mail okay?"

"Great, thanks."

I tried to remember what Buster had said about his facial-recognition software. Certain parts of the face remained constant even throughout life and death. Jaw lines, cheekbones, space between the nostrils. That was how the computers aged the pictures of those poor lost children on the milk cartons.

The e-mail came through. I printed a copy and looked closely at Frank Bascomb. Both he and Larry looked like they might be of Italian descent, with a lean, horsey face. The long chin should be a clue.

I traced Frank Bascomb's forehead with my finger, trying to gauge the amount of space between his eyes. I looked at the picture I had of Larry from the sidewalk sale. The size of Larry's face was too small. I couldn't really tell. The scale was wrong.

I pulled up the computer screen with the jpeg of the sidewalk sale. With my photo software, I cut Larry out of the landscape and enlarged the image until it was about the same size as the picture of the dead man from the alley. His face filled the screen.

I printed the enlargement, superimposed the picture of Larry over the picture of Frank and held it up to the light. The picture of Larry was blurred from being blown up, so the match was not perfect.

I squinted into the light. The jaw was a little fleshier, but the basic shape was there. His nose matched up. The forehead was the right width.

I couldn't be sure, but it looked like Larry Ferguson very well might be Frank Bascomb.

FIFTEEN

I DIDN'T WANT FRANK BASCOMB to be Larry. That would mean that Celeste's boyfriend was dead. It was one thing to break up with a man, quite another if he was the guy found murdered in my alley. I hoped I was wrong.

I needed a better picture of Larry. And, I realized, I knew where to find one.

I grabbed my car keys and stuffed the laptop into my back-pack.

"I'm running an errand," I called to Vangie in the kitchen as I passed on my way out the back door.

Vangie looked up from the sink, where she was washing out a cup. "What's up? You look like you've seen a ghost."

A ghost. Bad choice of words. Or maybe the right choice. Frank Bascomb was coming back to haunt me. "I'm fine. I'll be back soon."

"Don't be long. We have to hang up the QPO samples as soon as the store closes. I've got bowling tonight." Vangie's imploring voice faded as I closed the door.

I tried to figure out when the last time was that anyone saw Larry alive. He'd picked up Gussie in his yellow Taurus on Tuesday. Celeste said he'd left that night. Gussie and I waited for him at the bank on Wednesday afternoon. He was a no-show and, by that evening, he was dead.

If Frank Bascomb was Larry, why would he be in my alley? It made more sense for a random guy to be cutting through, than for Larry to be there on purpose.

Unless he was meeting someone. After Celeste had thrown him out, he had to meet Gussie somewhere. Maybe they set up a rendezvous at the store, away from Celeste's prying eyes.

I pulled up in front of Celeste's. I had to take a moment to slow down. The house was like Celeste—imposing, but still beautiful. The native stone fireplace chimney was covered by a dead-looking wisteria vine. Hard to believe that such an ugly plant would bloom into delicate purple flowers in a few months.

Now that I was here, I realized I needed a strategy. I couldn't barge in there and tell Celeste her boyfriend was dead. I didn't think I'd get the words out. Celeste could intimidate me at my shop. On her own turf, I didn't stand a chance. I needed to know what I was going to say before I went in there.

I had to be sure. If I went off half-cocked and told Celeste that Larry was dead, and I was wrong, none of the Stitch 'n' Bitchers would ever talk to me again. Pearl would never forgive me for getting the police involved. Ina and Gussie would resent me getting into their business. No, I'd figure this out first and let Zorn handle it from there. Celeste would never have to know why I was there.

Maybe I was completely off-base. I opened my laptop to look at the pictures of Frank Bascomb and Larry again, to test my theory. A popup told me the laptop had found a wireless network and connected to it.

An alert sounded on my laptop. It was eBay, letting me know a higher bid had been placed on the pot I'd been tracking. I opened the site. A perverse need to know what the pot had sold for made me look. I needed reassurance that the final bid had been out of my fiscal league.

That was it. I would ask Celeste about the value of the pot. She loved to show off her superior knowledge. That would work as my access into the house. Once inside, I would look for the picture of Larry, grab it and get out without telling her why I was there.

I was jazzed. I minimized the pictures, left the site up, threw my backpack over my shoulder, and went up the walk.

She answered the door after one ring. She was impeccably dressed, her hair held up today by several Chinese jade hairpins. She wore a flowery skirt and coordinating coral sweater set. She always dressed as though she was expecting company. Her makeup and lipstick were discreet, but there. Soft leather moccasins were her only concession to loungewear.

"Dewey?"

I held up my laptop. "Sorry to bother you, but I have the chance to buy an Ohr piece. I would love to have your opinion."

She looked from me to the laptop. "I'm not sure . . ."

I threw back my shoulders, forced some cheer into my voice and moved forward. "You're not too busy, are you? This will only take a moment," I said, moving into the foyer.

Once over the threshold, I felt my heart race a little at the way the light filtered through the stained glass transom, leaving shards of color on the tile at my feet. Two more steps, and I was stopped by the beauty of the inlaid tile work on the mahogany hall stand. This house and its furnishings were like animate objects, and I responded to its life with an involuntary quickening. A beautiful combination of function and art.

It was so easy to get distracted. I did a quick glance around the living room beyond, hoping to see some of her treasured ceramic pieces.

Celeste's impeccable manners kicked in and interrupted my reverie. "Why don't you sit in the dining room?"

I shook my head. I started into the living room. "I'm buying it online. I just want to see what you think."

Her eyes strayed back to the laptop. I'd piqued her interest.

"I'm not sure what I can tell by looking at that screen," she said, doubtfully.

"I'll tell you everything you need to know," I said, seating myself on a Stickley rocker near the fireplace and putting the laptop on a small side table.

I opened the auction site. The picture of the pot appeared. "See? Do you know how things work? A person bids electronically, and…"

"I'm aware how an auction works, Dewey." Celeste had put on her reading glasses and was looking down her nose. "I'm not sure this is a real auction. There's no provenance, for instance," she said. "No way to prove how old it is."

For me that was a plus. "That keeps the price down."

Celeste did not approve. "What's the point in buying things without their history?"

"Just for the beauty." I looked around the room. There were so many wonderful decorative items, but not as many as I'd thought I remembered. Two Navajo rugs on the floor. A pair of silver candlesticks on the mantel. I responded to the look of them, but for Celeste, it was more complicated. She needed to know where each one came from.

"Do you think this is overpriced?" I asked. "Here, look." I handed Celeste the laptop. She studied the screen, giving me a chance to look around the room. If she had a picture of Larry, it would be in here. The mantel had photos on it, but I didn't see one that looked like Larry. I had to get closer.

I stood, wiggling away from Celeste and maneuvering her into sitting down. As I did, I bumped the mouse and the screen changed.

A long list of Ohr pottery showed up. There had to be twenty items, vases and pots and assorted kitchenware. I'd never seen so many for sale at one time.

I clicked on one of the items and heard Celeste gasp as a picture of a salt cellar came up on the screen. The unique glaze was just like the one I'd seen in her kitchen the other day.

I recognized the color. "That matches your mortar and pestle," I said.

Celeste's hand had come up to cover her mouth, and her forehead was creased. She looked like she was ready to cry.

"Celeste, are these yours?"

She nodded, biting on the inside of her cheek. I clicked on a few more. Each time, her head jerked in recognition. I would have bet she hadn't known her pieces were up for auction.

"Yours?" I asked. She nodded slowly, her eyes drawn to the screen like a magnet to the refrigerator. "Why are you selling them?"

She shook her head. "Not me. Larry." Her voice was humming with bitter surprise.

She glanced at the inglenook behind us. Benefiting from the fireplace's ambient heat, the bench in there should be a cozy place to read. But except for a shelf of old Reader's Digest Condensed books, the shelves were empty. That must have been where her precious pottery had been housed.

"Larry," she said, her voice dripping with regret. I felt her sadness in my bones.

She continued, "He has stolen all of my Ohr pieces."

My stomach dropped. Larry stole her most valuable pottery. That made sense if Larry was the dead man. Frank Bascomb had a criminal record. It looked more and more like Larry was a con man. More and more like Larry was Frank Bascomb. Dead.

Celeste turned away. "I don't want to see anymore." Her heart looked like it was breaking, seeing her most prized possessions up for auction.

I was desperate to give her some good news. She had so much pain on her face. "They're not sold yet. These are just pictures. The pottery has to be somewhere. Larry must have stored the pieces. We can get them back."

"I'm not interested," Celeste said. She stiffened her shoulders and lifted her chin. "I never want to see those pieces again," she said.

Now my heart ached. I would never see those pots again either.

Celeste walked across the room, her body unconsciously heading for the vacant inglenook. I followed her. It was like a little room next to the fireplace. Shelves on three sides and a built-in window seat, but no window. It was easy to imagine curling up with a cup of tea, a quilt, and a good book. Something by Sue Miller, that you could get lost in.

She ran her hand along the empty shelf. "Those weren't the first pieces he stole from me, Dewey. Last Easter, I discovered my full set of Revere silver was gone. Twelve place settings."

I didn't know what that would sell for, but it had to be a lot. This house was full of expensive pieces.

"Before that, it was the miniatures."

He'd been taking small valuables. I wondered how long it would have taken until he got to the furniture. I had visions of a truck pulling up while Celeste was at a Stitch 'n' Bitch meeting, her coming home to a house devoid of treasures.

"Didn't you confront him?" I asked. Easter had been six months ago.

She nodded, her head resting on her chest. Her eyes were slits. She seemed unable to open them wide, in case all of the pain entered and set up shop.

"Why didn't you throw him out then?"

Celeste sunk onto the corduroy cushion. "He said he had a business deal go bad, and was strapped. He promised never to do it again."

"And you believed him?" I asked, incredulous.

She lifted her head and gave me her death stare. "Not really. I knew Larry was a thief. I didn't care."

I couldn't believe what she was saying.

Celeste's waved a hand at me. "They're just things, Dewey. Objects."

Precious, one-of-a-kind things. The kind of things that give you joy to look at. It wasn't about the ownership. I treasured the feeling that came from looking at a pot thrown in Mississippi nearly a hundred years ago. Sensing the artistic freedom and single-minded vision of that particular artist conveyed in a fragile piece of dinnerware. Like quilts, these things gave us a sense of history and connectivity.

Celeste sank on the bench, her long legs folding around her like a praying mantis. She was limp, unable to keep her standing. She aged suddenly, her face a mass of wrinkles. She was mourning not the loss of her objects, but the loss of the man. The man she thought was still out there.

She pulled a throw pillow onto her lap, her hands running over the embroidered peacock.

"Larry Ferguson was a handsome man," she said. "A kind man."

"Kind?" I felt bad, the word blurting out of me.

She didn't hear me.

She was lost in her memories, in a place so tentative, I didn't want to disturb her. It felt dangerous, like waking up a sleepwalker. "I met him at an antique fair in Moss Landing. We were both trying to buy the same Tiffany piece."

She smiled faintly, the memory a ghost of true pleasure. The lines in her forehead eased. "He very graciously allowed me to have it."

He was a con man. He'd targeted her, maybe even knew who she was. She frequented all the antique fairs, and the dealers knew her.

"He took me out to lunch at Phil's Fish Market."

That was a surprise. I couldn't imagine Celeste at Phil's. Fish came directly off the boats and was battered and fried right in front of you. Picnic tables were the only place to eat, and the napkins were paper. Not her usual dining experience. But it was inexpensive, if Larry was paying.

As though she read my thoughts, she pushed her sleeves up on her sweater and looked at me defiantly. "He courted me. I don't suppose you know what that means," she said haughtily.

Courting? Sure I did. Buster was courting me. No sex. I suppressed a smile.

"He took me to the opera, to the ballet. Places I hadn't gone in years. I liked being with him."

As Celeste continued her revisionist history with Larry, I inched closer to the fireplace mantel, staying just outside the inglenook. The family pictures were lined up two on each side, in matching silver frames. Or possibly fake silver frames, if Larry had stolen the real ones.

The pictures were all old. A wedding photo of a young woman from the eighties, based on the lace hat she wore. A Christmas picture of a new family with a different woman, complete with standard poodle in Santa hat. An aged studio picture of Celeste and her husband.

No Larry.

That was a disappointment. I sat back down in the leather chair, half-listening to Celeste's accounts of wine tours in Napa with Larry and trips to Broadway. She was lost, back dating a man who was the best boyfriend she ever had.

I wiggled my laptop to life. The two pictures of Larry and Frank came up. I adjusted them so they were side-by-side on my laptop, making sure the screen was not visible to Celeste. I thought they were the same guy, but I couldn't be sure. The picture of Larry was not clear enough.

Wireless connectivity came back and the auction site came up. There was another way to connect Frank Bascomb and Larry Ferguson. I found the Ohr salt cellar and clicked on the seller's information. The seller was listed as Frankenstein. The profile said he'd been a seller since May 2007 and was in Milpitas, California. His feedback was all good, but he'd only had four transactions.

Not a real name and no picture, naturally. If Larry had used aliases in real life, most likely, he was using several seller names, too. I kept going, looking at piece after piece. The depth of the collection was breathtaking. The pottery should have been sold by Sotheby's, not online. There, it might have fetched a half-million dollars.

The last piece I clicked on was a free-form vase. There it was. The seller was Frank Bascomb. A link to Larry.

My throat closed. I had the proof I needed. I must have made an involuntary noise.

Celeste looked up. "What is this about, Dewey? Why do you care about Larry?"

I hadn't noticed that she'd stopped talking. I'd completely zoned out. I was busted. I shook my head. I struggled to get out of the armchair gracefully, holding my laptop like a pizza.

"It's not about Larry. I didn't come here to talk about Larry," I said, even though I knew I was protesting too much.

She narrowed her eyes at me, grabbed the computer. She was blocking my way out of the chair. She read the information on the screen. "Is this who's selling my things?"

She read further. "His address is Milpitas. Larry lived in Milpitas before he came to live with me. Why isn't Larry's name here?"

"I don't know, Celeste. You need to talk to the police."

Celeste said, "The police? Why?"

I suddenly felt even smaller with Celeste towering over me. I felt a catch in my throat. "You were robbed, weren't you?" I said meekly.

"Dewey," Celeste said, drawing out my name. "Tell me." Recognition was in her eyes. She just wanted me to say it out loud.

I looked around the room. This was a home where people would think they were safe. It was substantial, protective even. But all the natural beauty had not protected Celeste, and I could protect her no longer.

"I think Larry died in my alley," I said.

"You think that was Larry in your alley?" Her voice was trembling. "But the police know who he is. Was."

"Frank Bascomb was the name on the license. But it was an alias." I pulled up the picture of Frank's seller picture on eBay. "Isn't that Larry?"

Celeste's hands flew over her face.

"I'm sorry," I said. Really sorry. Then I remembered Celeste wasn't the only one involved with this con guy.

"What about Gussie? Why didn't you warn her about Larry?" I said. She could have told Gussie what Larry was about and saved me a lot of headaches. "Did he rob her, too?"

Her eyes were glowing. Tears gathered in the corners, but didn't fall. She was stoic. "I fought to give my kids their autonomy when they were younger, and now I wanted mine. It's hard earned, and I wasn't ready to give it up. Gussie is the same way. Her daughter has no time for her. We have to take care of ourselves."

Her face crumpled, the fine lines that crisscrossed her face looking like they were growing deeper by the moment. I patted her hand's wasp-wing skin. So thin, I felt like I could touch her vulnerable veins. My mother would never get this old and this vulnerable and, for a moment, I was glad.

She'd given up everything she'd once cherished to keep a man in her life. Her favorite things, her friends. Her self-respect. Now that he was dead, how could she look herself in the mirror? There was no chance for redemption.

Celeste made a tight noise as though her throat was too closed up to allow sound to escape. She stood, back straight as a ruler. She seemed to glide on the wood floor with her leather shoes. Without another word, she climbed the stairs to the second story. I heard the door shut and the lock turn. Celeste was going to grieve in solitude.

My phone beeped. Vangie was texting me that she needed me to get back. I looked at my watch. It was four. I texted back, "Soon."

I had some money to retrieve first.

I went to Gussie's through the fence between the two yards, again struck by the difference. Celeste's garden orderly and neat, Gussie's pure chaos. On Gussie's side, the pile of weeds was still up against the fence. I could see Gussie's three-leafed plants and wondered if Vangie knew where her pot brownies were coming from.

I was almost to the back door before I saw her. Her back to me, Gussie was on her knees in the far corner of the yard, away from Celeste's, digging in a loamy pile of dirt. She was dressed in baggy elastic-waist jeans and a purple jacket made from a sweatshirt. A faded splintery picnic bench served as her garden table. She was spooning dark mounds into a two-quart pitcher that read Country Style Lemonade on the side. She was happily humming to herself.

"Gussie?" My voice rose as she lifted the pitcher. A pumpkin vine wrapped around my foot and nearly tripped me. I took several steps before righting myself.

Gussie sat back on her haunches. The pitcher tipped, and I reached out and set it upright. Brownish liquid seeped out onto the weathered bench.

She fanned herself. "Oh, my dear, you mustn't sneak up on an old lady like that. It's not good for the heart." She smiled at me to take away the sting of her words.

I was dismayed. "I'm sorry. What are you doing?"

"I'm making tea." She picked up the pitcher, and checked the level. She added more water and stirred. The dirt swirled to the surface.

I was horrified. "Tea? You're not going to drink that?"

Gussie laughed. "Really, Dewey. Compost and water. It makes the best fungicide tea. Best of all, it's free. I'm spraying my roses for the winter."

Silly me. I knew zilch about gardening. I had great plans for my garden at my house, but that was all they were. Plans.

Many of my quilting customers were skilled gardeners. The two crafts seemed to attract creative people who didn't mind getting their hands dirty.

Gussie looked at me. "Dear, I'm surprised to see you here. Don't you have so much to do for the sale?"

I didn't answer her. "Did you hear about a man being found dead in the alley behind my store?"

"Oh, yes," she said, shaking the pitcher vigorously. Her upper arms were ropy and strong. "God bless his soul."

Indeed. God bless his rotten little soul.

I took the pitcher out of her hand. The color was disgusting, although the smell was not as bad as I expected. It was kind of pleasant, like freshly turned-over earth. "It was Larry, Gussie."

When she didn't respond right away, I repeated myself. "He didn't leave town after all. Larry's dead."

"Really? I'd heard the man's name was …" She got a faraway look in her eye, trying to remember what she'd been told.

"Trust me, it was Larry. He had a fake driver's license."

Her eyes were wide and innocent. "Why?"

This was the hard part. "He was a con man, Gussie. He was stealing your money."

She was lagging behind the conversation a sentence or two. "He's coming. He's coming to take Jeremy his down payment."

I slowed down. "No, he's not. The only place that money was going was in his pocket."

I waited for the news to sink in. I'd given her a lot to process. This was taking too long, but I'd learned one thing working at the store. It was always faster to let my older customers go at their own pace.

She steepled her hands. Her nails had dirt under them. "You're saying Jeremy is not buying a house?"

I shrugged. "I doubt it. Did Larry talk to him?"

"Sometimes, if we were all in the backyard, he'd answer my phone. I could never get inside in time. Sometimes I didn't even hear it ring. He liked talking to Jeremy. They became good buddies. Jeremy never had a dad, you know and ..."

I stopped listening and sensed something moving in Celeste's yard. I moved closer to the gap in the fence. Was Celeste coming over to tell Gussie herself about Larry? But there was no more movement. It must have been a bird or a squirrel. Celeste was lost in her own world, too broken to consider her friend.

"What have you done with Jeremy's money?" I asked.

"It's still in the shed. I thought Larry would be coming today. But you're saying he's dead."

I watched her face change as she looked at the house next door. Her own concerns erased when she thought about her friend.

"Celeste, oh, dear. Does Celeste know he's dead?" Her hands flew up to her face, her dirty fingers leaving streaks on her face.

"She figured it out," I said.

"And you left her alone? She can't be alone now. She'll be brokenhearted." She pushed herself off the bench, tipping the pitcher of compost tea and dumping it on the ground. I half-expected flowers to spring up immediately.

She started toward the gate between her house and Celeste's.

I reached out to stop her, grabbing the sleeve of her shirt. "Wait, Gussie. What about the cash?"

She gathered her sweatshirt closer to her, swaddling herself. "You know where it is, Dewey." She gave me the combination to the lock. "Right 12, left 3, right 4."

I repeated the numbers. My phone beeped again urgently. "I'll put it in my safe, and we can put it back in the bank later," I told her.

"You mean, we'll take it to Jeremy." She waved me off and was gone, distracted by her grief for her friend. She still believed Larry's story that Jeremy needed the money for a down payment. I doubted Larry ever talked to Jeremy about him buying a house. All he needed to know was that Gussie had a grandson who was estranged from his family. He took it from there.

She could believe what she wanted. There was no harm in that, as long as I had the money, her savings were secure. I walked over to the shed. The door came open easily, practically falling off the rusted hinges. I knelt by the footlocker. Right, 12, left, 3, right, 4. I tugged on the padlock, but it was holding fast. Dammit. My fingers started to sweat. I tried again. The lock wouldn't budge. I went out of the shed, starting toward Celeste's. I took a few steps. I didn't really want to go over there.

I went back to the footlocker and pulled on the padlock again. No give. I looked around the shed. There was an old axe, the handle nearly orange with rust. I swung it at the lock, and missed, nearly hitting my foot. I jumped, adrenaline pumping.

I took a breath, waiting for my heart to stop racing. I coughed, the mildewy contents of the shed stirring up allergies. I needed to get out of here, but I wasn't going without the money.

I took a short swing, putting all my muscle behind it. The lock broke in two, and I pulled open the lid.

There was the twenty-nine thousand dollars. I fit the money in my backpack around my laptop. The laptop had never been worth so much.

SIXTEEN

I CALLED ZORN AS I drove back to the office. What was the greater sin, driving while talking on the phone or not letting him in on what I knew? I'd risk the ticket.

"Anton Zorn," he barked into the phone.

"It's Dewey Pellicano," I said. "I have some information for you about the dead man in my alley."

"I'm listening," he said. I heard him pull out a pad.

I filled him in. "He's been going by the name of Larry Ferguson, living with one of my customers. An elderly woman, Celeste Radcliffe. And he was bilking her. I found some of her possessions on eBay. He seems to have discovered how valuable her pottery was and taken a large amount out of her home."

Zorn asked for Celeste's name and address. "I will want her to identify the body," he said.

I wished him silent good luck in getting past Gussie to talk to her.

"Do you have any more information about his cause of death?" I asked.

There was silence. "This is an ongoing investigation, Ms. Pellicano."

"I just wondered if he was poisoned, after all."

He said briskly. "The coroner has not ruled on the cause of death—only that the manner of death was homicide. I don't know where your information is coming from."

I had to set him straight, before Buster took the heat for telling me things he hadn't told me. "I don't have any inside information. I've heard from some people that this was a possibility. My boyfriend and I have not discussed this."

"Your information is sketchy at best." I could hear Zorn clicking on a keyboard. "Well, it looks like Larry Ferguson has much more of a history than Frank Bascomb," Zorn said.

"Like what?" I asked. He'd never given me this much before.

He caught himself. "Suffice it to say Larry Ferguson is well acquainted with the penal system," he said.

I waited for more, but nothing was forthcoming. Zorn remembered who he was talking to. He thanked me and hung up.

I didn't know what I'd expected from him. Gratitude? If he didn't want to acknowledge that I was the one who found out who Larry was, then so be it. We never took in much cash, and what we did went right into the bank.

At the store, I stashed Gussie's money, unloading my backpack into the safe. I dug out my laptop.

Vangie was out on the store floor with Jenn and Kym. They were filling goodie bags to be handed to the customers.

"Hey," I said. "I'd like a store meeting in five minutes. We'll do it out here as soon as I do this one thing."

I had to tell Ina and Pearl about Celeste. I found them in the classroom. Pearl wasn't hand quilting. She was adding paint to one of her small quilts.

She looked up guiltily. "I gave up," she said, as I walked in. "I'm not stitching another stitch on that Old Maid's Puzzle. My fingers are killing me."

"It's okay," I said. "I never intended for you to be hand quilting all week. Especially if you don't like to."

I was quiet for a few minutes. The two women watched me, reading the expression on my face and knowing that something was wrong. They exchanged a glance. Pearl put down her paint brushes, and Ina watched me from the quilting frame.

"I have some bad news," I finally said. Pearl and Ina clearly feared the worst.

"It's Larry, Celeste's guy. He's Frank Bascomb. He was the dead man in the alley."

Ina poked the needle into the quilt and pushed away from the frame. She was winding thread back on the spool, as she stood. "We'll go to her," she said.

"Gussie's there," I said. "Celeste took herself to bed."

"You were there?" Pearl said. Pearl jammed the lid on her small paint pot and stored it in a purple plastic pencil box.

I nodded. "Long story."

Ina said, "We'll get the scoop from Celeste. Let's go."

Pearl and Ina left in a flurry. I was touched by their leap into action. Celeste had wonderful friends. She would be okay.

Enough about Larry or Frank. I'd spent more time on him this week than on my shop. Now the sale was less than thirty-six hours away. I tried to quell the butterflies in my stomach.

I went out front. "Okay, I'd like a progress report from everyone. Where do we stand on the jobs done for the sale? We only have the remainder of today, and then tomorrow, to get done, so tell me what still needs to be done."

Vangie spoke first. "My special project is nearly complete."

"Okay," I said, knowing I'd put her on the spot. I didn't want to talk about the online store just yet. "The e-mail hasn't gone out about the sale yet, but I will do that tonight. The big shipment of notions got checked in this morning. Finally."

Jenn said, "We've put those all out already. We've finished bagging all the kits. We're just about done with the goodie bags."

"We could make some favors to go in them," Kym suggested.

There was no way. "Have all the shelves been dusted? Have you set aside the door prizes? Are the bathrooms cleaned?" I said, making my point. "The front window could use a fresh look, too."

"What about the QP Originals?" Kym said.

"Vangie and I will hang up the samples tonight," I said.

Jenn was busy taking notes. Kym just looked at me sourly. Life at Quilter Paradiso was getting back to normal.

"All right, then," I said. "There's plenty to do between now and the sale. We're going to need every last minute."

I returned to my office. The e-mail icon was up, so I checked my inbox. Another digest of messages from the guild. I scanned through.

I breathed a sigh of relief. There was a question about natural dyes, using hibiscus. Another looking for a source of ivory buttons.

There was a hue and cry about someone's dog dying from tainted food. No mention of dead bodies. No mention of the store.

Finally things were back to normal.

The poisoning of the dog made me think about Mrs. Unites's theory about Frank, no, Larry's death.

Mrs. Unites had said that the face of the dead man looked like someone who died of DDT. San Jose had once been farmland. Orchards still existed, although they were harder to find. Redevelopment had paved the valley of the heart's delight and put up condos.

I went online to see if the chemical was still being used. It had been banned in the sixties.

Larry's face had been contorted. I remember thinking he must have died a painful death. According to the witnesses, he'd been lurching around the neighborhood for at least a half-hour before ending up in my alley. It sounded like a slow, torturous way to die.

I looked up poisonings, checking for the usual reactions. Vomiting seemed like a common denominator, but no one had reported Frank throwing up on his way to the alley.

Vangie appeared in the doorway, with the twenty-foot ladder.

"Ready to hang some quilts?" she asked.

I glanced at the clock. The store was still open.

She read my mind. "We haven't had a customer in hours. Only those people scouting out the stuff they want to buy when it's discounted. I found two bolts of Moda stashed behind the book display. Someone was thinking ahead."

Mindless work, just what I needed to keep my mind off Celeste's mourning.

SEVENTEEN

LATER THAT NIGHT, I tugged on the long silver handle, making the door rattle. It was locked tight. I was here alone, and I wanted to be sure I was safe.

Jenn and Kym left as soon as the store closed. Vangie had helped me hang the QP Original quilts, and then left for her bowling league.

Turning around, I walked into my store, following the path a new customer would take. I tried to look at the place with fresh eyes. In the clip from *Wonderful World of Quilts*, the store had looked to me like we could use some sprucing up. The Vineyard quilt, hung high, was in the same position that it was in when my mother was alive. Even with the quilts Vangie and I had just finished hanging, the store looked stale. We needed a change. I needed a change.

I'd put Vangie's poster on the front door, to set up some anticipation about the QP Originals. The loft railing was the perfect place for Ina's "Over Easy." Her pattern was just the thing for beginners.

Eye-catching colors, simple shapes. The quilt looked great viewed from a distance.

Pearl's quilt was small, so it needed to be at eye level and securely fastened. We'd made a display board and placed the landscape near the cash register, so it'd be the last thing people would see. If we had a line of customers waiting to pay, as I hoped, her quilt would get a lot of attention.

Celeste's Garden quilt was intricate and needed to be seen up close to be appreciated. Redwork was an old-fashioned craft, but I was counting on the fact that many of my customers remembered their mothers or grandmothers embroidering and so might be tempted to try it themselves. Vangie had climbed the ladder, and we'd suspended the redwork quilt right over the cutting table. That would give the customers time to scrutinize it while they waited for their fabric to be cut.

Jenn's Home for the Holiday Quilt and Vangie's Starry Nights were hung along the alley wall, with their kits underneath. That was as far as Vangie and I had gotten before it was time for her to leave. I'd stayed behind. Buster was in L.A., and I had no desire to go home to an empty house.

I walked backward, trying to decide what I wanted to move. I wasn't the great merchandiser. Making things pretty was not my forte. That's why I'd let Kym continue in the role she'd had when my mother was alive. The problem was I didn't like her end product.

I tripped over a white wicker baby doll carriage that housed the flannel pre-printed panels. I heard a loud crack as I caught myself on the shelving nearby. I was okay, just a sore shin, but the doll carriage wasn't so lucky. It was listing badly to one side. I'd broken the wheel. I felt a moment of guilt. This was one of Kym's props.

I picked up the fallen fabric and looked at the panel barcodes. I could see they were over a year old. Since I'd already destroyed the display, I might as well mark them down. I found a red pen and reduced the price to three dollars. I put them in a flat wicker basket. I dragged the broken carriage up to the loft and surveyed the store from above. Already it looked less cluttered. I looked for more things I could change.

From here, I could see everything. My favorite items, the paint sticks and pots of dyes and the art quilt books were stuck on a rack, near the hall. This stuff was expensive. And popular. I would move it up front.

I felt a surge of energy. I ran down the steps, emptied the wooden rack and moved it to where the baby carriage had been. It was heavy, but I didn't mind.

I loaded it back up again and stood back. That looked better.

I polished the front glass case and filled it with beads, and the one-of-a-kind buttons that had been languishing in the drawers behind the cash register. I cleared a space for the fancy scissors. I mentally designed a sign announcing "As Seen on *Wonderful World of Quilts.*"

Turning my attention to the fabric, I gathered all the florals I could find and grouped them together. Than all the landscape types. I color-coordinated the batiks and moved them to the wall behind the cutting table. A new line of exotic-looking Amy Butler fabrics replaced the nineteenth-century reproduction line that Celeste had been admiring.

I wondered how Celeste was doing. She'd already outlived her husband, now she'd be burying another love.

My phone rang. I mopped the sweat off my neck. Moving fabric was an aerobic activity.

I dropped a bolt when I reached for the phone, and it set up a domino effect, until at least thirty bolts had fallen.

"Sorry for the racket," I said to Buster when I answered. "I just knocked over a mess of fabrics."

"You still at work?" he asked. "It's after eleven." I picked up one bolt and undid the pin holding it together. I pulled the fabric tauter and re-pinned. All the bolts that had fallen now needed straightening. I put in my earbud so I could use both hands.

"Of course, what about you? Sanchez there?" I said.

"Out like a light. Man can't stay up past nine."

There was a moment of silence. I panicked. I didn't want Buster to talk about anything substantive. I'd keep the conversation light.

"Is the weather nice there in L.A?" I asked.

"It's Lala land. Perfect sun, perfect bodies, perfect faces. Even the cops look like they belong on TV or in the movies."

"They're all fake, you know," I said, keeping my voice light.

"The cops?"

"The boobs. All the boobs in L.A. are fake."

My attempt at humor fell flat. There was another awkward silence.

"About last night—," Buster began.

My stomach tightened. I felt the hurt and uncertainty come rushing back. I wasn't ready for that discussion yet. I'd spent the day ignoring any worry that I'd lost Buster.

I diverted him yet again. "Did you get in to see your inmate?"

"Yup."

"Is he the one that committed the murder here?" I asked.

Buster sounded happy, but restrained. "Looks like it. All the surveillance footage I looked at paid off. I finally found a shot that matched the regression I'd done of his current mug shot. It had to be him."

"Congratulations. You worked hard." His task reminded me of my own news. "Guess what?" I said. "I figured out who the dead guy in my alley was."

Buster sounded incredulous. "What do you mean—you figured it out?"

"I used your facial recognition points. I found a picture in the shop's photos that looked like him, and matched him to the dead guy's picture."

"He was one of your customers?" Buster asked.

"Worse. He was Celeste's boyfriend, Larry," I said.

He whistled. "That explains what he was doing in your alley. Probably looking for her. Nice work, Holmes."

I warmed to his praise. "It's bittersweet. He'd been robbing Celeste blind. He was selling her Ohr."

"Not the Ohr," Buster said, with exaggerated fake horror in his voice.

I laughed, which I knew was what he intended. Despite the distance between us, he could make me laugh. "Your ignorance of Arts and Crafts pottery is forgivable, but barely. Let me put it in perspective for you. One piece can bring as much as fifty thousand dollars."

Buster was admiring. "So you ID'ed the guy, and broke up a pottery-fencing ring. Dewey Pellicano, investigator extraordinaire to the quilt world."

"Now if I could just solve his murder," I said. "My life could get back to normal."

Buster was philosophical. "He probably had a partner. Those con guys often do. Fallout between thieves is nasty stuff. Especially with so much money involved."

Now that the talk about work was out of the way, we were quiet again. I thought I heard Buster sigh.

He spoke first. "Last night, I was an idiot. I shouldn't have walked out on you."

That was true. "Apology accepted," I said tentatively. I wished I could see his face.

Buster continued, "I thought about what you said, and I do understand. It's like my job. I like to be the one that discovers the truth. It's not very satisfying if someone hands me the answers."

I wasn't sure I liked having my love life compared to homicide work, but I knew how his mind worked. I had to give him an A for effort.

He said, "You know I never meant to torture you. The six-month celibacy timetable was just to give us enough time."

"You wanted to woo me, you said."

"Exactly, so we could get to know one another."

I took a pin out of my mouth to answer. "And we did." Truth be told, for the first few months, I'd liked it. Our energies were focused on other aspects of our personalities. We both worked a little harder to make our time together memorable, knowing it wasn't going to end up in bed.

But our sexual natures could not be denied. The foreplay got bolder and longer and more involved. Better, yet less satisfying.

And the march to sex began. Why not? We were adults in a committed monogamous relationship. Sex was the next step.

Buster said, "Do you know why I haven't made love to you yet?"

"Because you admire Harry Truman, and he courted his wife for seven years?" I asked, laughing. No reply. Not funny to him. I continued more seriously, "I never thought the celibacy would last the entire six months."

"I was trying to remove my lust from the equation."

"What's wrong with lust?" I asked.

"I wanted the lust to have a context," he said seriously.

"Now you're losing me," I said.

"Don't get me wrong, lust is great. Lust is what we had the first couple of times. That was seriously great. I wanted more than that."

"More?"

He was quiet. I could hear him breathing. He'd been thinking about this a lot.

He said, "I didn't ever want you to feel like I don't want everything about you. Your body, yes, but your mind, your heart, your laugh, too. I wanted you to be completely secure in my love for you. Of course, I want you. But I wanted you to know that I wanted *you.*"

I let his words sink into me. Spending the afternoon with Celeste had made me leery of love. She'd spent all of her love on a man who didn't deserve her trust, never mind her love.

Buster spoke, his voice husky. The timbre went straight to the pit of my stomach, making my knees wobble. "The ban is officially over. My timetable is over. Whenever you're ready, all you have to do is ask."

I found myself whispering, "Is there a secret code word I need to use?"

"Yes."

I waited for the rest. He said nothing more.

"That's it?"

Buster said, "Just say yes. Yes means yes."

Finally.

I hung up the phone. I'd lost my appetite for rearranging, seeing it for what it was—a way to avoid thinking about our relationship. But now, all I had to do was to say yes. The next time I saw Buster, I would give him a resounding, *Yes*. I couldn't wait.

It was two o'clock in the morning. I should have been tired but I was exhilarated. I took a final walk through the store. I liked the way it looked. This was not my mother's store anymore. This was my store now.

I wasn't ready to go home, even though I had to be back early to watch *Wonderful World of Quilts*. I ran the feather duster over the register one more time. The display of Pearl's QPO quilt kits caught my eye. I opened one of the kits and laid out all the pieces. It was an ocean scene, and the hand-dyed blues and oranges attracted me. I ran my fingers over the fabric while I read the directions that came with the kit. According to her blurb on the envelope, all I needed was four hours, fusible webbing, and an iron.

I gathered up the pieces and headed for the classroom. I had a date with Petey.

EIGHTEEN

I waylaid Jenn on her way to the kitchen in the morning.

"Everything go okay with Zorn the other day?" I asked, watching her face. Her mouth looked a little more strained than usual. She must have let her husband know about Frank Bascomb. Dragging up long-buried hurts is rough business.

She nodded, continuing into the kitchen and hanging up her purse. "It just brought up a lot of old drama. I could have gone without it."

"Well, Frank is out of your life for good now."

She shrugged. "I guess."

Kym grabbed her and pulled her into the classroom. It was too bad that Frank's death didn't bring her more closure.

I went back to my computer.

"Hey, kiddo, the store looks great."

I looked up from the promotional e-mail I was composing to see Pearl and Ina entering my office. They were both smiling at me, but their eyes were soft, and Ina had black circles under her eyes. Pearl looked pale under her usual tawny skin.

"Thanks," I said. "I didn't expect you to be here to watch *Wonderful World of Quilts*?"

"Wouldn't miss it," Ina said.

I said, "How's Celeste? And Gussie? Have you seen them this morning?"

Ina shook her head. "We left Celeste's around midnight. I called Gussie this morning. They'll be over soon."

Pearl gave my chair a little shove. She glanced at Vangie, who was counting yesterday's receipts. She lowered her voice. "Why didn't you tell us about Gussie and all that money?"

Ina put in, "No wonder you were ready to call the cops."

I shrugged. "She made me swear I wouldn't. Besides, you told me that old ladies didn't need my help."

Pearl gave me a disgusted look. Old ladies was not a politically correct term.

Ina said, "Having all that money in the house, that's nuts."

I skipped the *told you so*. "It's okay. It's not at her place anymore." I nodded to the safe behind the door. Vangie'd had it open while she was working on the bank deposit. The key dangled from the lock.

I could see the stacks of cash. I said, "She gave the money to me to hold. If Jeremy does need it for a down payment on the house, he can come and get it."

Pearl and Ian exchanged puzzled looks.

"House? What house?" Ina said.

"The one that Jeremy's buying."

"No-uh." Pearl talked over her. "Is that what she told you? Jeremy needs bail money."

What? Bail money? I looked from one to the other. Neither one looked very surprised at the idea of Jeremy in jail.

"We were at Gussie's when somebody called her last night and said Jeremy needed money to get out," Pearl said.

Before I had a chance to react, Kym poked her head in my office. Her cheeks were rosy with excitement. Being on TV was going to be the highlight of her life. "The show's on."

I glanced at the clock. "We've got ten minutes," I said. I wanted to find out more about Jeremy and Gussie.

"Let's go," Kym said. She stood in the doorway, staring at Vangie until she put her work away.

"Come on, everybody," she said, hands on hips. She herded Pearl and Ina out of my office. "I want everyone seated before the show starts. No interruptions."

"Wait," I called to Pearl. "Tell me about Jeremy."

Kym had her arms around both women. Ina said over her shoulder, "Gussie will be here. Let her tell you."

I went back to my computer to save the e-mail I'd been working on. I needed to proofread it one more time before I sent it out.

"Oh, dang," Vangie said, putting our cash back into the safe in the plastic zipper bag. "I wanted to finish the bank deposit." She gave no indication she'd heard the conversation about Jeremy.

"Later," I said.

"Later, I will be too busy" she said, exaggerating grandly. "The phone will be ringing off the hook and the computer will be pinging me with new orders from QP Online. I won't have time to take a breath."

Her enthusiasm was contagious. I forgot about Celeste, Jeremy, and Buster. I crossed my fingers, and kissed her. "From your mouth to the gods' ears."

She grabbed me and started singing, "QP is on TV," again, forcing me to conga into the classroom.

Kym must have sent out engraved invitations. The classroom was buzzing. There were at least two dozen people in there. I waved to her parents and said hi to some of our old-time customers. Kym's small quilt group, the Appliqué Girlz, was well represented.

Kevin had set up the TV in the far corner under the windows that faced the alley. They'd taken down some of the tables to make room for all our folding chairs. Kym hadn't been happy to work around the Stitch 'n' Bitch quilting frame but I'd told her putting the TV out on the store floor was impossible.

Wonderful World of Quilts aired at 1:30 p.m. on the East Coast, 10:30 a.m. our time. Everyone was smiling and happy, chatting. I felt my own excitement rise. This wasn't just about Kym. Being on national TV was a big deal for the store. If things went the way we hoped, and the phone calls and online hits started coming in, we'd be getting orders as soon as the show finished airing. In less than a half hour, everything about QP could change.

Kym flitted from person to person, bestowing her hand like she was the queen. She was flying so high, you'd have thought she was going to be on the Jumbotron at the Arena.

Vangie watched her with amusement. She let go of me with one more high kick as though we were still conga-ing and sat herself on one of the remaining classroom tables, swinging her legs like a little kid. I went over and leaned against the table near her.

"I have one word for you. Reruns," I said reverently. The craft channel ran its shows over and over again.

Vangie high-fived me. "Here's one more. YouTube," she said.

I laughed. There wasn't time to fill Vangie in on what I was going to do next, but I knew she'd roll with it. I glanced at the clock. Three minutes until air.

I stood in front of the TV. The chatter continued until I held up my hand for attention. Kym made a shushing noise that was unnecessary as the room quieted.

I said, "Thanks for coming. Vangie's made extra coffee, so after the show is over, please help yourself. I think there's Krispy Kremes, too."

Vangie nodded, and rubbed her tummy and licked her lips. The group laughed. None of us needed sugar to be high this morning. We were one donut hole short of giddy as it was.

I waited for the laughter to die out. "I have an announcement I'd like to make. You know tomorrow is our big anniversary sale. In fact," I said, pausing for effect, "today is the actual date my mother opened the doors twenty years ago."

Applause started with Pearl and the others joined in. Vangie pounded the table next to her and whistled, her thumb and fore-finger in her teeth. I wasn't going to miss the opportunity to steal a little of Kym's thunder.

"This date will also be the anniversary of our newest venture." I paused, looking around the room at the expectant faces. I took a deep breath.

The door to the classroom opened. Gussie and Celeste slid in. Gussie looked like she'd slept in her clothes, and she couldn't keep her eyes off her friend. Celeste, in a purple knit that made her gray hair shine, was impeccably dressed and made up.

I waited until they were seated near the front. "Today is the official opening of Quilter Paradiso OnLine, our new web-based store. Now you can shop twenty-four, seven."

There was silence at first, as people took in the news, then more applause. I looked for Kym's reaction, but didn't see her. Where had she disappeared to?

When the applause died down, I said, "Any questions about how to access the store, ask Vangie. She's the one that made it possible."

Murmuring went through the crowd as I took my seat in the back of the room. The clock was getting close to starting time.

I said, "Let's watch some TV."

I turned on the set. *Stamping Special*, the show that came on before *Wonderful World of Quilts*, was showing its ending credits. Jenn's head swiveled. "Where's Kym?" she said.

Sure enough, her seat next to Kevin was empty. I hadn't seen her leave. My future plans were lost on her. Had she even heard my announcement about the online store? Did she even care?

"Where is she? Kevin?" I asked. He shrugged, his face unreadable.

The logo for the production company came on the screen. The show was about to begin. Still no Kym.

Just as the happy sounding, tinkling theme music began, the closet door opened dramatically. I gasped.

It was only Kym. I clutched my chest where my heart was still beating wildly. The crowd laughed nervously.

"Are you ready for me?" Kym asked, batting her eyelashes. I couldn't believe my eyes. She'd changed into the same clothes she'd been wearing on the show. I wondered if this was the equivalent of wearing your Giants T-shirt when the team was playing.

I looked at my brother in disbelief, but he was grinning at her. Kevin patted the chair next to him, and she seated herself slowly, enjoying all eyes on her. Her parents beamed. I thought about apples falling not far from their trees. She'd learned how precious she was at their knees.

Kym said. "All right, here we go. Vangie, would you flip off the lights?"

Vangie dimmed the lights and the *Wonderful World of Quilts* logo filled the screen. Lark's voice teased that we would be taken to a premiere quilt shop in the next half-hour, learn a new way to appliqué, and answer viewers' questions.

Gussie approached me, "Dewey, I need…"

"I heard," I said. "As soon as this is over, we'll talk."

Gussie returned to her spot next to Celeste, who was staring straight ahead. I wondered why she'd come. It was obvious Celeste was a million miles away.

A commercial for floor cleaner blasted us, the volume of the strident, stressed-out mom's voice at an eleven. I muted the TV.

A stab of loneliness pierced me. I was surrounded by people, but I felt alone. This was Kym's time. I swallowed an irrational jealousy.

A second commercial, this time for a local car dealer, had started when the door opened and light from the hall crossed the TV screen. A groan went up from the group, and everyone turned to look to see who'd spoiled the darkness.

Buster. I shot up from my seat and waved him over. I was thrilled to see him. Vangie shot me a look that told me the joy was written all over my face, and I shrugged. I didn't care who knew I was happy to see him.

Kym wasn't pleased. "Hurry up and sit," Kym said. "We're going to miss the beginning."

He dragged a chair alongside me, straddling it, so he was leaning against the back, his arm along the edge. He hadn't shaved this morning, and one lock of black hair dipped over his forehead. He looked so hot. I savored the tingling I was feeling just below my belly button.

"I heard there was a big show this morning," he whispered. "'I didn't want to miss it."

I pushed the hair off his face just to touch him. "Kym's happy you're here," I teased.

He took my hand and kissed it. He pulled my chair closer to his, so only I heard what he said next. "I did *not* get up at the crack of dawn and drive for five hours, exceeding the speed limit in at least eight jurisdictions, getting crappy gas mileage for Kym."

My eyes filled with tears as his knee bumped mine. "Get it?" he said.

I nodded. I got it. Healy was here for me. Only me. I grabbed his knee and squeezed.

Turning back around, I caught a look from Celeste. She was so miserable.

Kym wheeled her arms and yelled, near hysterics. "Dewey, un-mute! Hurry!"

I turned away from Buster's smiling face to see the show had begun.

232

Without sound. I pointed the remote and pushed up the volume.

Lark was pointing at the brick façade of Quilter Paradiso. I felt a chill run through me. What would my mother think of this? Her quilting business, housed in the store built by her great-grandfather, on national television. I was so proud.

Mom would have been thrilled. A wave of sadness flooded me as I missed my mother. She would have been the first person I'd called to share news like this. I patted Buster's knee again and was rewarded with a smile.

I looked at Kevin's profile to see if he was feeling it, too, but his eyes were on Kym. All of his sense of pride was tied up in her. The lonely feeling threatened to come back. I leaned closer to Buster.

I pushed the mute in time to hear Lark say, "…Kym Pellicano of Quilter Paradiso…"

A cheer went up in the crowd.

"Go, Kymster," Jenn cheered.

Kym said, "Ssssh."

I settled back. Buster left his hand in my lap, and I played with his thumb. On the screen, Lark interviewed Kym about her unique method of appliqué. Vangie turned and gave me another thumbs-up when the camera zoomed in on the palm-tree-handled scissors Kym was using. I returned the gesture.

The camera lingered on Kym's hand and the scissors. I heard the whispering of desire in the crowd. Looks like we had a chance of selling all 144 pairs.

I was having an out-of-body experience, not really hearing what Kym was saying. She and Lark were standing next to each other behind the cutting table as Kym trimmed the back out of her appliqué piece. Lark was smiling and nodding, the consummate professional, probably bored, but never showing anything but extreme interest.

I stopped listening to Kym. Behind Lark was the wall of cherry drawers that had been installed in the 1920s when the Dewey Mercantile store became Dewey's Hardware. The drawer fronts next to the pulls were worn smooth from years of hands. As the camera panned back to Kym, I saw the Accounts Payable window into my office. This was my heritage. I was so filled with delight seeing it on TV, I almost missed what came next.

The camera panned through the store, resting on a quilt I'd never seen before. Hackles raised on the back of my neck. I sat up straight and tuned into what Kym was saying on the TV. Buster gave a surprised, "Hey," when I dropped his hand. His eyes alternated between the screen and me as I leaned forward, not wanting to miss anything.

In the show, Kym pointed to the unfamiliar rose and blue quilt laid out on the cutting table. "This is my 'Joyous Hearts' quilt," she said. Kym's lips were moving along with her image on the television. "Part of the new line of original patterns at Quilter Paradiso. Complete quilt kits are available."

My ears were filled with a rushing noise. I didn't believe what I'd just heard. She'd told the entire viewing audience, potentially a million quilters, that I was selling kits for her quilt. Kits I did not have.

Kym turned, smiling like a cat that ate all the carp in the koi pond.

In two steps, I crossed to the room to where Kym sat. Kym ignored me. As I walked, I muted the volume. That had the desired effect.

"Hey!" Kym said. Kevin watched me warily.

I was toe to toe with Kym now. I said, "Are you fucking kidding me?'

The obscenity flew out of my mouth. I heard the room gasp. I was finished holding my feelings in. "Tell me you did not just do that. You have got to be kidding me, Kym."

Kevin and Buster exchanged a look. Kevin moved closer to Kym. Buster headed my way. I heard noises from the crowd, but the words did not reach my brain for comprehension. All I could hear was Kym's voice.

"Problem, Dewey?" She was smug.

My throat hurt from the giant lump that had taken up residence there. "You just told a national audience that we had a pattern and kit we don't have. How am I supposed to sell that?"

If Vangie's predictions were right, the phone and Internet orders would be coming in soon. Only now it was for quilt kits we didn't have.

Kym was unrepentant. "Just print out the instructions that Kevin e-mailed the other day."

I put my hands on my hips. "Those instructions have to be tested and corrected. Vangie has to put in our graphics, the store's contact information …" My voice trailed off. I was exhausted from having to explain this to her again. I was done. I couldn't do this anymore.

"Kevin, get her out of here, please," I said.

He pulled out her chair as she protested. "I didn't do anything wrong," she said, looking around the room for support. Her parents and appliqué group frowned in my direction. Gussie looked confused. Ina was explaining things to her. Pearl looked angry. Celeste had remained seated. Her face was unreadable.

"I know, Kym," Kevin said. "Let's just go."

Even Buster's face had turned dark. He shook his head at me slightly, as though warning me Kym was not worth the trouble.

Kevin held the classroom door open for her. Her parents, her friends, the Stitch 'n' Bitch group were all watching. I couldn't let that stop me from doing what I needed to do. They might not understand, but this was the time. I had the grounds and I had the opportunity.

Vangie turned on the lights, and the fluorescents put us under a harsh glow.

"Kym," I called.

She took a step back in the classroom, hopefully. She was sure I'd called her back to make amends. Kevin let the door shut and moved behind his wife. He was looking at me like the day I'd overfed his fish.

Anger coursed through me. Every procedure not followed, every suggestion ignored, every directive scoffed. Every insinuation that she was better at running a quilt store than I was flooded into my brain. I was through with torturing myself with my sister-in-law.

"Don't bother to clock in. Get your things out of the cubbie and go home. You're fired."

Kym stared at me. Kevin's face tightened. He put an arm around his wife. I felt Buster behind me.

"It's time," I said. "Kym, your tenure at QP is over."

She turned on her heel and ran out of the room. Kevin didn't look back. I waited until I heard the back door clear before I turned to the room. No one had moved.

"Thanks for coming," I started, but the words didn't get out, before the stampede started. The room emptied, Kym's friends moving angrily past me.

When the dust cleared, Buster, Vangie, and the Stitch 'n' Bitch group were still in their seats. To my surprise, so was Jenn.

I smiled weakly. "Okay, I guess we're going to be a little short-handed today. Do the best you can."

Pearl said, "We can help."

I looked around the room. "I've got to make some calls."

Firing Kym was so big, I couldn't get my mind around it yet. I could only think about what I needed to do to get through the next few minutes.

But Saturday was another story. I needed every hand I could get. I'd probably lose Kevin, despite the fact that he'd worked more of these sales than I had.

I needed to get on the quilt guild e-mail list and ask, no, beg for help. I was so far behind now, I didn't know how I'd break through. Kym's little trick meant we'd all be spending time making Joyous Hearts quilt kits or excuses.

Vangie had left the safe door open, and I shoved it shut. It wasn't very satisfying as it closed silently, slowly, laboriously, like a lumbering old man.

Buster followed me in the office. He was looking at me as if I might break. I took a deep breath. I wasn't that easily defeated.

"You going to be okay?" Buster said.

I nodded. "I need to get to work."

"Me, too," he said. He kissed my cheek, squeezed my hand, and he was gone to the police station.

I stood in the middle of my office, trying to decide what to do first. I rubbed my forehead, hoping to conjure up a plan.

I glanced at the time. Our segment on the *Wonderful World of Quilts* show had ended, but the phone wasn't ringing. Nor did I hear Vangie's computer ping. Customers were not virtually beating down the doors as we'd hoped. No one was clamoring for the scissors or any other QP product. I'd completely miscalculated.

Gussie came in and closed the office door. "I need my money back, Dewey," she said, pulling me toward the safe. "I've got to get it to Redding."

"Oh, please, not now, Gussie." I took a breath, reminding myself to be kind. "Pearl told me about this notion that Jeremy is in jail."

"He *is* in jail." Gussie's eyes were flashing.

I lost patience with her. My nerves were frayed. "Who told you that? He is not. Larry was lying and, whoever this new guy is, he's lying too. Did you ever think Larry might have a partner, who knew about your money?"

"No, this guy was Jeremy's friend. Larry lied about the mortgage, that's true. But he was trying to protect me. Jeremy knew I couldn't bear to know that he was in jail."

I scrubbed at my face. "Gussie, it's not that difficult to get bail money to Jeremy. Call your daughter."

Gussie shrank back. "I can't. Her new husband has forbidden me from calling the house."

I needed to convince her to drop this once and for all, but I could see the conviction in her face. She really believed Jeremy was in jail and that she was his only hope.

I patted her arms and modulated my tone to a gentle one. "Listen. I'll call Buster and he'll arrange things. If Jeremy is in jail, he can get the bail bond here. No one has to drive to Redding."

She pulled on the bottom of her sweatshirt, stretching the fabric and releasing it. "That'll take time," she said nervously.

"Not as long as driving up there." Or giving your money to a total stranger.

I eased her toward the door. I could appeal to her sense of loyalty to the store. "You know I could really use you this morning, right?"

She nodded. "I want to help."

"Just give me some time while I get Buster to straighten this out."

I led her to the classroom. The TV was off. Jenn was wielding the box cutter, slitting open the scissors shipment. I hadn't heard the FedEx guy make the delivery. *Thank you, Felix*, I thought.

The Stitch 'n' Bitch group was armed with barcodes and was slapping them on the packages of scissors as fast as Jenn got them out of the boxes.

Vangie had erased my to-do list on the whiteboard and was writing on it.

"What's going on?" I asked.

Gussie joined the group pricing the scissors. The worry lines had eased from her forehead a little. She liked Buster and was willing to wait for him.

"We're figuring out how to get everything done by tomorrow," Vangie said. She pointed to the new to-do list on the board. "Re-prioritizing. I'm going to print out the directions to Kym's quilt."

I was not convinced. "What about the kits? She said there were going to be kits."

Jenn said, "I'll make them. I can stay late tonight if I have to. In fact, my kids can come over and help me bag up the kits. My daughter's totally into scrapbooking. She can make them look pretty. We can make at least two or three kits. We can take orders for the rest."

Vangie was writing while the others threw out ideas. Everyone was brainstorming. I was amazed by the energy in the room.

Ina said, "How's this? An incentive for people who wait until next week to get the kit. We'll give a free class to put the kit together."

I cringed. That meant less profit if I had to pay for a teacher. "I can't afford that."

Ina was adamant. "It won't cost you anything. I volunteer to teach the class. I'll show the kit buyers how to do the quilt. Just one night, but—"

I wanted to catch their optimism, but there seemed like so much to do. My mind buzzed with so many undone chores, I was afraid I'd blow a circuit. It was too late.

"I appreciate you guys stepping up, but . . . Vangie you have the banking to do, and the online store. And Pearl and Ina, weren't you going to work on the Old Maid's Puzzle?" And Celeste, deep in her grief, shouldn't even be here. At least Gussie had let go of the idea of taking the bail money, for now.

The six of them gathered around me, drawing me closer to the whiteboard. Vangie's eyes flashed with determination.

Pearl spoke softly. "Let us help you, Dewey. If we say we can do this, we will."

My eyes filled with tears. "You really think this'll work?"

They all nodded. I was lucky to have them in my corner. I had to let them try.

I agreed. "Okay, get to it. I'll be in my office if you need me."

From there, I called Buster and asked him to check on Jeremy and see if he was in jail in Redding. He promised to call me back soon.

Jenn and Pearl went to the front of the store and pulled fabrics to match the ones in Kym's quilt. She'd used a particular line of fabric that we didn't carry anymore, but by the looks of what they had stacked up on the cutting table, they were finding great substitutes.

I opened the e-mail program. I'd send out the note to my customers reminding them of the sale tomorrow. Forget correcting the typos. Forget drawing the cute graphics. Forget embedding the video that Lark had sent me. I sent out the e-mail with just the times of the sale and the live link to the QP online store.

I also logged on the guild listserv and asked for people to volunteer to work tomorrow. I could only pay in fabric, but that should attract a few takers. The list was quiet. Thankfully. No more talk about a man dying in my alley.

About one o'clock, Celeste came out of the classroom. She looked drained, like she'd been running on adrenaline and her supply was suddenly cut.

"I'm going to take myself home," she told me.

I got up from my desk and went to her in the hall. "Thank you for helping. It means a lot to me that you were here today."

She waved me off.

"Need a ride?" Gussie called from the classroom.

Celeste shook her head. "The walk'll do me good."

Ina said, "Let one of us go with you."

"No," she said, shaking her head. "Dewey needs all the help she can get. Without Kym."

I sensed her disapproval, but shook it off.

Celeste said, "I'm just going to go to bed."

I walked Celeste to the back door. I wanted to be sure she was doing okay. She'd lost her boyfriend, after all. Even if he was a creep.

I asked, "Did you talk to the police yet?"

She shook her head, a long lock of gray hair coming loose from her bun. She didn't seem to notice. "I told them I wouldn't be available until this afternoon."

We stood in the hall, the open door allowing the cool October air in. It felt good on my overheated skin. I thought I could smell wood burning. It was the aroma of fall, of leaves falling and trees reinventing themselves for a new season. I needed to drop a few leaves, if QP was going to survive.

Celeste sighed deeply. She ignored my question about Zorn. "The whole thing is overwhelming." Celeste sagged against the door jamb.

I was alarmed at such un-Celeste-like behavior. I glanced back to the classroom to see if Ina or Pearl was coming. I would gladly let one of them take care of her.

I said softly, "Ina?" No one came. I guessed they couldn't hear me in the classroom.

Celeste continued, "I couldn't sleep last night." She seemed to pale further, and I was getting worried. She needed someone more nurturing. I threw my head in the door and called for Gussie a little louder.

To my relief, I turned to see Gussie coming with her keys in hand, carrying a full tote bag. I saw a Diet Coke can peeking out. Even today, Gussie was recycling. The sight made me smile.

Gussie said. "Come on, Celeste. I changed my mind. I'm ready for a nap, too."

"Thanks, Gussie," I said, the relief that Celeste would not be alone like a weight lifted off me. I followed them out, watching Gussie and Celeste walk arm in arm to her car. "Buster will call us and let us know what to do with the bail money."

Gussie waved me off, her concentration on her friend now.

I stood on the back porch. I closed my eyes, breathing deeply. When I opened my eyes, Celeste and Gussie were gone and the back of Shore's ugly van was in my face. I was so tired of looking at it. I'd call my father right now and ask him to tow it out of here. Now. I wanted Tim Shore out of my life once and for all.

I pulled my cell out of my pocket and dialed him. "Hi, Dad," I said. "I need a favor."

He didn't answer. I'd heard him pick up. He still didn't trust his cell phone, so I spoke louder. "Dad?"

But he'd heard me. He said, "Is this about Kym? Because I don't want to get caught in the middle."

I saw red. Kevin and Kym must have gone straight to the Pellicano Construction office and filled him in. "Dammit, Dad, no. That's business. My business. Nothing to do with you."

I'd thought he'd understand. He'd had his own contracting concern for forty years. Surely he had had to fire people. "Dad…"

"I mean it, Dewey," he warned.

243

"I just need to borrow a truck and a couple of your men."

He listened to my plea to get rid of the derelict van in my parking lot. He said he couldn't promise me anything until after work. All his men were out on jobs. I hung up, feeling less like a Pellicano, and more like an unwanted stepchild.

I went back to my office, sitting heavily at my desk and checked my e-mail. Several new messages had been posted on the guild list since this morning. One was from ruthbequiltin, promising to come in and help out tomorrow. She had a friend she'd bring along.

That was a step in the right direction. I felt a little better. Quilters were good people, always ready to jump in and lend a hand.

I opened another e-mail from the guild list.

"My favorite quilt shop has just become the worst," the first post began. "Kym Pellicano, one of the original owners, was fired today. I will never set foot in that store again."

My heart sank to a new low. There were several more e-mails in the same vein. Misinformation abounded. Kym was the daughter of the owner. Kym was the owner. Kym was the heart and soul and main contributor to the shop. I got sicker as I looked. I clicked off, and sat back in my chair. I had never appreciated the power of e-mail until this moment. Word of mouth was nothing compared to word of e-mail.

The office walls closed in on me. I didn't want to look at any more e-mails, but if I sat here, I knew I couldn't help myself. I shut down the program and went up front to get away from the invading computer.

Jenn was working out on paper the dimensions she needed to cut. Each kit had to have enough fabric in it to make the complete quilt, but no more. If we accidentally shorted a kit, the customer would be upset. Of course if we included too much fabric, I would lose money.

Jenn had laid out the pieces that Kevin had sent in his e-mail. At least Kym had drawn all her appliqué figures. Once Jenn'd figured out what fabrics went into each kit, then I had to figure out the price based on the fabric used. It was tedious, time-consuming work. Not something to be done in a rush. Of course, time was not something we had today. Thank you, Kym.

I helped Jenn measure. We talked quietly while we worked. She told me she appreciated the new look of the store. I thanked her for helping out. She seemed to have put thoughts of Frank Bascomb out of her mind.

"My kids are going to come here after school, if that's okay. I'll work until five."

I was truly grateful. "Thanks, Jenn."

A customer came in, and Jenn moved on to help her. I glanced on the whiteboard and saw one job that suited my current frame of mind. Cleaning the bathrooms had been on Jenn's to-do list, but there was no way she was going to have time.

I was scrubbing out the toilet, wondering how many years I was cutting off my life breathing in the acrid smell of the toilet cleaner, when I heard Jenn call to me from the front of the store.

"I can't make change. I need more ones, Dewey."

I told her I'd be right there, and went into the office. Vangie could have gotten the change, but she was concentrating on writing Kym's instructions. She cracked her knuckles and stared at the screen. I opened the safe. I'd pulled out the pack of twenty ones and closed the door again before I realized something was wrong.

I panicked, opening the door again. Gussie's money was gone. "Where's the money?" I said.

Vangie picked her head up from the computer. "Gussie's money?" she said, "She took it when she left. Didn't you see her go?"

"Damn!" I yelled. Gussie had been carrying her tote bag when she left with Celeste. I'd just assumed it was full of cans.

I looked from Vangie to Pearl to Ina who'd come in from the classroom when they heard me shout. "Gussie! She's got the money and gone to get her grandson out of jail," I said. "I'm calling the police."

"Hang on," Pearl said. "Maybe she's home."

Or maybe she's already given her money away. The man that called last night had to be another con man. Larry's partner.

Pearl used her cell to call Gussie, but there was no answer. She tried Celeste. Same thing. No answer.

I looked from Pearl to Ina to Vangie. No one knew what to do.

I did. I said, "I'll go look for her at her place, but first I'm letting the police know. They can look for her, too."

I called Buster back. "Hey," I said.

He immediately said, "I'm still waiting on a call back from Redding."

"Forget it," I said. "Gussie took off with the money. She might be driving herself there. Can you track her down?"

"How long has she been gone?"

I looked at Vangie. "Two to three hours?" She nodded.

Buster said, all business-like. "I'll send out an endangered senior alert, and everyone on the force will be on the lookout for her car. It won't take long to catch up with her."

"The police will find her," I said to the three women in my office. They looked relieved. I hung up after thanking Buster.

"I can't just sit here. I'll go to her place and see if she's there," I said, grabbing my keys and my cell. "Call me if you hear anything."

I walked out the back door, knees shaking at the thought of Gussie out there alone with that kind of money. And a bad guy. I hoped the police would get to her before he did.

Shore's van was the first thing I saw. My blood boiled. This bastard was still here. I kicked a tire. That didn't begin to relive my stress. I banged on the side panel, my hand hurting satisfactorily. There was no answer.

I knew he didn't lock his doors, so I yanked hard on the back door handle.

To my horror, Tim Shore was lying in the back of his van, dead.

NINETEEN

OH, MY GOD. I covered my mouth. I thought I screamed, but only a tiny squeak came out. I stared at his body, sprawled on the dirty mattress. The stale smell of marijuana floated out along with another smell. Eau du death. I tried not to inhale.

My eyes adjusted to the dark interior. Tim Shore was dressed in his underwear and a T-shirt. The boxers were printed with dollar bills. He looked like he'd bedded down outside my store for the night again. I hadn't seen his van last night when I'd left because I'd gone out the front door to admire my handiwork. He must have pocketed the money Buster had given him for a hotel and slept out here again. And died.

I looked to see if he had the telltale expression that Frank Bascomb had had, but Shore's expression was smooth. If he'd been poisoned, it wasn't evident on his face.

A very white bare foot was right in front of me.

I touched him. His foot was icy. Like at a Halloween party, the freezing cold burned me and I drew my hand back as though it was on fire.

I wiped my hand on my pants. Past Shore's head, I saw Gussie's "You're nobody til someone bunny loves you" tote bag, flat and empty, ears flopping, lying on the back seat. The last time I'd seen it was in my office, full of zucchini.

I got angry. What was he doing with her bag? What else did he have that didn't belong to him? I went around to the passenger side. I was going to have a look before the police arrived. I wanted to know what this guy had been up to in my parking lot. I glanced at the shop. As long as no one came out the back door, I'd be okay.

I pulled open the front passenger door. Another decaying stench wafted out, but this one wasn't human. Squash lay in a pile, split open and rotting on the floor. A familiar key lay next to the zucchini, shiny and unused. the store key. Shore had stolen one of my keys and made a duplicate, just like Wong had suggested.

He'd broken into the store Wednesday night. Why? To steal a bag of zucchini?

I tried to remember where I'd seen Tim in the last few days. He'd been at the bank the morning Gussie and I were there. He might have overheard the conversation about the cash. Gussie had used that tote bag to carry the money. He must have been really frustrated when he didn't find the cash in the tote bag.

I picked up the PG&E bill that I'd seen on the front seat earlier in the week. The address was Milpitas. The same town that Larry had lived in, and where Frank Bascomb had his eBay account. Shore didn't live in Santa Cruz after all.

249

Tim Shore must have been Larry's partner. He was the "friend" who called Gussie last night. He attempted to extort her, but he'd died before he had the chance. From the looks of his clothes, he'd been dead for hours. I shivered. Gussie was out of danger, for now.

I dreaded making the next call—to the police. My insides felt like ice.

Another murder in the parking lot of QP. Did Shore kill Frank Bascomb? Poison him and watch him die before coming to class? I shivered at the idea of sitting in the same room with a murderer.

I headed back inside, but stopped as I remembered why I'd come out. Gussie was somewhere with nearly thirty thousand dollars. She could be at some rendezvous point, waiting for him to show. An awful thought crossed my mind as the wind blew through the van, refreshing the smell of marijuana.

For the third time in as many days, I headed over to Gussie's. I texted Zorn on my cell and told him there was a dead body in a van outside my store. I didn't correct him when he said he'd meet me there. I'd be there, but first I was going to find Gussie.

I parked on the street in front of her house. There was no sign of her car. It was getting dark. The porch light was on over Gussie's front door. Frugal Gussie would never leave a light burning unnecessarily. She must be home.

I rang the doorbell and banged on Gussie's door. No answer. I reached into the grinning mouth of the ceramic frog, checking for an extra key. I found nothing.

I paced off the small walkway and glanced over at Celeste's. No lights were on there. She must have gone to bed. Could Gussie be asleep? I had to know.

My years of sneaking in and out of my parents' house were about to pay off.

I went around to the back, knocking at the kitchen door and peering into the windows. I could see a new puzzle half done on the card table. She must have started one last night.

I stopped in her garden. The night jasmine gave off a sickening smell that turned my stomach. Celeste's house cast a long shadow into Gussie's backyard. It seemed to be in mourning, just like its owner.

The window to Gussie's kitchen was low to the ground. I managed to pry off the old-style screen without breaking a nail and opened the window. I pushed it up without a problem, and pulled myself inside. I overshot and landed butt first, with a thud, next to the old refrigerator. It started up with a wheeze, causing me to cry out. And clamp my hand over my mouth.

Light from the streetlight outside flooded the living room. I maneuvered through the shadowy shapes in the kitchen. The stainless steel bread box, now empty, caught the light and shimmered. It was empty. I picked my way carefully, remembering the cats who liked to trip up humans.

I didn't hear a sound. I turned on a light, further illuminating the front room. She wasn't here. I took a peek into her bedroom. I banged my shin on a plant stand, rocking the cactus and pricking myself in the process of righting it. I sucked on my finger.

I'd thought for sure I'd find Gussie here.

My phone rang. It was Buster, but I didn't answer. He'd have heard about Shore's body by now. I was sure Zorn was wondering why I wasn't at the store.

Zorn had said Larry had been struck on the head. Probably by Tim right before he came into my class. But he'd died of poison.

Gussie had a garden full of toxins. What if Tim had convinced Gussie that her grandson was in jail, but instead of handing her money over again, she'd killed him. She could have fed him the compost tea. Or given him marijuana laced with something. If I went back in that shed, would I find DDT?

I sank into Gussie's chair, like I'd been shot. The idea that Gussie, sweet Gussie, had killed someone made me weak. But I'd seen her fierce loyalty. To her grandson. To Celeste.

I glanced to the house next door. From here, I could see directly into Celeste's dining room. A light was on now. I sat up.

I could see her shadow drifting elegantly across the plain white curtains. Even alone, she was dressed in silky pajamas. I wondered what someone looking in my window would see. Ragged flannel boxers, tank top so stretched out it was dangerously close to being obscene and me, slumped in my armchair, eating right out of the cereal box.

Celeste picked up a china cup and saucer, heading for the kitchen. As she moved away, another figure was revealed, seated at the dining room table. This face was in complete profile to me. It was a very familiar silhouette. I looked at the honeymoon souvenir plaques on the kitchen wall. The same nose. That same chin.

Gussie *was* at Celeste's.

Relief flooded me. I'd get to her before the police did. Find her a good lawyer. Get her some help.

I let myself out of the back door. I walked through the split in the fence, thinking about these two women, so close, yet so different. Celeste and Gussie proved that quilting brought people to-

252

gether. There was no way that they would have become friends without their mutual interest in sewing. Celeste was too lady-of-the-manor type, Gussie too frugal and middle class to be part of her social scene. But Gussie had gone to Celeste when Celeste needed her.

I knocked on Celeste's back door. A curtain twitched, but I couldn't catch sight of Celeste's face. When she didn't open the door right away, I knocked again.

"Celeste, it's Dewey," I called out. I know she didn't want company, but I needed to talk to Gussie. I tried the door. It was locked. I peered in the side windows, seeing only the slice of the kitchen visible from there. No activity. Just the still beauty of the wood and slate, illuminated by the under-counter lights.

I stamped my feet on the porch. I wasn't dressed for an October night. The temperature had dropped, the air had grown chilly. I shivered.

My phone rang. It was a text from Buster. "Where are you?"

Not where I was supposed to be. I put the phone back in my pocket and banged on the door again. I wasn't going back to QP until I'd settled things with Gussie.

Celeste opened the door slightly. "Dewey, what are you doing out there? Please stop."

"Celeste, thanks." I made a step to cross the threshold, but Celeste kept the door mostly closed. She was in bare feet, and had added a floor-length, navy blue quilted robe. Yellow silk pajama pants peeked from under the hem.

Her hair was down, flowing around her shoulders. The long white tresses made her look like an ethereal fairy godmother.

"I need to talk to Gussie," I said. "I've got news about Jeremy." I didn't, but I knew it would get me in the door.

"Gussie's not here."

Celeste was protecting her friend. From me? "I saw her, just a few moments ago. Sitting at your dining room table. I could see her clearly."

Celeste shrugged, her elegant shoulders lifting slightly. "You're mistaken, Dewey. Go home." She began to close the door in my face. I stuck my foot out and stopped the door.

"Wait, Celeste," I said. The door was squashing my toes. I fought not to pull away. I squared my foot, trying to jam it in farther. The door opened a fraction more. I leaned in. Celeste's face was grim.

A sharp noise emanated from the kitchen. I started, and Celeste looked sharply over her shoulder. We both let out a sigh of relief when it became apparent that it was only the automatic ice maker, cubes tumbling inside the refrigerator with a clang. I took advantage of Celeste's loosened hold, and pushed open the door. She stumbled back, but she was no match for me.

I skirted her and headed for the dining room. The Mackintosh dining room table and chairs were majestic. Straight backed, and elegant. Like Celeste. But empty.

One of the chairs was pulled away from the table. A delicate tea cup sat on the matching saucer. A slightly sweet smell came out of the cup.

"There. That's where I saw her!" I said.

Celeste was unfazed. Her arms crossed over her chest. Her earlier fatigue seemed to have gone, replaced by keen, glittering eyes and hardened resolve.

She said, "You saw me, having a cup of tea. Can't I have a snack in my own home? You should leave, Dewey. I told you I didn't want company."

"I can help Gussie," I said. "She'll be okay."

"She's not here." Celeste insisted. She held the kitchen door open as though I should scoot outside.

I ignored her and walked into the living room. I stood in the middle, turning slowly, trying to figure out where Gussie could have gone. Something about this room was out of whack, I could feel it. Celeste watched me from under the dining room arch. Her eyes tracked to the upstairs. The crown molding was at least twelve inches deep. The wood shimmered.

I headed for the magnificent mahogany staircase and listened. I didn't hear anything. "Mind if I look upstairs?"

Celeste shrugged, an elegant shrug. Her outfit looked some something a Katharine Hepburn character would wear in an AMC movie. Or maybe Barbara Stanwyck.

"Suit yourself. You know what's up there. Four bedrooms, two baths," she said.

Plenty of places to hide. Was Celeste hiding Gussie?

I walked carefully up the stairs. I listened, but didn't hear the floors creak as though someone was up there.

Celeste called up the stairs, "Be warned. I didn't make my bed today."

The first door off the hall was her bedroom. Not only had she not made her bed, but the clothes I'd seen her wearing earlier were in a heap on the floor. Celeste must really be distraught.

"Would you like a divining rod, Dewey?" Celeste called pleasantly, as though I was a favored grandchild on a scavenger hunt. "Are you looking for oil or water?"

I didn't let her needling bother me, but I was beginning to wonder if Gussie was on the road to Redding with her money. Surely if she'd been driving, the police would have picked her up by now.

No. She had to be here. I'd seen her. But what if she didn't want to be found?

The rest of the rooms were in perfect order, looking more like museum dioramas than lived-in spaces. I opened closets, wardrobes, armoires, anything big enough to hide a person. No sign of Gussie.

Larry's clothes were still in the closet in the spare room. Two tan corduroy jackets, Hawaiian shirts, shoes on the floor. It looked like he'd never left. Poor Celeste, having to deal with his debris.

Celeste was waiting for me when I came out of the guest room, eyes narrowed.

"I'm sure Gussie will turn up in the morning," she said. "She's probably gone to her daughter's."

"You think?" If so, what had I seen through Gussie's window? A shadow? A figment of my imagination? I'd been so sure.

Celeste opened the door to her bedroom. "Dewey, I'm tired and I'm going to bed. I haven't forgotten I'm to be at the store tomorrow to quilt on the Old Maid's Puzzle."

The Old Maid's Puzzle. "Why were you so willing to give Gussie up to keep your man?" I asked her.

Celeste sneered at me. "You don't know the first thing about it."

"I know that Gussie loved you and you betrayed her. Gave her up to a con man." Driving her to murder.

Celeste grimaced and held her side as though in pain. "You have no idea how I tried to protect that woman. She wouldn't listen to me. She insisted she knew what she was doing. Insisted that Larry had all the answers. Long after I knew what he was, she couldn't accept it."

Celeste's pain seemed to get stronger. She was nearly doubled over now. Her voice was raspy. "It's worse than you know. Selling the pottery and the silver wasn't all that Larry inflicted on me."

She rubbed her hand along the door, the jamb darkened by the hands that had passed over it. Her pride of ownership was palpable.

In a soft voice, eyes unfocused, she continued. "He forged my name on a new deed of trust and mortgaged the house without my permission."

I froze. A house like this should be worth over a million dollars.

Her eyes flitted down the wainscoted hall. "I don't own this house anymore, Dewey. It's going into foreclosure next month."

The house. That struck me like a blow. She loved her house as much as I loved mine. How would I feel if my house was ripped out from under me? What would I do?

A chill shuddered down my spine, making me wince from the force of it. I felt the specter of losing my own house. Not being able to pay my bills. Forced to sell.

I knew Celeste had been hiding something. I just didn't know what. The truth of it was making me queasy.

I felt nauseous and turned away. I needed to orient myself. Celeste had opened the double doors to her bedroom, behind me. The low railing overlooked the living room below. I had a clear view of the downstairs from here.

She moved farther into her bedroom, picking up the clothes she'd shed earlier. Her voice was icy and carried in the stillness of the rooms. "Do you think I care about the things that he took? I would have given him anything. Furnishing this house used to be my life. But when you get old, you lose your lust for objects. When you have everything, what more do you need? I needed Larry. He screwed that up."

I felt dizzy. I grabbed the railing for support. The living room looked out of whack to me. There was an imperfection in the room. The fireplace inglenook was lopsided.

A log dropped into the fireplace, sending up a shower of red cinders. I stared at the fire, feeling my equilibrium return.

Behind me, I heard a closet door open and close. I forced myself to focus on the fireplace and realized what was wrong. There had been two cozy spaces on either side of the fireplace when I'd been here as a teen.

I said, "You only have one inglenook. All of these houses have two, one on each side of the fireplace."

Celeste crossed the room quickly and joined me at the railing. "The architect was into asymmetry," she said.

"But you're not," I said.

The inglenook would be big enough to conceal a person.

I started down the stairs when I heard a grunt and felt the air move as something flew by my head. I ducked instinctively. I turned. Celeste was wielding a closet rod, the iron bar raised again. I stumbled, and she hit me square on the back of the head.

I saw stars. She was closing the space between us, growling now, a primal sound coming from deep within her.

In that instant, I realized how wrong I was about Gussie.

Celeste knew which plants could be used for evil. She was a master botanist. She'd poisoned Larry, Tim Shore, and now Gussie. That was the smell coming from the tea cup. Poison.

There had been no chance to save Larry or Tim Shore, but Gussie was a different story. With a different ending, if I got to her fast enough.

I pulled on the banister to help me get upright. Celeste was rearing back, the rod held high. I threw my shoulder into her belly, and heard the rod fall down each step.

Celeste was quiet. She'd had the wind knocked out of her and was lying in a heap on the landing. I raced down the steps and to the blank wall on the right side of the fireplace.

I rapped on the paneling. It was a good match, very close to the wood everywhere else in the room, but now I could see the grain was more striated, the color a deeper shade of red.

I held my breath and leaned against the paneling, trying desperately to hear anything. Blood was coursing down my neck from my head. I fought off dizziness.

"Gussie," I yelled. I thought I heard a whimper. "Gussie!" I said louder.

I pushed desperately on the paneling. There had to be a hidden door. I could hear Celeste breathing heavily. I took a quick look. She was lying on the landing, trying to pull herself down the steps.

I didn't think she'd be able to get to me, but I picked up a fireplace poker, just in case.

I pushed on the paneling again and a door sprang open. Perfectly cut into the paneling, the seam of the door matched the seams of paneling. I crawled into the space.

Gussie was snoring lightly, her small form stretched out on the built-in bench. She was dressed in sweats. I was glad to hear her snoring. She was alive!

I pulled my cell out of my pocket. This time I skipped Zorn and called Buster directly.

"Come. I need your help."

———

Hours later, I lay in bed next to Buster. He was murmuring gently, trying to lull me to sleep. He avoided my head after I'd cried out when he'd accidentally brushed past my stitches. I'd refused to stay overnight at the hospital and he'd told the paramedics he'd look after me. Any dizziness or vomiting, he'd promised to bring me straight back.

He'd been quiet most of the night. I knew he hated seeing me in danger, but there was nothing he could do about it. I knew he was struggling with his inner demon. The one that wanted to lock me in an ivory tower and leave me there. I didn't want to deal with that particular demon tonight.

We'd been lying on my bed for an hour. I was flat on my back, and he was on one elbow, rubbing my arms, my feet, my belly. He was fully clothed, although he'd taken off his tie. I was in my rattiest pair of pajamas. The good ones, a cute baseball-style shirt and matching pin-striped pants were lying on the end of the bed. I'd laid them out for the sale that was starting in five hours.

I'd given my story to Zorn and checked in on Gussie, who was recovering from a dose of digitalis, and came home to sleep. But sleep wouldn't come.

I was almost relaxed. Each stroke of Buster's lured me close to releasing the tension inside me. My skin, which had felt like it was on fire, calmed as he soothed me.

I zoned out, trying to keep myself from thinking too much about the night's events.

"Want to talk?" Buster said. He delivered a soft kiss on my forehead.

I told Buster what I was thinking. About the ultimate sadness of these two friends torn apart by a scheming man. A woman disintegrated by her love for the wrong man.

My voice was small and quiet. Buster leaned in to hear.

I said, "You were right. A relationship is not about the sex. The sex is beyond the point. You being with me tonight. Caring for me. This is what counts."

He kissed the back of my neck.

I continued, "I'm sorry I was so focused on what was missing."

Buster laughed a little. "I'm not sure I thought about it quite that much. I just wanted to get to know you while not being blinded by lust."

"How about now?" I said, my voice husky.

Buster's hand stilled on my belly. He leaned in, and I felt his breath tickle my neck. "What about now?"

"Are you blinded by lust?"

He didn't answer right away. I turned on my side so I was face to face with him. His chin was dark with the day's beard, his lips a deep red in contrast. In his eyes, I saw concern. And now confusion.

I could feel his heart beating wildly in his chest, faster than it was a minute ago.

"Nooo…" he said, so carefully I had to laugh.

I pushed myself up on my elbow. "It's okay if you are. A girl likes to be able to blind her guy once in a while."

He didn't answer me. I undid my top button. "You have to admit this is pretty sexy. You and me alone on my bed in the middle of the night."

"You with your possible concussion," Buster said. "So damn hot."

I kissed him. "It was a lucky hit. I was only out for a couple of seconds."

Talking about tonight was not the route to take. Buster closed his eyes and groaned. The thought of me lying on Celeste's floor was too much for him. I had to bring him back to the present.

I kissed him again, this time slowly and deeply. I crept closer, entwined his strong legs with mine. I felt him surge and knew I was getting somewhere.

I reached for him. He moved back so quickly, his knee hit me painfully.

Ow!" I said, laughing.

He turned red. "I'm sorry, I didn't mean to."

I kissed him again, until he gasped for breath. His eyes were bright and shiny, and a tiny bead of sweat trickled down his cheek. I licked it off.

"Too hot?" I said.

He lay back and let me unbuckle his pants. I unbuttoned his shirt, taking my time. His chest rose and fell. He closed his eyes, savoring my touch.

"Are you feeling okay?" he asked. He was trying again to be the super-considerate boyfriend, although by the look on his face, I didn't think he really cared. He was pretty close to being beyond control.

I kissed his bare chest where the V-neck of his undershirt left it bare.

"Buster?"

"Hmmm..." he said, unable to put together a coherent word.

"Yes," I whispered in his ear. "Yes, yes, yes."

TWENTY

I GOT TO THE store about five minutes before the "Butt Crack of Dawn" sale was to start. It was still dark. The parking lot looked strangely empty without Shore's van or the CSI van. It hadn't been this quiet since the beginning of the week. All tangible evidence of the havoc that Frank Bascomb and Tim Shore had visited on the shop was gone. The long-term damage had yet to be measured.

From the emptiness of the lot, the QP anniversary sale was the latest casualty.

There should have been a long queue of quilters in their pajamas here by now. There should have been giddy laughter at being up and out so early, and take-out cups of coffee. There should be women, ready to spend their money on their favorite hobby, in my parking lot.

I had the key in the lock when a figure came up the sidewalk and turned into the parking lot. My heart set up a hammering sound. I tried to cry out but no noise came. I was wishing I hadn't snuck out on Buster, leaving him asleep in my bed.

A familiar voice cut through the morning gloom. "Hey, sis."

My heart was pounding so hard I thought it would jump out of my chest. I pressed on my sternum. "Jeez, Kevin. You scared me."

He took the key from my hand and opened the back door. I passed him and set the security code to turn off the alarm.

"Sorry," he said.

I said, "I didn't think you'd be coming."

Kevin tried for a light tone. "I haven't missed a big sale at QP since I was sixteen."

Without good sales, today, this would be the last big sale. Or second-to-last. There would always be the Going-Out-of-Business sale.

Kevin said, "Who would help Mrs. Cook out to the car with her purchases? She buys enough fabric to fill her Mini to the roof."

He stopped in the hall, backlit by the parking lot's lights.

"We're family, Dewey."

Kym would make him pay for being here, I knew. Tears pricked my eyes. He moved past me and turned on the store lights.

Vangie came rattling up on her bike. She had on a tie-dyed shirt and pajama pants printed with bright green frogs on chrome-detailed motorcycles. Her long brown hair was tied back with a red print bandanna. She looked like a hippie, if hippies wore pjs.

I smiled at her. With Vangie and Kevin here, my mood began to lighten. Now all I needed was customers.

"Let's get this party started," she said. Her huge yawn swallowed her words and gave away her true feelings.

"You'd rather be in bed," I said.

She smiled. "But I'm here, aren't I?"

We did our usual opening routine, while Kevin unlocked the front door and lit the open sign. Vangie put the till money in the drawer. I thought about how yesterday's request for change had led to a chain reaction of events.

We usually had an extra cash-only pay station open on sale days, letting people check out at the office window, but I told her not to bother setting it up. We wouldn't need it today. Lines of paying customers were not going to happen.

At quarter past six, five women arrived in pajamas, robes, and slippers. These were the hard-core bargain seekers. I let them in and turned them over to Vangie and Kevin. I positioned myself in the office, not wanting to witness firsthand the failure of the sale.

I ignored the pressure in my chest and tried to immerse myself in work. The database had not been completely updated, and I saw a new shipment of bolts that had never been checked in.

Instead, I found myself on the Internet, going to the eBay site over and over, looking at Celeste's pottery. Bids were suspended. Both of the would-be sellers were dead. And their owner in jail.

Another kind of failure.

Those first customers made their purchases and left by six-thirty. No one else came in.

Online, I stayed away from anything quilt-related, especially the guild e-mail list. I left my inbox unopened. I was sure ruthbequiltin and her friend would not be coming in to help out. I didn't want to know what the other women were saying about QP. I would be forever known as the quilt store with the murders in her alley. And a murderer as a regular customer. Not exactly the image to attract the average quilter.

I didn't have the heart to update the database. It wouldn't matter if we weren't open for business.

Vangie came into the office a little after seven. The deepest discount period was over; now the discount was only twenty-five percent.

"Did the scissors sales pick up after I left yesterday?" I asked her. Maybe the online store had produced some sales that I didn't know about.

She shook her head. "I don't get it. The sales didn't roll in. I'm sorry. I was so sure..."

"Hey, we tried, kiddo. That's what matters."

I tried smiling at her, failing dismally. I wandered out front. Kevin was dusting the highest shelves. He'd already found ways to make himself useful. The very top of our shelving units were over six feet tall, out of reach for me and most of my employees, but for Kevin it was an easy stretch to use the feather duster.

"Pink's not really your color," I said. I looked around the empty store. "Some sale, huh?"

"It'll get better," he said. At least he didn't remind me that this was probably the worst sale he'd ever attended.

"Mom's legacy," I said, pointing to the scissors display. The pretty scissors shone. "There's a hundred more where those came from." It hurt to think of how much money I'd spent.

Kevin squinted. "Kym has a pair of those."

"Yes, and because she used them on the TV show, I decided to buy as many as I could. I used the money from Mom's life insurance policy. Bad call, wouldn't you say?"

Kevin leaned in. "Know what I used my insurance money for?" he asked conspiratorially.

I steeled myself, praying my sister-in-law hadn't talked him into paying for a boob job.

He said gleefully, "Fantasy Baseball Camp. I leave next week."

I burst out laughing. "Kevin, you did not."

"Mom would approve," he defended himself. I got it that Kym didn't.

He was right about Mom. I gave him a hug, feeling the solid warmth that came from knowing my brother was on my side. Feeling better, I went back to my office.

"So how's it looking for the online store?" I asked.

Vangie said carefully. "There are a few orders in there."

That didn't sound good. "How many?"

Her voice was defeated. "Two."

My jaw dropped. "Two? That's it?"

Vangie nodded miserably. "I don't understand it," she said.

"I'm going on the guild listserv," Vangie said.

"No, don't!" I yelled. I started toward her. "I can't stand the thought of those biddies talking about us. I can just hear quilting-sassy now. 'Murdering quilters are having a field day at Quilter Paradiso. Don't set foot over there unless you want your throat cut.'" I ended with a snorting laugh that sounded even to me more like a sob. I took a breath. I had to keep it together.

Vangie kept her mouse moving, ignoring me. "Oh, boy."

Her voice sounded strangled. My heart skipped a beat. "Vangie, please…" I began.

She said, "You're going to want to read this."

The front door chimed and I heard Kevin cheerily greet a customer. I looked out there. To my surprise, a group of seven was right behind her. The back door opened and four more quilters came in.

What was going on?

"Vang," I said slowly. "We better get back on the floor."

She looked up. "That's what I've been trying to tell you. Read some of these messages. They're rallying the guild to come out and support you."

I slid over to her machine. She went out of the office to greet the customers. She had a digest version of the guild list up.

Ruthbequiltin wrote, "Dewey is the one who found Gussie before she was killed."

Mamma71 said, "Let's put our money where our mouth is. Go to Quilter Paradiso and spend, spend, spend."

The messages were running like that. One quilter offered to pick up anyone who lived in the Villages, a local retirement community and quilting hotbed. She had room for six.

I looked at the clock. Just about eight. The discount period was almost down to twenty percent. I could maintain a good profit at that discount.

Ina and Jenn were due in any minute, but I would need more help than that. I called my father. He didn't answer. This was his swimming time at the YMCA.

I left a message on his machine. "Dad, I need you to come to work today. We're getting busy and it looks like it's going to stay that way."

I was afraid he'd consider helping me out to be taking sides, but I hoped he'd show up.

I parked several bolts of fabrics on the shelves where they belonged, and answered a tiny lady's question about fat-quarter packs. The door chimed continually as customers flowed in and out. I went back for another stack. We couldn't cut fabric fast enough.

"What can I do?"

Buster appeared at my side and took the bolt out of my hands. I felt my burden lessen. This was the first time I'd seen him since I'd left him in my bed this morning. He'd shaved and showered and slept a little longer. The worry lines of last night were gone. His shoulders were relaxed. Our nighttime encounter had done us both a world of good.

"I see you engaged in a little recreational ironing," I said, laughing. His red plaid shirt was stiff with starch.

He looked down, and shot his cuffs. "What can I say? My day just goes better when I start with a sharp crease."

He frowned as I unbuttoned the top four buttons on his shirt. He was wearing a Quilter Paradiso T-shirt underneath. I unbuttoned one more.

"Got to let that logo show." I patted his chest.

He looked around guiltily, then leered at me. "You had me worried for a moment. I thought you were going to ravish me on the floor of the kitchen."

I put on a coy look. "Actually, last night was great and all, but I was thinking of imposing a moratorium on sex …" I said, laughing at my own joke and spoiling the punch line.

"That genie is out of the bottle," he laughed.

"So to speak," I said. I fought the urge to kiss him and settled for a more appropriate peck on the cheek. He squeezed my arm.

"Let me get to work. Show me where this stuff goes," he said.

I followed him, pointing out the places to put the bolts.

When we were in the back corner of the store where there were no customers, I said, "What's the word on Celeste?"

"She's not talking, but we found Gussie's money in a tapestry bag by the front door. She was ready to leave town."

I shuddered at how close Celeste had come to making a clean getaway after killing Larry and Tim Shore, and almost killing Gussie as well.

"The CSI unit found poisonous seeds in her house. I take it they came from the weeds next door. A few seeds in the marijuana cigarette was all it took to kill Tim Shore. There's evidence that she'd hidden Larry in the inglenook before Gussie, but he got away. That's who people saw in the neighborhood. Not a drunk. Larry, feeling the effects of the poison."

I shook my head and sighed.

Buster continued, "Zorn thinks she knew she wouldn't be able to dispose of the bodies, so she figured she'd just lock them in there, let them die from the poison, and then leave town. Luckily, she didn't give Gussie much."

"Yikes."

"If you hadn't gotten to her when you did, she'd have been a goner. When the tox screens come back, we'll have enough to put Celeste away for the rest of her life."

I felt a stab of sadness. This was Celeste, one of the original Stitch 'n' Bitch group. "Oh, Buster, she's an old lady."

He put on a fake gangster accent. "Who tried to kill my best girl. For that alone, she should go down the river."

I laughed at his attempt to cheer me up. He rubbed his hands together. "You've got a boatload of people here. What's next?"

"Can you cut fabric?"

Buster rolled his eyes in my direction. "I can handle a gun, I think I can use a rotary cutter."

I said, "Yeah, well, don't come crying to me when you cut your fingertip off."

A stubby blonde stopped me to ask questions about the Home for Christmas quilt kit. When I looked up, Buster was standing behind the second cutting table. A group of women had gathered and were giving him advice. One pushed him out of the way and cut her own piece.

I caught his eye, and flashed my eyebrows at him. "Oh brother," I said, laughing. "You really know how to work this crowd." He shrugged happily.

The rest of the morning flew by. I helped Vangie bag the customers' purchases. It was close to noon, and there were at least forty customers milling about. The noise level was high with happy talk. Despite the fact that the discount was a mere 20 percent by now, they were all spending money freely. Most had armloads of fabric, kits, patterns, and notions.

And scissors. The palm-handled scissors were one of the most popular items of the day. I sent up a silent thanks to my mother. I'd be able to replace the insurance money in my account, saving it for another rainy day.

The hair on the back of my neck stood up as a memory of her, standing in just this spot during another sale long ago, flitted across my mind. She'd loved to bag herself, so she could exclaim over their brilliant ideas and exhort them to return with the finished products. Quilter Paradiso had been her dream, had been her store, and she'd been happy here.

But now it was mine. I felt myself take my place in the store, alongside my mother. In my store. Quilter Paradiso was now QP.

In a short lull, Vangie pulled up a sales report.

She said, "The sale *is* going well. At this rate, we should be able to pay off all our bills, and have enough left over to get us through to the new year."

I held up a warning hand. "Don't jinx it."

"Are you putting a flyer in every bag about the new QP Online?" she asked, worry lines growing on her forehead.

"I am," I said. "The online store business should pick up soon."

"And then we can work twenty-four hours a day," Vangie sing-songed. "Gotta love that Internet."

My father arrived with sandwiches. I felt my ears burn as I wondered if he would stay. Behind him, Sean was carrying a case of bottled water. My other brother, Tony, was toting a huge cheese-cake. One after the other, they kissed and hugged me. It felt so good to be in the circle of my family. I choked back happy tears.

Kevin looked over at me. He looked sad, and I knew he was missing Kym. My heart broke a little for him, but I also knew that Kym didn't belong here anymore.

"Looks great, kid," Dad said, looking around the store. I know he noticed every change I'd made. "Okay if I stick around for a bit?"

I smiled at him. It wasn't much, but it meant a lot coming from him.

Dad piled the sandwiches in my arms and said, "Take these into the kitchen. I want to be in on the action."

"Hey, Mr. Pellicano," Vangie said. "What's this about wanting a little action? I bet I know a couple of women in this room who would give you a tumble."

"Okay, that's it," I said, pointing at Vangie. "You go eat lunch." Vangie and my dad grinned, enjoying my discomfort way too much.

Vangie took a sandwich into our office.

Kevin found me. "I've got to go, sis."

I hugged him. "Thanks for coming, Kev."

He hugged me back. "We're okay," he said. "You're my family. I'll always be here for you."

I kissed his cheek and rubbed the back of his head. "Same here."

Vangie shouted. I made my way quickly over to her.

"You okay?" Buster was right behind me, carrying a bolt of fabric under each arm.

"I'm fine," Vangie said.

"Hey, that's my fabric," a spiky redhead called after him. She blocked his way. I smiled at him, and he followed her back to a cutting table.

In the office, Vangie was pounding the desk, making her mouse jump.

She said, "I'm an idiot. I can't believe what I did," she said. She grinned from ear to ear and crowed. "I screwed up the confirmation button on the QP Online site. All of the orders have been going to the wrong e-mail address. I just checked the old inbox and it's full of messages. There must be at least fifty orders in here."

I looked over her shoulder. E-mails had come in from all over. I saw plenty from the East Coast, then Germany, New Zealand. Paris, France.

"I'm going to be filling these orders until the middle of next week," she said, her voice higher than usual.

"Are you okay with that?" I said tentatively.

She looked at me with a huge grin. "Are you kidding? I'm ecstatic."

———

Ruthbequiltin and her friend, Karen, came to help out so everyone could have a lunch break. When traffic eased after three, I was ready to sit down. I should have been exhausted, but I was giddy from the contagious laughter of my customers.

I grabbed a sandwich and went into the relative quiet of the classroom.

I found Ina and Pearl sitting by the Old Maid's Puzzle quilt. I joined them at the nearest table and unwrapped my sandwich. I'd ended up with salami and cheese instead of turkey and it was slimy from having sat out for most of the afternoon, but I was too hungry to care. Besides, eating a lousy sandwich would mean I'd feel more entitled to follow it with the cheesecake. That would be my real sustenance later when things calmed down.

I said to Pearl, "I'm sorry that you ended up with the hand-quilting detail. I know that's not your favorite thing to do."

Pearl smiled at me. "I'll let you in on a secret. I'm faking it. I haven't quilted at all today. My fingers are too sore. I shove the needle over to anyone who walks in here. At least thirty people have quilted on it. Get this. I recruited one of your customers to finish it up for us next week."

I high-fived her. "Nice job. You're a trip."

She smiled at me. "No, just too old to do anything I don't want to do."

"What a concept. When do I get to be that old?" I asked.

"You're just a babe in the woods," Ina said.

I pointed to their envelope of cash. "How many tickets have you sold?"

Ina said, "Three hundred and sixty-four at last count."

My mouth fell open. I covered it to avoid giving them a bird's-eye view of half-chewed lunch meat. "That's wonderful," I said. "Gussie will be so proud of you."

At the mention of their friend, the two women exchanged a sad glance.

I asked, "Is Gussie okay?"

Ina nodded. "The hospital said she was resting comfortably."

Pearl said testily, "Whatever that means. I mean, do they ever tell you she's resting *uncomfortably*? Isn't rest by its very nature comfortable? But hospitals are not comfortable by definition."

Pearl was back in form, ready to take on the medical community. It struck me that these two women would rather be with their friend than stuck in the QP classroom. "Do you want to go visit her?"

Ina said, "With that crowd out there? As soon as I finish my tea, I'm going back on the floor. It's fun. We'll see her after the store closes. Her daughter came down last night anyhow."

"Really?" That was a surprise. Maybe Gussie and Donna could start to repair their relationship.

I chewed my sandwich, feeling my belly fill up. The food was reviving me.

I had one thing to settle with Pearl. "No more hash brownies from you. Gussie's going to have to destroy the marijuana Celeste was growing in her garden."

Pearl made a face.

"Thank you both. For being here when I needed you. My mother had such good friends."

I swallowed hard, the salami a salty lump in my throat.

Ina said, gruffly, "We're not here for your mother, silly. We're here because you needed us. *You.*"

I got misty-eyed and gave them both a big hug.

Pearl spoke first. "We want to thank you, Dewey. You brought our Gussie back to us."

"But Celeste …" I said.

Ina said sternly, "Celeste was lost. That was her choice. There was nothing you could do to prevent that. Don't lose sight of the fact that, because of your actions, Gussie didn't die."

I let their acceptance wash over me. For the first time, I felt their peer.

"I want to show you something," I said. I ran into my office and pulled out the landscape quilt from the desk drawer. I was a little nervous that Ina wouldn't approve, but I really wanted Pearl to see it.

"Look what I did," I said tentatively.

Ina took the small piece from me, and showed it to Pearl. Both women broke into large smiles that thrilled me.

"This is marvelous, Dewey," Ina said.

"I just followed Pearl's pattern."

Pearl said, "Your individuality shows through."

I laughed. "If by individuality, you mean mistakes, I agree with you."

Ina frowned. "If I taught you one thing, Dewey, it's that false humility is not at all attractive. Be proud of what you did."

Ina grabbed me and hugged me, hard. Pearl joined in, patting my back. I squeezed them both.

"What about me?" a shaky voice said. "Can I get in on the hug?"

We turned, arms still entwined. I tripped over Pearl's feet, and looked up to see Gussie, leaning on a walker in the doorway. Her hair was in complete disarray, the front frizzy and the back flattened as though she'd just gotten her head off a pillow. She was wearing slippers and baggy pants and a sweatshirt that read, "If you can't be a good example, be a dire warning."

Pearl let out a whoop, and using her heelies, beat Ina and me over to Gussie's side. We hugged again, this time including Gussie and her walker. Tears, laughter, and incomprehensible words tumbled out.

Finally Ina said, "Sit down, Gussie. How did you get here?"

"Called me a cab," she said. We exchanged a mystified look over her head as she settled into the chair next to the quilt frame. She was shaking, but picked up the needle Pearl had been using and took several stitches.

"Aren't cabs expensive?" I asked tentatively.

Gussie said, "I wanted to work on the raffle quilt. Besides, it's cheaper than another night in the hospital," she said. She set the needle down as though it weighed five pounds and leaned back in the chair, catching her breath.

Ina fussed, "Are you sure you're okay?"

"I'll be fine. Nothing like sleeping in your own bed to make you feel better."

Home, even a home in the shadow of the woman who tried to kill her, was better than a hospital room.

I patted her arm. "You rest up here. I've got to get back to work. I'm glad you came."

At five, I closed the shop. There were still customers inside, but I was too exhausted to face anyone else. I leaned on the door and looked back at my store. Buster was leaning down, getting an earful from a pretty, middle-aged woman in orange Crocs. All of his attention was on her, and I smiled. I knew what a good feeling that was, being on the receiving end of that focus.

Dad and Vangie were bagging a customer's purchases. Vangie tossing it to Dad after she scanned it, and Dad pretending to dunk it in the bag. The woman was laughing, a high whinnying laugh. Others in line were getting a kick out of their performance.

The store looked decimated. Fabric bolts were everywhere, stacked behind the cutting table, in rows three and four deep. We hadn't been able to keep up with putting things away, but it didn't matter. There was always tomorrow.

I'd be here, first thing, opening QP.

THE END

ABOUT THE AUTHOR

Terri Thayer is busy writing, quilting, and keeping an eye out for murderers at quilt shows. So as not to disappoint her fans, she is still trying to figure out a way to bring Buster to the guild's show and tell.

Ocean Waves—Coming Soon from Midnight Ink

I shivered in the night air. A cool breeze was blowing straight off the Pacific Ocean. I wasn't close enough to see it, but I could hear the waves breaking, and I pulled my old quilt tighter around my shoulders. The only pay phone in the conference center was outside on a wall of the building.

"I heard a woman scream," I said to Buster, for the second time. "A long, drawn-out scream."

His voice was strong and reassuring. "Dewey, babe, you're not in San Jose. Asilomar is in a wildlife preserve. Animals make weird noises. That's all you heard."

"Stop!" A sharp voice cut in. I turned, tangling myself in the phone cord and nearly strangling myself.